Will of the Alpha

Edited by Rechan and Kandrel

Will of the Alpha

Edited by Rechan and Kandrel
2012

Cover line work by Kadath
http://www.furaffinity.net/user/kadath

Interior Illustrations by Timothy Dzon a.k.a. Dbull
http://www.furaffinity.net/user/tkddbull/

Published by FurPlanet Productions
Dallas, Texas
www.furplanet.com

Print ISBN 978-1-61450-049-0
eBook ISBN 978-1-61450-076-6

Printed in the United States of America
First Edition Trade Paperback 2012

Table of Contents

Forward

A little over a year ago I noticed that there was very few furry media products aimed specifically at titillating the audience's kinks. Sure, artists may specialize in one or two things like macros or paws, but aside from Flinter's transformation comic or a themed portfolio here and there, you have very limited options for getting your kink fix. I set out to correct that problem, and after a year of hard work, you hold in your paws the fruits of many talented individuals' efforts to satisfy you. Hopefully *Will of the Alpha* will be the first of many books designed to scratch your particular itch.

This book has a little something for everyone, be it orientation or fetish. Within these pages you'll find extensive bondage, pony play, puppy play, flogging, objectification and power exchange. While "Memories" and "Furlough" may be focused more on hot action, other stories are about the lives of the characters themselves. "Dinner Theatre" explores what happens when work lives and the lifestyle collide. Self discovery and new experience are at the root of "The New Toy", "Attachments", "The Leather's Always Blacker", and "Breaking In". "Missed" is about the importance of defining a relationship. In "Savage Toys" a fox finds himself in the dangerous game of dominating a dragon. And "Infinite Loop" is a 'who done it' set in the dark near-future. Finally the book is rounded out with the poems "Pets and Amour" and "Sweetly Sadistic" by Elijah Lapso.

I want to take a moment to thank all the authors and artists who contributed to this project, and the hard work of FurPlanet for putting it all together. But my biggest thanks go out to Kandrel, who helped from day one with story selection and editing. Without him this project would have been far more grievous an effort.

For your comfort, the stories have been organized by severity, with the first, "Savage Toys", being the lightest, and the final story "Attachments" being the most intense.

Now read on, and may you find your fantasies inside.

- Rechan

Savage Toys
by Kandrel

The implements of Sir Humphrey's decadence lay scattered around us like a toddler's toys, thrown carelessly about his cave as he graduated from one to the next. He sprawled in the center, his four massive limbs thrown skywards, awaiting my pleasure. Using his thickly scaled tail to climb to his belly, I brandished the very first of my delights for his eager eyes, which gazed down at me from color-speckled orbs as large as saucers. He held his forelegs out to me, wrists pressed together, and wordlessly I fit the cuffs into place.

The cuffs had been the first thing Sir Humphrey had requested. We had taken tea, sat prim and proper like gentlemen, when he had asked the question. "Tell me of the southern savages, Rupert." It was his favorite topic: salacious news of recently-discovered tribes, with customs so alien and fashions so unique. I shared the gossip from the capital, where ships arrived in dock laden with the wonders of distant lands, all available at a premium to the highest bidder. So often, that highest bidder was me, backed by the financial weight of Sir Humphrey's hoard.

So I sat on a rocky outcropping that Sir Humphrey used as his table and shared the gossip of the Ngona-Ngona tribe of the savage continent. He drank in the lurid tales of dark-furred natives in between sips of his tea. His tail thrashed as I spun the tale of cultures who trussed up their partners in elaborate restraints, cuffs for the hands and hobbles for the feet. I watched his eyes go wide as I wove the story of the sailor who had been caught, and the ordeals he was put through, only to be claimed as a "bride" of one savage.

"Rupert, my dear fox. You must acquire this for me at once!" he had bellowed, his enthusiastic voice rattling the stalactites that hung precariously overhead. I nodded and said I would have them for him on my very next visit. I would have to; who would say no to a dragon?

The cuffs in my hands had taken leather from a whole cow, and as much steel as went into the harness from my wagon. They had taken skilled craftsmen a week to coax from the raw materials. Completed, they were truly a piece of art. Inside, they were made from the softest of leathers, delicate so as to be a caress across his scales, yet outside they were bound in the strongest of hardened steels. "Impervious!" The blacksmith had said. "The most durable alloy known. Strong enough to hold back even a rampaging dragon!" It had been an idle boast, but pray he had been right.

I closed the clasps around Sir Humphrey's wrists and pulled it taut. Leather groaned as it stretched tight around his forelegs, and he gave the customary tug to make sure they held tight. True to the blacksmith's words, they did. The steel made no complaint as the dragon twisted and pulled. Truly, they were a work of art.

He gazed down at me, eyes wide and desperate. More, his gaze seemed to cry to me. He needed more. It had been the same look he'd given me when I presented the cuffs for the very first time. He felt how they tugged at his wrists, how the steel glinted coldly from around his warm red-scaled hide, how the restraint left his arms useless, powerless, even in the face of one measly fox - myself.

Oh, how carefully he played the gentleman, how delicately he controlled his emotions to seem the paragon of modern society, regardless of how remote his mountain lair was from even the paltriest of civilized cities. The gold he spent to import tea from the orient to serve to his few guests when they arrived would have bought a small village; I should know, it was I who had imported it for him. His delicate china was cast to enormous proportions, large enough to sate a dragon's appetite, and it had cost more than a skilled laborer would earn in a year. Then there were the wonders and novelties, bought at dockside by yours truly with gold carefully portioned off from the dragon's hoard. Oh yes, Sir Humphrey was the paragon of society: prim, proper, and controlled.

As soon as I had fit those cuffs to his legs the very first time, though, I caught a glimpse of something in his eyes as he struggled. The cultured veneer slipped, just slightly, enough for me to see some of the dragon's more uncivilized features. Greed and avarice, a pride in his possessions of which the artful restraints were now one. They rose like ghostly apparitions on his expressive scaled face as he tugged at the tempered steel, burning through the gentleman's mask.

And there was lust. It rose slowly, like a beast awakened from a long slumber, but soon it subsumed the greed and avarice, devouring them as it filled the dragon's countenance. The cuffs were just a glimmer of things to come, but already they hinted to Sir Humphrey of what he would feel. The tug of his limbs, caught by the ingenious restraints, left his legs immobile, paralyzed, useless and powerless. It was not a feeling often felt by dragons of his stature, and the lust that rose from the sensation was readily apparent with just one glimpse between his hind legs.

Sir Humphrey had jumped when I first touched him, then. It wasn't the gentlemanly thing to do to even acknowledge the dragon's state, but to reach out and lay hand on that gently throbbing length... It was unthinkable. In that moment, as I stared down his shocked gullet, glowing softly with the embers of dragon's fire, I realized that I was one wrong word from a very quick and fiery death.

"You are restrained and helpless, Sir Humphrey, are you not?" It was a bold thing to say, to imply that a dragon was powerless in the face of a lowly merchant such as myself. Only his forelegs were hobbled, and with his teeth and hind legs and dragon's breath, he would surely defeat even those cleverly designed cuffs eventually. However, it wasn't the actual restraint that kept him from snuffing me out of existence in that moment. It was the idea of restraint, the feeling of helplessness, of submission to whoever happened to hold the keys, that made him shut his gaping maw and whimper. Then, as the idea slowly percolated through his cavernous skull, that length that hung between his hind legs gave a throb beneath my hand. In that moment, that very first inkling of torments and pleasures to come, he was mine.

The next visit, he rushed through tea with only the barest of nods to civilized behavior before he allowed me to truss his hind legs with custom made hobbles to match his cuffs. This time he allowed me to crawl beneath him and grasp his length with both hands. I could barely make my fingers meet around its girth. I let him rock against my grip, his limbs tugging at their respective restraints as his flesh glided against my palms.

He teetered uncertainly on his bound limbs, and I only barely managed to escape before he crashed to his side. While I let my heart slowly calm back down, he humped and speared through the cool cave air.

"Rupert, oh my dear Rupert, I need your-"

I interrupted him. "But you are trapped, Sir Humphrey. What would you do now if I chose not to?" There was another flash of anger, another calculated risk, a bold action that could easily have ended messily for me. But the rage fled quickly, and the dragon flailed against the cuffs and hobbles.

"Please, Rupert, you wouldn't leave a friend in such a state." His hips jerked in a quick spasm, and some of the dragon's excitement leaked onto the cave floor as he lay helpless on his side.

My heart beat a tattoo against my ribcage, but the act had to be maintained. If I was going to keep my position, both figuratively and literally, I had to play this to the hilt. "Ask me again, Sir Humphrey, but ask me as someone who is caught, someone who is well and truly trapped as you are. Beg me to help you, Sir Humphrey."

The dragon's features fell, and his long, whip-like tail curled up to his bound limbs. I was ready to call it off, to apologize for my arrogance. Then I saw his length throb, hidden by his hobbled hind legs and the tail that'd drawn up to his chest. Then, I knew I'd been right.

"Rupert, I-"

"Sir. Call me Sir, now."

"Sir Rupert, I beg of you to finish this. I..." He closed his eyes, and I saw him give another spasmodic jerk of his hips. "I'm so close. I'm begging you, please, just another touch, sir..."

I approached him and pulled at his tail. He allowed me to lever it away from his chest, revealing his desperately throbbing length. His hind legs fought at their restraints momentarily, but stilled when my hand found his shaft again. The dragon gave a low, rumbling call just as my palm met him, and his hips gave a jerk as I closed fingers around him. It only took that one thrust within my grip, as long ropy spurts of his seed painted his cave floor.

He rewarded me well after that trip, a bag as large as my fist. On that alone I could have bought a small townhouse in the city, but I didn't. This wasn't the end, that I was sure of. Cuffs and hobbles were only the start, and the reward promised more, much more if I played my cards right.

Next came a gag for his mouth; comfortable leather around his snout and a shaped plank of expensive rock maple to dig his teeth into, all supported with the same ruthlessly strong steel. When I delivered that, he allowed me to strip, and after he came I took my own pleasure across his snout. The next month I delivered to him strong chains to attach the cuffs and hobbles, and while his limbs were bound together and useless above him, I used just my tongue to bring him to climax.

Each time, he gave me a handful of gold from his horde. Half went to the craftsmen to forge for me each new marvel, delivered the next month in an escalating display of submission to myself. The other half I secreted away, saving for, well, who knows what? Saving was what mattered, for some day in the future when the game ended, and I needed to escape.

For I knew this game was limited. Each time I ascended to the mountains with a new wonder for Sir Humphrey's delight, he watched me with eager eyes as I displayed the new piece of decadence: straps for his wings, a steel collar with attachments for various gags, a spreader bar as wide as I was tall to keep his hind legs held apart. He had narrowed his eyes shrewdly at that last one, but I heard no complaints from around the wooden gag as I took my pleasure from his tail slit for the first time.

But the dragon's eagerness would not last indefinitely. I was running out of innovative ways to restrain him, and when the wonders ceased arriving, I had no doubts that my tenure as "Sir" would be short-lived. So I saved half of each handful of gold, depositing with various banks and moneylenders in the capital for that fateful day when I would need to make good my retreat.

All of this leads up to today. When I arrived, he hadn't even bothered with tea. Leaving my mule still tethered to my cart outside his cave, he ushered me inside, and before I could even unveil my newest wonder, he had flipped himself over onto his back, wings outstretched and forelegs held up in obvious demand. I disrobed quickly, throwing my traveling clothes outside the ring of the dragon's discarded toys. Then, with lust clouding the dragon's normally bright and intelligent eyes, I began.

By the time I'd secured the cuffs, he was already half-hard, the length laying across his belly scales and twitching every few seconds. I hopped down near his head and ran my fingers under his chin. He rocked his head back and bared his throat in shameless submission.

"So, what does my dragon wish today?"

Sir Humphrey shivered against my tentative touch, and then rumbled back in what he must have thought was a whisper. "All of it. Everything you've made and whatever you've brought. I want it all together this time."

Who was I to refuse? Who would say no to a dragon? I stood next to his head and pulled the collar over his throat. As I snapped the steel lock shut around his neck, I rolled my hips against his snout. He tried to turn his head away, but I tugged at the horn-like scales that adorned his head.

He let out a soft whine, but I knew it was all act. "Don't whine at me, you're mine to play with. Open your mouth." There was no reluctance as his fanged maw opened at my demand, and his serpentine tongue slithered out and caressed my sheath.

I took longer than was absolutely necessary adjusting and securing the collar, pausing every few seconds to roll my hips against his snout. By the time I slid the last lock closed, he had me hard, and his tongue was sliding around my knot. I didn't want to finish there, though. There was so much more to assemble first.

Next came his gag, fit precisely behind his eighth row of fangs. I then secured his wings, locking them closed and strapped to his back by a harness about his midsection. After that came his tail, curled up along his side and strapped to his collar. With each piece of this erotic puzzle, more and more of his body became powerless to resist.

I fetched the spreader bar from the floor of the cave and stepped back up onto Sir Humphrey's tail. He made a pretense of kicking his hind legs, but allowed himself to be "caught" within moments. First one thick ankle into the restraint, then the other, couched in the soft leather. Then I connected the bar to his forelegs to keep his legs all in place, and all of the dragon's many limbs were finally restrained.

There were more toys, not to mention the piece de resistance I had carted up from the capital with me this month, but as I slid myself down from his belly, I couldn't resist. With his tail curled off to the side and his hind legs strapped up above, he looked so vulnerable, so usable, that I couldn't restrain myself. I straddled the base of his tail, and as he struggled, all four of his limbs above me, I angled myself down and pushed into his tailslit.

There was almost no resistance. The scales to either side of his slit were smooth, and parted almost effortlessly around my own excitement. He was loose, though that wasn't a surprise given the difference in sizes, but lord was he hot. His slit gripped as best it could as Sir Humphrey cried his mock "complaints" into the uncaring maple of his gag. It felt wonderful, blissful even as I dipped my hips, and he wordlessly crowed enthusiasm as I ground my knot against him.

My length, yes, that was loose inside the dragon. The motion was almost frictionless as I rocked my hips, just a whisper of motion, and a heat like basking next to an open fire. But when I pushed my knot against that sublimely scaled slit, then I felt resistance. Then, I felt him grip me. I could feel each and every one of his motions as he wriggled and writhed in his restraints, traveling up my body from my much more modest endowment as I plunged into the dragon.

Perhaps I should have waited; should have held my pleasure until his kit was complete, but with such a luscious dragon tugging at your need, who could resist? I barked my approval as I took my pleasure in him. He purred beneath me like an indulgent cat as he felt me twitch. He gripped, but he was much too large for a proper tie, so I pulled free to paint him with my pleasure at the height of my peak. White streaks coated his warm ruby scales, save for where my seed splattered across his own desperately twitching length. In the character of "Sir", I marked him as mine. True, no fox could ever truly claim a dragon, not completely, not forever, but "for now" was good enough for me. For now, he twitched and danced at the end of his ropes like a puppet—*my* puppet. For now, he moaned and gurgled from behind his gag as I drizzled him with my dominance.

Adorned and restrained as he was, though, Sir Humphrey's savage attire wasn't yet complete. True, the next pieces hadn't been part of the sailor's tale of the Ngona-Ngona tribe, but I was a resourceful fox. I had worked and sweated over the designs, and the next pieces had been made in secret, with clever stories told to hide their function from the curious craftsmen. Out of the package I'd brought first came a tapered wooden phallus, slightly curved and ridged along its length like Sir Humphrey himself. His head swung around to watch as I fit the piece to its straps and lines, running a durable leather cord to the spreader bar here, and strap to his hind leg there, and a collar around his tail to steady the whole piece.

I ran fingers over the lacquered wood, one last careful check to make sure it was absolutely smooth, flawless in its design, but it wasn't truly necessary. I'd examined it a hundred times looking for flaws or imperfections, but there were none to be found. It was the proper surrogate lover that Sir Humphrey needed, a size to finally match his own, rather than my own diminutive form. Confident in my work, I stretched the straps to fit the length against Sir Humphrey's slit, and let the taut cords do their work. They bent and bowed as the dragon tensed in shock, but the more he struggled, the deeper the cords pushed the faux-erection into his rump.

There was one more piece to the ensemble, but I waited for my dragon to recover from the shock of the first of his new playthings. It responded to his every impulse, spreading his slit almost obscenely wide around its girth as his gyrations tugged the toy until it sank to its base. At first, he started slowly, just a twitch here or there to learn how it would react, but within minutes, the dragon had learned to control it. He relaxed his tail and arched his back, and the toy retreated until all but one of its ridges glistened in the cool air of the cave. Then he tensed his limbs and tilted them forward towards his head, and the phallus slid deep, until all I could see of it was the grain of its hilt.

Then I extracted the very last of my creations from its bag. I had based it on tools I had seen stables use to "harvest" their prize stallions. Sir Humphrey almost didn't notice me until I'd climbed up to his chest again, balancing precariously as he rolled beneath me. With a careful knock on his keel bone from my fist, though, he immediately quieted and stilled his eager motions. His eyes were glazed with the same lust I'd seen when I first fit cuffs to him, the feral, bestial instincts that his gentleman's exterior hid so obsessively. I'm not sure if he understood what I was doing when I fit the leather sheath over his excitement, and hooked the last cords to the harness.

The reaction, though, was both immediate and overwhelming. I was thrown from his chest as he rolled beneath me. My first reaction was panic; something had gone wrong. Something had pinched, something had stung... But nothing had gone wrong. Instead, they'd gone right, oh so right. The dragon trumpeted his approval through the gag as his body strained against the bonds. The last piece I'd fit to him was a sheath made from the softest fawn leather. It rode his length as his hips bucked.

Sir Humphrey's serpentine neck stretched to its limit as his body undulated in the harness I'd made him. Cords pulled, and lines drew taut, and the hardened steel held as the dragon tensed. He was gorgeous to watch, now that he didn't need my hands to bring him to this point. I could see his shaft strain in its artificial sheath as he hit the peak I was now so familiar with. Thick jets of his own seed splattered against the lines of the harness, dripping down over his twisted body. His body writhed in its steel and leather embrace, then went still.

I don't know if he was unconscious, or sleeping, or some other state unique only to dragons, but he took no notice as I stood over him, or at least over his head. I leaned down and ran my fingers over the horns that adorned his crown. It had been special, but it could never last forever, me and my dragon.

By the time he woke again, I was packed and ready to leave. His head lifted and swiveled towards me. I could see the beginnings of a smile around his gag, but the smile slowly faded as his eyes strayed from me to the fully laden cart behind me. My mule trod at the cave floor nervously.

"I hope you've enjoyed my gifts, Sir Humphrey." His eyes narrowed as they locked onto my face. "Forgive me, though, if I don't wait for a 'Thank you', this time."

The neck slithered like a snake. He twisted, and even though his limbs were bound, he moved as sinuously as a deadly viper. As his legs touched the floor, though, the lines pulled taut, and his harness flexed. At one end, something slid deep enough to make him whimper, and at the other, something squeezed to make him twitch.

"It'd never last, you and me." I continued as he glared up at me, "One day, one fateful day, you'd remember that you're a dragon, and I..." He lurched again, and this time the whimper twisted up an octave into a moan. The leather and steel held. "You'll remember that I'm just a fox."

He bit at his gag and scraped at the floor, but moved no more than a foot before the results of the movement caught up with him. He was hard again; my creation had done its work. I could see the dragon's greatest needs well in his eyes. He wanted me to stop, oh yes, his eyes begged me to stop, but there he was confused. In the steel of his gaze, I could see the avarice of his race rising; he would tear me asunder. Then the lust rose, spurred by my device, spurred by my casual dominance, but spurred most by his longing to submit. He was hard again, erection in its leather sheath spearing skyward as he twisted in the restraints. Every instinct told me to flee, but I had no need to run. The device had taken him prisoner.

My cards had been dealt, though, and regardless of what fate they won me, my only choice was forward. I turned away from Sir Humphrey and tugged at the reins of my mule, and behind him my cart was laden to the brim with dragon's gold. It was a fortune, so vast that I doubt I even a merchant of my caliber could truly comprehend it. The cart wobbled a bit on suddenly shaky wheels, but then they started to roll. With the dragon roaring and moaning his protest around the rock maple gag, I left his cave and trundled my way towards the capital.

***

Life is kind to those who can afford it. Wealth bought me passage aboard a luxury sea-liner, bound for distant lands, but even distant isn't distant enough when you're hiding from a dragon. Every day cost more than gold. It cost me one day during which Sir Humphrey would seek me out. So on the wealth the dragon gold had brought me, every day was lived as if it could very well be my last.

In the gem of the far coast, Farleigh, three gold coins bought me a day and a night in the skilled hands of Mistress Harell and her harem of otters. Then six more bought me passage across the endless sands, guided by a small tribe of jackals who showed me the way during the hot days, then showed me their own ways during the cold nights. A glittering jewel from the pilfered hoard saw me invited to the sultan's palace when I reached far Ahmu Dhira, the pearl of the desert. At each stop, a small token of good will from Sir

Humphrey's last (and unintentional) gift delivered me to the lap of luxury. I tasted the finest foods and sampled the finest hospitality.

In the end, it was a competition between which would run out first: my time, or my wealth. It was a question only answered when I finally found myself far from where I'd started, on a continent not on any map I'd ever seen. My native guide, paid from the last remnants of the pile of gold that now fit in one belt pouch, led me to the mouth of the river M'Gala, to where a certain tribe lived. They called themselves the Ngona-Ngona, and had some very unique customs.

It was here that Sir Humphrey waited for me. Perhaps he had also only just arrived, chasing my trail. Or perhaps he had sought this place out at once, sure that my trail would lead here, eventually. He was curled around the chieftain's hut like a cat preparing to pounce. In his eyes, I saw the same battle I'd seen so long ago when I'd left him, trussed up in his elaborate restraints. My life balanced on the knife edge. He could so simply snuff me out, and his self-imposed quest would be at an end. But equally, I saw the need, the silent desperation peering out at me from behind his slitted irises. I knew he remembered it as vividly as I did, that moment when he was bound and helpless in his toys; when he first looked up and saw not the lowly fox merchant that'd been his servant for so long, but instead he saw Sir.

Regardless of which future he chose, which end fate had chosen for me, the next moment was already decided. Like a cat at the very end of its hunt, he pounced, and I was his.

The New Toy
by Ianus J. Wolf

Simon ran a finger under the collar, wondering again if the black leather really went well against his white and tan fur. His eyes scanned the club once more, and even in the dim lighting, it was easy to notice just how many guys in collars looked better than he did. Once again he was self-conscious of the extra pounds he was still sporting, made all too visible by the simple mesh underwear with the leather front that he wore. Standing in the corner, his tail twitching, the cougar worried that this would be another wasted night.

The last time he had tried "Collars and Leads" night at the club had been a few months before. It had been an awkward first attempt during which no one showed the slightest interest and Simon hadn't been able to work up the courage to directly talk to anyone. He'd left halfway through the evening feeling depressed and spent a long night at home alone. Again.

Today he'd finally tired of the idea of another night sitting at the computer fantasizing about being someone's slave and decided to give it another try. He'd been hitting the gym in just about all his spare time and felt some improvement in the last few weeks. He knew that as cougars went, he certainly wasn't bad looking and would look better once he lost a few pounds. But as soon as he changed into the simple collar and underwear outfit, he'd realized that he still couldn't hold a candle to all the fit, beautiful people that also wanted to belong to someone for a night. And once again, every male or female holding a lead or leash was claiming up the skinny, fit, and toned ones and leaving him to stand quietly in the corner.

Simon's hand went nervously to his belly, feeling the soft paunch there, remembering that his backside had also looked a little too big in the mirror at home. He let out a little sigh. It had only been an hour, but he already knew that it wasn't going to work out again. Watching a svelte little fox that had been there only about ten minutes get picked up almost immediately by a leather-clad, muscled wolf, he decided it was time to gather his clothes from the locker he'd used and just head home. Maybe six months in the gym would be enough time and he could try then. Taking one more glance around the room and dreaming of someone dragging him off to the back room where the beds waited, Simon pushed away from the wall where he'd been leaning and started to walk toward the lockers to get his clothes.

"Excuse me," said a feminine voice to his side, "can I ask you a couple questions?"

Turning his head, Simon felt his heart skip a beat. At his left stood an athletic female rabbit with a confident smile on her face and the most beautiful blue eyes he'd ever seen. Looking splendid against her gray fur, a tight black leather bikini top hugged pert, rounded breasts and left the smooth cream fur of her belly exposed. A lacey garter belt barely covered her hips and held her net stockings in place over her strong, shapely legs. Underneath, black lace panties barely hid her sex, allowing him to almost make out a vague impression. Her hip cocked against her right paw while her left idly twirled a short, red lead.

"Um…" Simon managed to respond, "Of course… uh… mistress. Anything you want."

"Ah, ah, ah, I haven't claimed you yet. No need for that." Her eyes glanced up and down his body, constantly appraising. "What's your name?"

"Simon."

"Well, Simon, I'm looking for a present for my husband tonight. Something I can enjoy too. How do you feel about other males?"

Face flushing, he stammered, "I-I'm fine with other males. I'm bi."

"Hmm, good, good," she stepped a little closer and gently touched a soft-furred finger to his chest, slowly running it through his own fur down to his pudgy belly, "And what are you really looking for? What are your limits?"

Simon had known for a long time what he wanted and where his lines were, but in the moment, he didn't want to risk losing this. Despite a few relationships before, it was the first time anyone had shown interest in him within any of the clubs or the community at large. "Oh, you know… anything."

The rabbit immediately took her paw away and fixed Simon with a stern gaze. It was only then that he realized that she was at least five years older than him, possibly ten. The thought of it and the firm look both made him shiver slightly, even as he worried that he'd just made an irredeemable mistake.

"Simon, I'm going to tell you something, and you need to listen and take this very seriously. You need to be completely honest when you're talking things over in situations like this. Otherwise, you are going to get into situations that you don't want to be in. Beyond being frustrating, it could be dangerous for you. Do you understand?"

Wilting just a bit under the force of her eyes and her words, Simon nodded. "I... uh... I guess mostly I like the idea of serving someone else. Of being used for their pleasure. I don't... really like the idea of real pain though. I'm okay with a little punishment if I'm not doing good, but I've read about people that draw blood and I don't want anything like that. Really I just want to be a good boy for whoever claims me."

Face softening slightly, the rabbit nodded. "Much better, Simon. So what about a little flogging or the sting of a crop?"

"Oh, that would be okay. Just nothing too heavy."

"And what about sexually? Any particular limits there?"

Simon thought for a moment. "No, I'm honestly pretty open when it comes to that."

Her face brightened and the soft smile suddenly turned dark and mischievous. With steady practiced motion, she reached up and took the d-ring on Simon's collar, attaching her lead to it with a soft click. She gave him a gentle tug.

"I think you'll make a fine toy tonight, unless you want to dispute the claim. My name is Michelle, but you will call me mistress."

His entire body tingling in excitement, the cougar nodded once. "Yes, mistress."

"Good. Now let's go see what your new master Terry thinks of his present."

Without another word to him, Michelle began to walk off towards a group of tables, pulling the lead. Simon followed readily with the pressure on the back of his neck, his heart pounding. Soon they approached a round table where a large, dark brown stallion sat alone, seemingly engrossed in his drink and scanning the room.

The horse was dressed in a skintight t-shirt stretched over a broad, muscled chest and dark blue jeans.

"Dear," the rabbit said, "look what I found for you."

As the horse looked up and set his eyes to coldly appraising the cougar, Simon shivered. He'd thought the mistress's husband would be another rabbit. He'd never been with a horse, and at the moment the idea of the master's equipment made him nervous.

"Oooh, that's pretty cute," the horse said in a deep baritone as his eyes roamed approvingly over the cougar's frame, "Yes, a nice find indeed. Does it have a name?"

"This is Simon," the rabbit spoke before Simon could answer for himself. "Sit down, Simon."

Obediently, quietly, Simon took the chair across from the horse, keeping his eyes lowered. As soon as he was in the seat, Simon suddenly felt a large rabbit's foot plopped up onto his thigh, followed by a second. Looking over, he saw Michelle draped back over her chair and watching him expectantly.

"Well… rub them."

Shaking out of his momentary stupor, Simon set his paws to work, gently squeezing and massaging the large feet. His new mistress moaned at the rubbing and made happy churring noises when he let his claws brush through the fur at the top of her feet. Ears falling back, she closed her eyes and basked in the attention.

The horse chuckled approvingly. "Simon, I'm Terry. Let's talk candidly for just a few minutes while you do that."

Both horse and rabbit looked at him seriously. Terry began talking with Simon about the cougar's history and when he'd last been tested as he and Michelle shared their general history with him. Remembering the rabbit's earlier admonition, Simon was as honest as possible about his meager collection of experience despite his shyness on the topic. They discussed limits, expectations, and safe words, and when an appropriate system had been selected, Terry leaned back to give the cougar a leering grin.

"I feel satisfied with that," the horse said, "Honey, I think we should take our new toy home to play."

Taking her feet slowly out of his lap, Michelle reached over and lightly rubbed the back of Simon's head. Leaning close, she whispered in the cougar's ear, "As long as you feel comfortable coming home with us, we'd love to use you for the night. Only if you're ready."

Simon's heart fluttered in his chest. He hadn't expected to be invited to anyone's home; he'd barely hoped to be pulled back into the back room for a short time. The thought made him a little nervous, but he already liked the two of them, and they were a good-looking, nice couple. He looked up at Terry and saw the horse casually waiting, smiling at him. A brief look at Michelle's warm eyes and he looked down again.

"I… I'm yours, Master. Mistress. May I have time to get my things?"

Terry chuckled gently and nodded. "Of course. Your mistress can take you to get your clothes. I'm going to go start the car."

The horse rose and headed for the door while the rabbit gave a gentle tug on Simon's lead, pulling him towards the lockers in the corner. The cougar fumbled his clothes out of the locker and started to dress, his entire body trembling in nervous anticipation. From a different locker, his mistress pulled a long, red coat and wrapped it around herself, adding a pair of slip on shoes to her feet. Once Simon was finally dressed enough for the short trip out, Michelle gave another firm tug on his lead.

"Come along, toy. I'm in no mood to wait tonight."

"Yes, Mistress."

***

The sedan pulled up to an elegant two-story house and turned into a large garage as Simon watched from the back seat. He still wore the collar with the lead attached, a basic t-shirt and shorts covering the rest of his frame. As the garage door closed behind them and a light came on, the cougar felt butterflies in his stomach and body shivering with nerves and anticipation. It was actually happening; he would be used tonight by the horse and the rabbit that were just now leaving the car. He couldn't shake the small fear that he would say or do the wrong thing and screw this up somehow.

Terry leaned in and smirked at him as Michelle went to the door leading into the house. "Come along, toy. We have to get you inside to play."

A lump in his throat, the cougar nodded, slowly opened the car door and slipped out, following dutifully behind the large horse. The door the rabbit had unlocked led from the garage into a large, immaculate kitchen. Simon followed them to the right and into a short passage that led to a large, well-furnished living room. A leather couch and loveseat sat before a flat-screen TV and a glass-top coffee table, with a large fireplace in the corner. The cougar looked around, wondering if this was where they wanted him, or if he would be taken upstairs to a bedroom.

The horse turned, his eyes staring directly into Simon's before the cougar quickly averted his gaze down. He could see the rabbit watching him as she shed her coat and tossed it over the leather sofa. Terry was already pulling off his shirt as he spoke.

"The clothes. Get rid of them." He did not raise his voice or sound cruel, but his words carried unquestionable authority.

With trembling hands, the cougar pulled up his shirt, exposing himself once again to the master and mistress. He watched them as he slid his shorts down, never daring to look them in the eye as they stared almost hungrily at him. Trying to avoid shuffling his feet, the cougar stood there, his portly gut once again hanging slightly over the leather and mesh briefs.

"The underwear too, toy. We don't need those in the way."

Immediately the cougar obeyed his master, already feeling his own will diminishing as he clumsily worked the tight fitting mesh down his legs. He'd always picture getting undressed with much more grace, but he could not stop his tail flipping about and getting in the way. He almost toppled over a few times before he finally managed to stumble his way out of the tight mesh. He almost worried that his master would laugh at him now, or that his mistress would decide she'd made a mistake and they'd tell him to go home.

Instead, the large, muscled horse stepped over to him, still grinning wide, and slowly reached his hands out to the plump cougar. With no shirt, the equine's thick, well-defined body became more apparent, and as the powerful hands touched his fur, Simon shivered. Everywhere the horse touched him, little tingles of pleasure shot straight through his body to stir his loins.

Fingers ran through the fur of his back, stroked his chest, and rubbed softly along the paunch of his belly to knead the flesh there.

Where his master's eyes had appraised him, now the large hands did the some, holding and caressing the timid feline and exploring every bit of his body that they could find. As the horse pulled him closer, one of those questing hands slipped down under his belly and slowly cupped his groin to give a gentle squeeze. All the while the rabbit leaned back against the couch and looked on with a steady smirk, her paws running through her own fur.

"Hmm, feels so good, nice and soft," the horse rumbled as he held the cougar.

With Terry's hands stroking and brushing all through his soft fur, Simon stood almost rigidly still. Unsure what was expected, he finally attempted to reach out and stroke his master in return. Suddenly, the master's hands were at his wrists and holding them gently but firmly as the mistress took a warning step forward.

"Not until you're told, my little toy," the horse said with a stern tone, "Never touch your master or your mistress until they tell you to. Do you understand?"

"Yes, master. I… I'm sorry, sir, I didn't know."

The mistress spoke up then, "You seem to know your place, toy, but you will have to learn what it means. Or I will instruct you as harshly as needed." She reached out past the master and gave the lead a firm yank downward. "Is that understood?"

"Y-yes, mistress," he said, his head bowed. "I promise I'll learn. I'll do better."

"See that you do," she replied as she gave him a little slack.

The horse stepped back and smiled again, his tail flicking softly behind him. "I think it'll be alright, dear. It seems to be a smart enough toy, probably it'll learn quick. I'm going to get ready downstairs. Would you be so kind as to bring him to the door and take him down for me when I'm ready?"

"Certainly, my sweet. Just call out when you want him."

With a last satisfied smirk to his new plaything, the horse moved down a hallway and the rabbit grabbed the lead and pulled, forcing the toy to follow. He moved dutifully a step behind her, not wanting to displease. He was aware enough to watch his master take a key from the top of the doorjamb and unlock the door at the end of the hallway. The master closed the door behind him, and the toy's mistress turned.

"He'll be a few minutes." Her paw moved and stroked the back of his head, sending more waves of gentle pleasure down his body. "No sense having you standing idle."

Her breath heavy, his mistress slowly moved her paw to her breast and began massaging through the leather. Soft eyes drowsing for a moment, she stroked herself, and he felt his loins stirring as he was forced to look without touching. His tail swished in the air, and the cougar felt a little purr rise in his throat. The paw at her chest pulled down the side of the leather bikini top in a slow, graceful motion that exposed a single plump breast, the nub of the nipple already erect amidst the soft fluff of her cream-colored fur.

Soft purring slipped through the rabbit's teeth as her paw pushed up against the breast. "Suck it, toy. Show me what you can do."

The cougar hesitated for a moment, unsure if it would really be appropriate while the master was getting ready. The moment earned him a sharp tug downward on his collar as the rabbit pulled his face down to her breast.

"You may be a present for him, but you also belong to me, toy! Now suck!"

Immediately the cougar opened his muzzle and pushed it slowly around the breast and the erect nipple. Inhaling deeply, he savored the scent of her fur as it washed over him with the taste of her on his tongue. He suckled as if he were a hungry cub and let his tongue gently dart over the stiff, delicate button, careful to keep the strokes of his tongue smooth for her and avoid any roughness. The mistress sighed as he did as he was told, the cougar careful to listen for any sounds of pleasure so that he could know what he was doing right. Her groans, her panting, the more she pushed the supple breast into his muzzle were the only praise that told him he was being a good toy and doing well.

His own stirring arousal grew as the soft flesh pushed against his muzzle and the fur tickled inside his lips, the cougar bathing in every sensation. Musk rose on the air as he licked and sucked for several long moments, her moans growing in intensity before he felt the pull on his collar shift backwards. The barest choking was enough of a signal from mistress, and he pulled his head back to stand and wait for his next instruction.

Holding his lead firmly in her paw, the Mistress leaned against the wall and panted softly. Her ears drooped just a little as a wide smile covered her face. Eyes closing, her other paw softly rubbed where his muzzle had been, brushing over where his saliva slicked all around the hard nub.

The powerful blue eyes opened again and regarded him almost kindly. "Very good job." Her paw reached up to stroke and scratch just under his chin. "When a toy does that well and reacts that quickly, it gets rewards."

The thought that he had brought mistress pleasure and done well gave the cougar almost as much pleasure as the delightful rubs along his muzzle. The toy did not speak, but merely smiled and gave a light purr as he felt a growing hardness in his groin.

"We'll definitely have to put this to good use," she said with the last stroke along his muzzle, "but we can't have a toy getting too excited just yet."

And with that her paw slipped away, leaving him untouched but for the gentle pressure on his collar. He waited quietly, letting his arousal ebb as much as it could. It was hard not to look directly at the mistress's trim body or think of the softness of her fur and how it had felt to have her breast lodged in his muzzle. Longing to feel the touch of her paw anywhere on his fur again, he was almost ready to beg her for it as his tail swished back and forth behind.

The master's voice finally came from behind the door, "Bring it down now please, my lady."

With the controlled strut back in her step, the rabbit tugged at him gently and without a word necessary the toy followed her to the door. Unable to avoid it, the cougar stared at the mistress as they walked the short distance. Her short bush tail swayed with her hips just above her perfectly sculpted rump, almost as if she were purposely taunting her toy. He felt half mesmerized as the door opened and the scents of leather, soft perfume, and musk wafted up to him. Concrete stairs lead down and turned to the right towards the end, and as the mistress lead him down that bend, the cougar's eyes widened and his heart once again fluttered in his chest.

His footpaws touched down onto lush red carpeting that brushed wonderfully against the pads as he entered a rectangular finished basement surrounded in brick wall. The far wall was dominated by a raised king-sized bed decorated in what could only be silk sheets. All along the long wall to his left hung various cuffs, crops, floggers, and other toys and attachments waiting for use, while to his right he could see an angled rack and a few tables lined against the brick. But the most striking thing in the room was his master.

The horse looked even bigger and stronger than before as he stood relaxed in the center of the room, naked but for a metal-studded black leather harness that crossed at his chest. Hugged tightly into the short brown fur, the straps accentuated the tone and strength in his broad frame while the glint of metal against the lighting helped to show off the healthy shine of his coat. Between his legs his thick, slightly flared cock hung down unabashed, simply waiting for the proper attention. In that moment he looked the paragon of male and the toy wanted nothing more than to worship before his master and bring him whatever pleasure he desired.

Next to the horse was what looked like a thin wooden cart about the height of his hips with a padded top covered in more soft leather. Thick beams comprised the base and supports that sat on four heavy casters. Each beam held various fasteners, and the cougar could see cuffs and belts attached all over the device.

The master's eyes were deep pools of lust, and his flared member twitched as he watched the toy step down from the stairs. A pleased grin was evident as one of his hands slipped to idly rub at his own member. "Looks so nice. Bring it closer, please."

The collar was tugged once more and the toy followed as his mistress pulled him up to stand before the master and wait. She released his lead and stepped off to the side, and one of those strong hands immediately took it up, the master holding it slack as he stared down at the cougar.

"You want to touch me, don't you, my little toy?" the horse asked.

The toy nodded slowly. "Yes, master. You're so handsome, so strong, I—"

"Hm, hm, that's enough. You may if you'd like. Show me how much you love your master."

Trembling, the cougar's paws slowly reached up and hesitated. The toy was unsure where he should start, it felt like such a privilege to lay one finger on his powerful master. Reverently, his paws settled against the strong chest and slowly ran across the equine flesh.

Beginning to feel the hard muscles beneath, his claws scratched lightly through the horse's soft, short fur while his pads roamed along the toned abs, up over the shoulders and to the corded arms, stroking as softly as he could. He could hear the horse nickering lightly in pleasure as he rubbed and began to gently knead around some of the muscles, glad that he was pleasing his master. As the equine musk rose, the scent began to fill his sensitive nose, and the cougar became lost in the feel of the horse's body. A paw slipped slowly down the master's belly, and his fingers dared to trail along the thick horse shaft and feel it slowly growing.

Instantly the paw was batted away from the swelling equine cock, and the toy paused instantly. He looked up at his master's face, not meeting the deep, dark eyes there as he wondered if he'd done wrong.

"Not yet, little toy," the horse said sternly, "You need special permission to touch there, only when you are commanded. Understood?"

"Yes, master."

"Good. Now paws behind your back."

More worried than ever that he had made a mistake and was no longer allowed to touch the beautiful master at all, the toy whimpered lightly. "Why, sir?"

He barely heard the whistling through the air behind him before the sting of the crop fell full across the center of his back, and the voice of the mistress rang in his ear.

"Your master did not make an idle request; he gave you an order, toy!"

The cougar quickly moved his paws behind his back, still feeling the burn from where the crop had struck. "I'm sorry, mistress. I'm so sorry, please don't punish me again."

"So long as you behave. But you must be trained."

As she spoke, the toy could feel soft padding wrapped tightly around one wrist then the other. Leather creaked as straps tightened, metal clicked against metal, and in only a few seconds, the cougar found his paws held behind his back by a pair of broad cuffs linked together. The horse sighed happily, his own hands touching himself where the cougar had just moments before, softly working his growing member as he watched his toy.

"That should keep its paws from wandering on their own, dear," the rabbit said as she slipped up against him from behind. Her breasts pressed against the toy's back, still bound in their soft leather bikini that rubbed wonderfully against his fur as her arms slipped around him. Furry fingers ran over the toy's chest and pinched at his nipples, softly at first, rubbing and teasing, then slowly increasing in pressure. Soon the mistress was twisting each nub hard, squeezing them tight as the toy whimpered from the mingled burning sting and the pleasure that shot straight from his chest to his loins.

Eyes closing as her mouth clamped around one triangle ear, the cougar struggled to avoid making any sounds that might displease her. As with the fingers at his chest, the mouth at his ear began gently, then slowly increased until the large, blunt front teeth were digging in against it. As she bit down on his ear and her fingers continued their torment at his chest and held him close against her, the toy felt himself getting steadily harder, his tail twitching madly against the mistress's thigh. Soon a strong hand wrapped around his rising shaft and he knew it was the master teasing him even further. The hand squeezed and caressed his growing erection gently, making his feline cock firm and throbbing between them.

The toy shuddered and panted in their mutual grip, brought almost to the edge of climax before the hand was taken away. As it slipped from his shaft, the pressure on his ear and burning twisting of his nipples slowly subsided, just as he felt himself almost to the tipping point. He whimpered as the attention ceased but dared not question it as his eyes struggled to open again with the equine looming over him.

"This toy is just too cute. I love the way it squirms like that. You picked well, my dear," the master said. "Any suggestions on what to do next?"

The mistress cooed softly as the cougar felt his body starting to wind down again, the erection almost painful as it softened slightly. "It's got an absolutely wonderful muzzle, especially for a cat. You should put it to good use."

"Ah, so you were playing with my present upstairs, hm?"

The mistress gave a musical laugh that the cougar felt against his back. "No sense in letting any time with it go to waste."

"Just what did it do for you that was so wonderful?"

"You should find out for yourself."

The toy stood quietly as the two talked, waiting and not willing to risk interruption. Finally the master looked down at him hungrily.

"Show me, toy. Let's see exactly how your mistress used you. Do for me what you did for her."

"Yes, master." He slipped slowly away from the mistress, his swishing tail brushing her thigh as he felt a paw gently gripping around it. The cougar leaned close to his equine master and slowly ran the tip of his tongue around the edge of the horse's large nipple. He could hear the labored intake of breath from the master while the mistress moaned lightly behind him and held the tip of his tail.

Muzzle pressing against the hard-muscled chest, the toy gently took the larger nub into his mouth, tongue stroking carefully along it as he felt it stiffening. The sound of his master moaning carried him forward as he sucked softly and took great care for the stronger male's pleasure, making sure his tongue was always smooth and soft against the sensitive skin. With his arms fastened behind his back, he leaned into his master's body, feeling his paunch rub softly against the hard belly. The thick, half-stiff horse cock brushed the fur of his thigh and his own malehood, causing the toy to grow harder yet again.

With every motion he could hear his mistress cooing softly behind him as she watched and stroked along his tail. Her paws deftly controlled the swaying, twitching tip as it was pressed and rubbed against her belly. Lost in the feel of the master's body against his, the cougar barely noticed the growing sighs of his mistress. His own hot breath sharply inhaled around the master's nub and brought forth a soft whinny of pleasure as he felt the rounded tip of his tail brushed down her fur and pressed against her soft, moist center. The mistress let out a high pitched grunt as the toy felt his tail pressed deeper into that warmth, the tip twitching inside of its own accord.

Grunts and whinnies of pleasure surrounded him now as his tongue and tail were put to the service of master and mistress. A large hand pressed and rubbed against the back of his head and spurred him on in his suckling, soon moving him firmly to the horse's other nipple. Knowing his duty, the toy delivered the same treatment, listening and feeling for each soft breath from his master that signaled he was performing his task well. His tongue flicked as madly around the hardened nub as his tail twitched, each end guided by the gentle paws of the owners that had claimed him. This was his purpose now, to bring them pleasure, and as he could feel their growing satisfaction, the toy felt his own pleasure rising.

"Oh god, so smooth," the horse murmured between panting breaths, "I have to have that muzzle on my cock. Get on your knees and suck like that, toy."

Immediately the toy obeyed, sliding slowly down his master's body and letting his soft frame rub against the horse's hard body, the feel of leather and muscle making him purr once again. Tailtip remaining in the grip of the mistress, he could feel a tugging at the base slightly as he began to kneel down. She moved closer now and pushed his tail in deeper, the mistress moaning all the while as it began to truly fill her.

That thick, flared member brushed up against his chest, and his paws struggled for a moment against the soft cuffs. The toy wanted to stroke his master slowly on the way down, prepare him for the bliss he hoped to bring. That was his hunger, even as he felt himself drooling at the thought of the thick cock filling his muzzle, he wanted more to know that he was giving his master the pleasure he deserved. The thought of the flavor of it on his tongue as he smelled the thick musk, the feel of it just beneath his chin paled next to the possibility that he might actually make his master fire a load of thick seed into his face while his mistress fulfilled herself with his tail.

Lovingly the toy nuzzled the slick shaft and rolled his muzzle against it, feeling the equine meat harden as the fur of his cheek tickled it. He slipped along its length as he was forced to lean back, planting slow careful licks along the side all the way down. The strong hand stroked his head again as the horse nickered above him.

The head was flaring wide as the toy opened his jaws and slid slowly and carefully down half the length of the thick, hard meat. He could feel the edges of that head brushing his palate as he closed around the wonderful malehood. The taste of musk and horse cock filled his senses until he was only dimly aware of the pressure at his wrists or the warm, moist squeezing around the end of his tail. The world shrank down to tending and lapping softly at the delicious member to please his master. Dutifully he suckled and pulled slowly deeper. As if from far away, he could hear both master and mistress moaning, whinnying, churring and making all manner of sounds that told him he was doing well.

The flare widened in his cheeks as he began to slide up and down the length as best he could. With each stroke, the toy worked to take the master's cock deeper and deeper into his muzzle. Finally he reached his goal as he felt the wide flare all but choking him and both strong hands at the back of his head, spurring him to keep working. Back and forth his muzzle moved, slipping the thick head in and out of his throat while his tail writhed in the warmth of the mistress's center. He could hear both of them starting to cry out, and the toy felt that soon he would probably be rewarded with a thick load of horse cream splattering his throat and face.

But just as suddenly as the cry came, a hand gripped at his forehead and the luscious cock was pulled from his muzzle and out of reach. As the flare popped out of his feline lips, the toy whimpered to have it back. Leaning for it would not be allowed though, because the toy knew the horse decided what a toy was allowed to have. He was Master.

"H-Have I displeased you, Master? I can do better, Master."

Master was panting now as the toy looked up, staring down at him with the large member just inches from his face. "Oh god… so incredible, that muzzle… Have to use it later. Dear… help me get it strapped in."

The toy felt his tail pulled free from the pressure around it, even as the warm wetness remained in his fur. Master and Mistress pulled him up, his head reeling for a moment. Barely conscious of a throbbing erection, it took a moment to be able to focus again. Master was looking him in the eyes.

"Dear, it's looking a little woozy. Our toy might be overwhelmed"

"Let's check." The mistress's hands were on him then as he gained his focus, feeling his head and along his neck.

"I'm okay, Master. You just have such a nice cock. It belongs in my muzzle, Master. Please, I want to be good and finish it, Master."

Master was looking at him intently, checking his eyes. The toy could almost see concern there before the look relaxed and the master grinned. "I have another place in mind for it, but I have to get my toy ready first."

Moving to his side, Master led him to the leather topped cart he had seen before. From behind, he felt Mistress working at his cuffs. Soon his paws were freed, the leather bindings still wrapped around his wrist.

"Lean over it, toy, and we'll get ready."

The toy did as he was told, leaning his body over and feeling the soft leather press against his fur. Hands gripped his rump and pushed up, while Mistress moved to the front and slowly pulled his wrists forward. The leather top was just large enough for his body, his head hanging over the edge as he watched Mistress take his arms down and attach the cuffs to points on the cart. Meanwhile, he felt similar wide cuffs pulled tight around his ankles, fixing them to the other end. Finally, his swaying tail was lifted and pressed to his back and he could feel Mistress leaning over him to bring a strap up around his waist that would keep it there out of the way, the cart now holding him tightly in place.

Hands fondled his soft rump for a moment before Master seemed to walk away and Mistress slipped out of his view. The toy waited, unable to see what was about to happen until he felt the cold, slick pressure against his tight pucker. Fingers rubbed against it and coated under his tail before one slipped neatly into the lubricated hole. He whimpered at the initial burn as he opened, but soon the finger was probing deeper and touching places that made the toy squirm and moan.

Unable to move or resist, the toy understood now. It knew now that Master deserved more than just its muzzle. Muzzle was good, but Master deserved to take its tight hole that had only ever seen lesser toys before. The toy knew it might hurt some, but it didn't matter if it served Master's delight. The finger inside was joined by another finger, then another, opening the toy wider and making it cringe and whimper. Discomfort as it stretched began to lessen slowly as the toy could feel that pressure against some button inside, more than a mere toy had ever done, and knew that Master's pleasure was its pleasure too.

As the fingers worked in and out to stretch the toy and the groans of Master filled the room, it could see Mistress slipping to the large bed now. Naked except for the stockings, her long ears twitched as Mistress sat on the bed to watch. Chest heaving, her nipples stood out hard and erect, and as Mistress's paws slowly began to roam over herself, the toy could feel its own sensations growing. The growing physical pleasure for the toy was only matched by the joy that Mistress would enjoy this too as her paws slowly slipped down her belly to touch herself, her eyes closing and her body leaning back.

After long moments, the fingers withdrew from it, and the toy knew what would happen next. It feared that Master's cock was too big to fit such a tight opening, no matter how much those fingers had worked at it. Even as the thought of watching Mistress while the thick meat plunged into it brought the toy almost to bliss, it feared that the flared head would split it apart. But it was just a toy there to be used, its entire purpose for the enjoyment of Master and Mistress. Soon it felt the thick flare pressing between its soft cheeks, pushing up to the waiting, slicked hole and bit down inside its lip, waiting for the push.

Mistress moaned and cried as she touched herself, opening her eyes to look at what Master was doing with the toy only to have them drift closed again in her pleasure, her paw working harder, faster against her sex. From behind, the flare pushed slowly at first, working to stretch the toy further, making it wince as it tried not to cry out. Hands gripped its rump to hold it steady while Master entered. Then the thick head gained purchase and shoved forward, spreading the toy wider than it ever had been, causing a moment of blinding discomfort as it sank quickly deeper inside, until the toy was full and stretched with thick equine cock.

Movement stopped deep within, and in a moment the pain faded for the toy. It couldn't help but moan as the burn was replaced by the incredible fullness, the intense pressure against that inner button, and the joy that it was serving Master so well. Eyes closing, the toy whimpered in pleasure and the slight, diminished pain as it felt the thick shaft beginning to slide in and out with steady, rhythmic thrusts. Master grunted and whinnied loudly, echoing in the basement as the toy felt the thrusts increase.

High pitched moans emitted between purring from Mistress on the bed until she suddenly cried, "Oh, bring it here! Bring it close, I need that tongue!"

The toy felt itself moving closer now as the thrusts stopped for a moment. Master's panting grew loud and he grunted as he pushed as deep as possible into the toy, making it let out a wincing groan. Moving forward to the bed where Mistress's strong legs were spread and waiting for it, the toy purred loudly, its body vibrating and bringing another whinny from Master. As it reached the edge of the bed, the thrusts inside began again even quicker now, the smell of Mistress so close causing the toy to tighten around the thick shaft as that vibrating purr continued.

Her paw grabbed the hank of fur on the back of its head hard and shoved the toy's muzzle into her sex. "Lick!" Mistress panted and growled at it. "Lick now!"

The toy obeyed, pressing its tongue deep into Mistress and tasting her even as it worked to stroke along her inner walls. Focus honed once again to tongue and rump, taking in every moan, every shudder, every whimper from her so that it knew where and how to lick again. Mistress fell back on the bed writhing and crying out, grinding her sex against its muzzle and spreading her warm moisture all across its face now. All the while, Master thrust into it, his passion pushing him deeper and deeper, putting more pressure on that internal button. Each press against the toy's inside spurred the fervor of its tongue, making Mistress moan and grind harder against the soft muzzle, one paw stroking her breast while another reached down and rubbed vigorously above where its muzzle worked.

Mistress's cry echoed in the basement first amidst the grunts and whinnies of Master's thrust. Grinding and gushing against the toy's muzzle, she filled its mouth with her essence as her body bucked and writhed on the bed to the tide of bliss crashing over her. High pitched wails erupted with every wave between the intense panting as she succumbed to ecstasy and bathed the toy's face in her flow.

The toy lapped against her quivering, swollen lips, tasting as much as it could of Mistress while Master's thrusts grew quicker and quicker, in and out of its tightly gripping tailhole. Soon after Mistress's pleasure began, Master gave a groan from deep within his chest that erupted into a loud neigh, and hot, thick cream flooded the depths of the toy. Wonderful warmth spread and pulsed deep into its belly, making it whimper at all the mingling pleasures of being so used. The toy felt its own satisfaction gather at its center and spurt forth, every inch of its skin tingling as if it were feeling Master and Mistress's orgasms across every nerve in its body. It became lost for a moment and rode the wave, barely noticing the warm stickiness that emptied against its belly as its entire being trembled in absolute bliss.

Then there was stillness. Everything had stopped and the only sound was the panting of three distinct breaths. It couldn't tell how long or how short the stillness lasted, but after a time that stretched and flowed, the toy felt the shrinking shaft slowly pull out of it. Its tailhole slowly constricted again, relieving a discomfort it hadn't even realized was there any more. Mistress moved from the bed out of its line of sight. It could hear them both moving about, and after another moment where it lulled on the cart, it could feel the cuffs at its wrists and ankles being removed. Strong hands tugged at its waist to help it down as more delicate paws helped at its own paws and shoulders to steady the toy.

Master was there in front of it, completely naked now and smiling warmly as it swayed a little on its feet. Mistress was behind, rubbing and helping to steady it as the toy regained its footing. One of those strong hands moved up delicately under the toy's chin and lifted its face up as Master's long face leaned down. The equine lips met the toy's muzzle for a deep, soft kiss. They lingered there, tasting Mistress's flavor on the toy, even as her paws stroked at its shoulders and rubbed gently down its back. The kiss deepened affectionately and the wide tongue pushed gently into the toy's mouth as Master's hand slipped around to cup the back of his toy's head. Suckling passionately at the tongue, the toy wondered if it would now be time to suck Master's cock again. After a long moment, the first kiss ended and the horse pulled his head back to look lovingly at the toy.

"Master, wha—?"

"Terry," the horse said with a smile, "Right now, you call me Terry, Simon."

The cougar blinked and gave his head a little shake, consciousness shifting as Terry drew him in close and held him, softly stroking his back. Without much thought, Simon wrapped his arms around the horse's waist and rested his head against the warm chest. He sighed at how nice it felt to just be held gently against the larger male now, and soon Michelle's softer fur wrapped around him from the other side. Nuzzling his ear as her warm body pressed against his back, her paws gently stroked the side of the cougar's belly.

"Let's all go to the bed," the rabbit's voice came as she petted Simon.

He could feel Terry nodding as they turned and walked him to the bed, Michelle's arm around his waist and the horse's arm across his shoulders. Simon followed easily, slowly coming back to himself as they laid him down between them. For a moment he was confused as this never seemed to be part of the fantasies, but it was incredible all the same.

Terry settled down to one side and gave him another kiss, one hand propping up his head while another rubbed softly over the cougar's side and belly. He could feel Michelle's hands on him from the other side, petting down his fur in long slow strokes. When the kiss broke, Simon felt her gently tugging at him and rolling him over to face her now. Her muzzle softly pressed to his while her paw slipped up to stroke the side of his face. All the while Terry's hands continued to roam over his body, while Simon and Michelle's tongues danced against one another. As they pressed in close around him and as his muzzle parted from hers, Simon soon lay on his back with the two cuddling him tight. He barely felt all the little aches from what had gone before as they lavished affection on him. The pudgy cougar sighed happily and relaxed nestled between the couple.

"How was that for you, Simon?" Terry asked as a hand softly cupped Simon's groin before stroking up his belly again, "Feels like you enjoyed it."

"Oh yes… Terry. You two are incredible."

"Hmm, you were a lot of fun too, Simon," Michelle said with a paw rubbing between his ears. "Definitely nice. So, hon, do I know how to pick 'em?"

Terry laughed and squeezed the cougar gently, "Oh yeah, he's definitely a keeper." He leaned over and kissed Simon again, the cougar responding eagerly. "As long as he's okay with that."

"That mean I'm invited over again?"

The horse nuzzled him. "Oh, definitely. I think I can speak for both of us when I say we really like you, Simon."

"Seconded," Michelle said as her fingers rubbed at his chest. "I hope you'll be around more often."

Sighing, Simon closed his eyes and lay contented in their attention. "I'd love that. Can I ask a question though? Why me?"

"Well, you're cute for one thing," Michelle said as he felt a blush beneath his fur, "And I don't think a sub should strut around. You looked just right, and you seemed like a nice guy."

"That and Michelle knows that I like my guys a bit more cuddly." Grinning, Terry gave the cougar's paunch a loving squeeze and kissed him on the cheek.

Simon couldn't help but purr. "So… what happens next?"

"Well," the horse said, "We snuggle like this for as long as we want, maybe all night. Probably breakfast when the time comes; I could make waffles. Maybe we play some more before we get you to your car. At some point we trade numbers and then we get together when we feel like it for whenever the mood takes us."

He'd never imagined it could be quite like this; it was better than anything he had dreamed to feel so loved and wanted afterwards. "Guess we'll have to really get to know each other."

Terry nodded and nuzzled, then glanced over Simon at his wife. "Dear, I think Simon is the best present ever."

Chuckling and still petting the cougar Michelle leaned over top of him to kiss her husband. "Glad you liked your new toy. Happy Anniversary, darling."

Simon's eyes widened for a moment. Then he just drifted back into their arms and purred long and loud as they held him tight.

Furlough

Furlough
by Mangi

"Okay boss, see you at 3."

The brown wolf hung up the phone, his tail dropping to the floor while he placed his muzzle in his paws. "What's he want now? This is why my work never gets done on time!" He looked up at the clock on the wall, the numbers displaying 2:30.

"What kind of crap is this?" The wolf's ears perked up at the sound. He stood and looked over the cubical wall, seeing his co-worker storming back to his desk. The eagle stopped, his feathers ruffled as he looked at the wolf.

"Charlie! Did you hear?"

"No, and do I even want to?"

"They're making us take an unpaid vacation next week."

"What!" Charlie exclaimed.

"Yeah, he just called you, didn't he?"

"How'd you guess," he said, a smirk of disgust on his face.

"Your face says all; have fun with him, he's in rare form today!"

Charlie slumped back into his chair, ears flattening against his head. "Fuck..." he grumbled under his breath. His eyes darted to the phone as it shrieked again, displaying the name of a client. "Not him again..." he said, his claws scraping the plastic of the handset.

"I swear, he can't open a door without a schematic, much less write a working spec!" He snarled as he looked at the clock again. The wolf's eyes went wide as he realized he was late for his meeting. Spinning quickly in his chair he dashed down the hall to his boss's office. Sheepishly he raised his fist, tapping at the closed door.

"Come in!" barked a voice through the thick door, making Charlie's ears flick. Charlie stepped inside and shut the door, leaning against it for security, his ears flat against his head and eyes locked on a worn spot on the carpet. He whimpered softly, a gentle note of submission as he kept himself meek.

Furlough

The bulldog stood up, ears fully forward and teeth fully bared. "I said 3; and when I say 3, what time do I mean Charlie?" His gruff voice filled the room as he snarled.

Charlie shrank back against the door and he continued to look at the floor. "It means 3, Sir," he whimpered softly as he shuffled his feet on the carpet. "I'm sorry Sir, a client called and it ran later than I expected."

"Sit!" The bulldog growled, his hand roughly indicating a chair sitting next to Charlie.

The wolf immediately sat in the chair. Keeping his paws folded in his lap he looked up towards his boss's muzzle, keeping focused on that rather than on his eyes.

The bulldog picked up a piece of paper. "So the whole company's on furlough next week. Here's your letter from HR making it official. Any questions?"

"No Sir," Charlie murmured, his response almost a whisper as he skimmed the letter, seeing buzz words about bottom lines and maintaining the budget.

"Good, now get back to work!"

Charlie walked back to his desk and read the letter. His ears flattened against his head while his lips pulled back, revealing sharp white teeth. "No money for a week, right when the mortgage is due, this blows." The phone shrieked again. "Oh boy, another one of my favorite clients. What's his problem this time...he can't find the any key?" He picked up the phone, lip curled and his teeth still showing. "How are you Steve, what can I do for you today?"

***

The engine revved on his truck as he pulled into the gravel lot of the Buffalo Bar; his oversized tires spinning and sputtering rocks as he came to a halt. "I really shouldn't spend the money here, but Mike said he'd split the tab," he thought.

The eagle stood out in the crowd as he made his way into the crush of people already there. Pop country music from the loud jukebox in the corner was ringing in Charlie's ears as he got to the high table, a beer waiting for him.

As his third glass of the evening clinked against the heavy tabletop, the wolf took a look around the bar, taking in the other patrons. The initial venting about the day passed, he started to relax.

"Hey Mike, who's the sexy panther over there?" He pointed to a feline at the bar, her tight clothing showing off her slender figure.

"Her? That's Betty; typical feline...thinks more of herself than she's probably worth, but I hear she's a demon in the sack."

The wolf's ears perked up. "Really..maybe I should go find out. See if she can keep up with me."

"Hah! Good luck, I doubt you're her type," said Mike.

Charlie grinned. "Oh yeah? Betcha I'll nail her tonight."

Mike chuckled. "Good luck there buddy. Tell ya what, you nail her and I'll pick up your tab for a month."

Charlie smirked as he surveyed the room around Betty, his eyes resting on an empty barstool to her left. Tail wagging, he moved across the crowded bar, squeezing around tables and patrons, his eye watching her tight gray dress contrasting against her stark black flicking tail. The wolf slid himself quietly into the seat while her back was turned, making a mental note of what she was drinking.

"Hi," he smiled big as he cleared his throat softly, getting her attention.

Betty turned, her golden eyes blinked once before she responded. "Oh, hello there," a sly smirk peered across her face as she looked him over, her eyes resting on his well proportioned torso.

The wolf tried to keep his tail from wagging too much, trying to create his own sense of mystery. "A lady as lovely as you should not be drinking alone. Mind if I buy you another round?" He gestured lightly at the bartender at the other end of the bar.

Betty smirked and her ears flicked in amusement as she lifted her martini to her lips. "Well aren't we being forward? You don't look like the subtle type, so it might be best if you tell me your name before I call the bouncer over here."

A sheepish grin spread across Charlie's muzzle. "My name's Charlie," he raised an eyebrow as he reached a paw out, a smile growing on his face, "and you are?".

"I'm Betty," she reached out and rested her paw on his, the back of her paw facing up towards his muzzle in a silent gesture for him to kiss in greeting.

"Nice to meet you Betty," he closed his paw around hers, shaking it, slightly oblivious to the social cues. "So what brought you here tonight?"

"I'm thinking of leaving soon, too little of interest going on," she absently tossed her head, eyeing the wolf slyly as she looked back at the bartender.

"That's a shame, I was going to buy us another round." His tail wagged faster, breaking the appearance of mystery.

"Did I say I was leaving yet?" She smiled as she gingerly lifted her glass, emptying her drink."

"A martini...neat, right?"

"So you were paying attention after all," she said.

The wolf raised a paw and waved, getting the attention of the bartender. The tiger's ears perked up as Charlie spoke, "another martini for the lady, and a Jack-n-Coke for me please?" He pushed a twenty in the tiger's direction as the drinks came together and were placed in front of him on the worn and polished bar.

Betty smirked. "At least I can get a decent martini here, they're so hard to find lately."

"Yeah, I've heard."

"Uh huh," the panther took another sip of her martini, her brow arched and her tail tip flicking slowly back and forth. "So what do you like to do?"

"I like to watch movies, sports, and you." He leaned forward, looking over his glass, locking his gaze with hers as a smug smile slid across his muzzle.

"Clever," she clicked her tongue as her class clinked against the bar. "Bet you say that to all the ladies."

"Nah," he shook his head slightly, trying to disguise the break in his demure facade. "I just try to be honest," his smile broadened, his tail swaying back and forth comfortably.

"You dogs are all alike, I've heard that one before."

The wolf's tail stopped, dropping back to a relaxed position. "Well can't blame a guy for trying, see you around," Charlie pushed back the stool, got up and and looked towards the door.

"Wait," she reached out, placing her hand gently on the wolf's paw, a smile surfacing.

Charlie's ears flicked as he turned to look at Betty again. "What?"

"You're cute, why don't we go back to my place? I'm sure I can think of something we can do."

***

"Fuck," the panther moaned, her hips twisting and writhing. "Get your tongue in there like a good doggie."

Charlie buried his muzzle between her legs, his tongue lapping at her silken lips. The wolf's thick black claws trailed down her inner thigh, lightly brushing her fur and making her shiver. The feline's musk grew stronger as the tip of his tongue flicked and teased her sweet spot. Charlie's hard cock pressed roughly against the satin sheets, spots of pre spread across the sheets with each taste of her. Pushing his tongue further inside her he greedily lapped at her juices; he winced as her claws dug into his shoulders.

"Yes! Right there! Don't stop!" she yelled, her body continuing to writhe and squirm.

Charlie grabbed her thighs, his tongue continued to push against her inner lips, tail wagging as her tail rapidly brushed over his chest. The wolf let go of one of her thighs and put a paw on her sweet spot; lightly teasing it at first before increasing the pressure. Betty yowled and pushed her hips against his muzzle, her screams now incoherent. With her thighs squeezing Charlie's head, he was thankful they were now blocking out some of the higher pitched yells that were coming from the panther. Without warning, Betty stopped. The wolf's ears perked up as he heard the muffled chorus of a cell phone ringer.

"What the..." Betty said, pushing Charlie's forehead back and sitting up. Reaching for the phone on the nightstand, she flipped it open.

"Hello? Oh hi honey, I thought you were going to call later!" exclaimed Betty. "What? You're at the airport? Home early? Well I'll see you in about half an hour then. Love you too, bye!"

The wolf's jaw dropped. "Wait what? You've got a man?"

"Yeah, I do...you should go. I need to shower before he gets home. Lock the door when you leave."

Betty walked out of the room, leaving Charlie sitting there with a look of confusion on his face. The wolf's ears perked up as the sound of rustling plastic was heard and the sound of running water started up. Sliding off the bed, Charlie fished his scattered clothes off the carpet. He pulled on his shirt and pants, sucking in his stomach so his pants could accommodate his still swollen cock. Charlie exited the bedroom and crossed the living room to the door, unlocking the deadbolt and knob. He turned around and craned his ears forward; he heard the shower still running.

"Bitch, wish I'd listened to Mike," he said as he turned the knob and walked out the door.

***

The moon rose over the houses on a suburban street. The brakes on the truck squealed as Charlie pulled into his driveway. Forcing open the door he stepped down, growling as his claws dug into the door and shoved it closed. The sweat dripped off his matted fur as he jumped up the two steps to his porch. He fished in his jeans for his keys before shoving them into the lock. Throwing the door of his house open he savored the blast of cold air hitting his body and starting to dry him off. He walked inside, tossing his keys on a nearby table before he stomped back towards the bedroom. Charlie pulled the black polo shirt off of his body before tossing it into the hamper. The wolf fell on the bed and lay on the cool sheets as his fur dried under the ceiling fan. Turning on the light, Charlie spotted his laptop on the nightstand and reached for it. He opened the laptop and waited, his paw drumming impatiently. Immediately after the OS booted he launched "Adult Chat" from the desktop. The laptop hummed as it powered on the webcam and mic. Charlie started looking down the list of names on the screen. His tail thumped against the bed as he found the one he was looking for. He tapped the touchpad and it brought up a new screen. A small icon in the corner turned green to indicate he was now connected to her computer.

"Hello Mistress," he said quietly, trying not to sound too eager to hear from her.

A sweet and seductive female voice purred, crackling through the laptop's speakers. "Hello pup, I haven't heard from you in a while. You know better than to ignore your mistress."

Charlie's tail pressed against the bed. "I'm sorry mistress."

"I assume you have a good reason pup," she said.

"Yes Mistress," he said quietly. "Permission to explain my absence Mistress?"

"You may explain pup."

"Work's been kicking my ass lately, and not in a good way." Charlie said. "Nothing I do seems to be good enough for the boss and it's meant late hours. The only thing I've had time for lately is work and going to the gym. It doesn't really matter now Mistress; today they told us that we're furloughed next week; some bullshit about saving money for the company. Never mind that we have bills to pay, ya know?" He stopped himself there and bowed his head, remembering who he was talking to.

There was a pause before Mistress spoke. "Aww you poor pup, is that all?"

"No Mistress. Tonight I picked up this chick at the bar and we went back to her place. We're fooling around, things are getting good...and her phone rings; turns out she has a boyfriend but she wanted some side action while he was not home. Stupid bitch blue-balled me," he growled.

"And now you're here." The sound of laughter came from the speakers. "The pups always come crawling back to me; so what does the puppy need, the usual?"

"Well..."

"Well what pup? Speak!"

Charlie bit his lip. "I...want to try a different scene, with Mistress's permission," he looked downward again, hoping he had not stepped out of line.

"What is the pup thinking of? You can tell Mistress," she cooed.

Charlie described the scene to her as his cock stirred inside its sheath. Rolling over on his side the wolf's paw grazed over the soft fur covering his abs. The wolf unbuttoned and slid his jeans off before rubbing the growing lump in his boxer shorts as they discussed the erotic thoughts drifting throughout his mind and making them into reality. Shutting his eyes, Charlie pictured the scene between he and Mistress unfolding. The wolf's tail thumped harder against the bed. He bit his lip as a paw snuck down the front of his shorts, wrapping itself around his thickening shaft. A moan escaped his lips as his paw freed his cock from its sheath and spread his pre from the tip down to the forming knot. A shrill chime rang out from the laptop's speakers, making Charlie wince from the sound. He opened his eyes and looked at the screen.

"One more thing pup," she said.

"Yes Mistress?"

The tone of voice coming from the laptop became firm. "Starting now, you are ordered not to cum until I say so."

Charlie grimaced, his ears flicking with irritation at the thought of the 'blue balls' he would have later. "But Mistress! I've had such a rough week..."

"Are you questioning me pup? No relief until I say so!"

The wolf sighed. "Yes Mistress."

Ignoring his now painfully throbbing member, Charlie ended the chat and brought up an e-mail program. Typing furiously he fired off a quick e-mail of his schedule to Mistress. He sent it off and shut down the laptop, knowing that she would take care of the rest.

***

Arriving home the next night, Charlie checked his e-mail and found a contract and quote from Mistress. The wolf skimmed over most of the contract since it was the standard stuff he had seen before. He stopped when he reached the newly added clause written in red near the end. It read that Mistress would choose the day and time of the scene during the week of his furlough. Charlie was required to inform her of any changes to his schedule from the one he had e-mailed her. He let out a low whistle as he read Mistress's price; it was more than he expected. He looked over his checking account balance, checking the math several times to make sure this was still going to work.

"Things are going to be tight this month," he sighed before nodding his head, satisfied that everything was correct. Claws tapping against the keyboard, he sent a reply to Mistress and consented to the contract.

The end of the workweek arrived and Charlie could barely sit still in his chair. His eyes would dart over to the clock, watching for 5:00 P.M. He was glad that most of the office decided to take the day off to start their forced vacation early; otherwise his co-workers might have wondered why he was wiggling so much. Reaching the end of the day he shut down his computer and ran for the door, tail wagging the whole way. The tires of his truck squealed as he pushed the accelerator to the floor and raced out of the parking lot. The wolf spent extra time doing cardio at the gym, pushing himself until the muscles in his legs trembled. After a long hot shower at home, the wolf collapsed on the bed, utterly exhausted, his ears drooping as his breathing slowed before falling fast asleep. Charlie was glad this week was finally over. Work sucked, he didn't get laid, and this furlough was not going to help him financially. However, for the next week, he didn't have to be Charlie...

***

The wolf walked towards the cubicle at the far end of the room. With a thud he dropped a brown leather briefcase on the desk before pressing the power button to boot up his computer. He settled into the chair as the monitor in front of him lit up with the login screen for Tungsten Aerospace. A few taps on the keyboard and the OS started to load, the computer furiously clicking as messages flashed past the screen.

"Jason? Oh good, you're here," a soft female voice said.

Jason turned around and looked up. An arctic fox stood there, holding a file folder against her blouse with a smile on her face.

"Hi Claudia, can I help you with something?" he said.

"No, just dropping by to see if we're doing lunch today."

"I'll be there, unless I get dragged into a meeting. Meet you at the usual place?"

"Sure, see you then," she said.

Claudia turned around to leave, walking down the hallway as Jason watched her tail swish back and forth, contrasting against the black skirt she wore.

"Nice vixen, I'd love to get a piece of that," the wolf whispered under his breath as he turned back to his computer. The screech of an alarm made Jason wince while he covered his ears.

***

Furlough

Jason opened his eyes to find himself staring at his bedroom walls, still holding his ears. The screeching of the nearby alarm clock continued before he slammed his paw on the snooze button.

"Stupid alarm clock, forgot to turn it off," he muttered. As the first rays of dawn crept across the ceiling, Jason reflected on the last few months.

"I can't wait until I'm done with this project, hate it." he said to the empty air.

The wolf was working on a special project at Tungsten Aerospace, code-named "Darius." His managers claimed they were going to blow the competition out of the water with the enhancements he had made. However, working on Project Darius was getting to him. The last few weeks of trying to prepare the project for a production prototype meant he was working 60 hours a week. An alarm clock didn't survive very long after being slammed or thrown across the room repeatedly. The ringing of his work phone was met with a growl before being answered. Some of his co-workers mentioned that he looked stressed. Fed up, he went to the project managers and managed to wrestle some time off to recuperate. Unfortunately they forbid him to leave town because he was considered essential, but he felt they had another reason. Rumors suggested, though nobody in Tungsten's upper management would confirm it, that Tungsten workers had been targeted by other corporations and the governments of a few rogue states in order to try to steal information. Jason laughed when people talked about those rumors. He figured that no one cared enough to target him.

Jason spent a few days around the house catching up on some personal projects. For the wolf it was glorious to get a full night's sleep and not hear the phone ring once. However, the novelty soon wore off and Jason found that he was bored. Besides boredom, he had this odd feeling he was being watched when he would walk outside the front door. He shook it off, obviously the paranoia of the upper management was seeping into his brain.

Wednesday morning found Jason yelling at the trashy talk show guests on TV. When the show was over he realized he needed to get out of the house and do something, anything, just not at home. He paced the living room as he tried to figure out what he could do that was halfway decent in town. He looked up and saw the beer poster on the wall, making his ears perk up. The wolf wanted to smack himself for not coming up with this idea before. Tonight would be a night to head to the Buffalo Bar to shoot some pool and have a few beers. He thought that he wouldn't be the only one interested in a night out; maybe someone from Tungsten would be interested in joining him, and he knew just the fox to ask. He sat down at his computer, tail wagging furiously as he banged out a quick e-mail to her.

Claudia,

How's things at the office? The vacation is nice but it sucks that the idiot managers told me I wasn't allowed to leave town. I'll be glad when things finally calm down with this stupid project and I can have a life again. The house looks nice and all, but I'm sick of looking at these walls. I need to get out for a bit so I'm going to go shoot some pool tonight at the Buffalo Bar. If you're not busy, you should drop by.

Jason

An hour later, he heard a chime from his computer speakers. Running to his desk he opened his e-mail to find a reply from Claudia:

Hey Jason,

I'm sorry but I have some prior plans. Thanks for thinking of me anyway and have fun tonight!

Claudia

Jason sighed and his ears drooped, betraying his disappointment. A lack of Claudia wasn't going to stop him from going though. That evening he pulled on a pair of blue jeans, black motorcycle boots, and a tight white t-shirt that showed off his chest and abs. Arriving at the nearby watering hole, Jason found that it was crowded for a weeknight. Most of the folks there were busy watching the hockey game on a large flat-screen TV placed at each end of the bar. Most of them had to stand as the few tables and stools around them were occupied. Ducking and weaving through the crowd Jason spotted the two pool tables that sat behind the bar. One had a game between two gray wolves that was just being set up; the other between a bear and a ferret that looked like it was almost done, with the ferret having the upper hand. There was a chalkboard up against the wall for folks to sign up to play. Jason didn't have to wait long for the next game after he signed his name on the board, now going up against the ferret.

Furlough

The wolf had a better night than he usually did, winning four of the five games he played. The last game was up against one of the wolves. Thanks to a lucky bank shot, he avoided hitting his opponent's striped ball before it knocked the 8-ball into the center pocket. Jason decided he needed a victory beer after getting that win. He strode over to the bar and raised his paw to catch the bartenders attention before hearing a voice behind him.

"Hello there handsome."

He turned and found himself staring into the greenest eyes he'd ever seen. He averted his gaze and lowered his ears, so as not to seem challenging or intimidating. The owner of those eyes was a tall, slender female wolf with fur that was such a light shade of gray that it bordered on white. The fur made her eyes seem that much more like tiny emeralds. He looked her over, his mind automatically taking note of her curves. He felt a little tingle of excitement between his legs.

"Were you talking to me," he said, tail twitching.

"Well, you're the only handsome guy I see here, so I'd say I was talking to you," she said.

A smile spread across Jason's face. "I'm Jason," he reached out a paw toward her, "and you are?"

The wolf gripped Jason's paw and shook it gently. "I'm Lana, it's nice to meet you Jason."

"It's nice to meet you too; can I buy a drink for a pretty lady such as yourself?"

A small smile crept across Lana's face. "That's sweet, but I'm being a good girl this evening...though I could always buy you a drink," she winked.

"Sure," Jason smiled. They got their drinks and went to find a table. There was a low table nearby that wasn't crowded with empty beer bottles left by other patrons so they settled into the slightly wobbly chairs. Jason took a swig of beer, the bottle clinking against the tabletop before he spoke. "So I haven't seen you before, are you new here?"

"Yes, I moved here a few months ago for work. Now I'm all settled in so I can finally have some fun." Her tail wagged as her claw absent-mindedly traced the grooves in the table.

Jason chuckled. "Well this is about it for fun on a Wednesday night. What kind of work do you do?"

Lana smiled. "I'm an administrative assistant."

They continued to make small talk and she bought him another beer. The hockey game ended and most of the other patrons left the bar. Jason glanced around and noticed that save for the bartender and a tiger and a fox sitting at the bar, he and Lana were the only other people there. The wolf decided to see if Lana wanted to head elsewhere or just call it a night. He stood up and put his paws on the table to steady himself as his head began to swim.

Slurring a bit Jason said, "Wow, it's late and I don't feel so hot, maybe I should call a taxi."

Lana looked at him with worry. "You look really tired, why don't I call a taxi for you?"

"Sure. I'm sorry to put you through this. I didn't expect that last beer to hit me so hard."

"Don't worry, it happens to everyone."

Lana pulled out her cell phone while Jason closed his eyes, trying to make the room stop spinning. The wolf sat down and leaned his head against the wall, resting against the cool wood. There was a tap on his shoulder.

"Come on, your taxi is here," said Lana.

Jason stood up and gripped Lana's shoulder as the two made their way to the exit. He saw a large silver sedan with the motor running and someone sitting inside. Lana brought him towards it and he saw the trunk pop open.

"Wait a minute, when did they get a silver taxi cab? Where's the company name?" he slurred.

Lana shook her head and chuckled. "Damn you're drunk. Here, we'll help you get in," she said.

His eyes went wide as he stared at Lana. "We?"

Hearing the sound of a car door opening, Jason turned to see the driver get out of the car and start to walk around the front towards him. His vision went black as something touched his muzzle and was pulled back, covering his eyes. It grew tight around his skull and the wolf reached out in front of him.

"Lana? Is this some kind of joke? It's not funny!"

Furlough

A pair of paws grabbed Jason's wrists and squeezed tight, making Jason nearly yelp from the pain. He tried to pull his wrists out before another set of paws grabbed his ankles and lifted him up. The wolf struggled weakly against whomever was holding him before he was lifted higher and then placed on something solid. The mystery paws pushed Jason's paws and feet further back and then he heard the slam of a car trunk. Jason banged his fist a few times against the trunk lid.

"Let me out of here! Help! Help!"

He continued to bang on the trunk lid, each hit growing weaker as his mind became hazy. His eyelids drooped as he lost consciousness; the last thing he heard was the engine revving.

***

"Wake up!" a voice screamed in Jason's ear, followed by an ice cold liquid being thrown in his face. The wolf snorted and shook his head to dry his fur, shivering as some of the liquid dripped down his sides and chest. He opened his eyes, but he couldn't see a thing! There was a now damp and clammy blindfold sticking to his head.

"What the hell?" he yelled.

Jason took a deep breath and the scent of menthol filled his nostrils. It reminded him of the medicine he had to use when his muzzle would inevitably get stuffed up during the winter. He tried to reach up to remove the blindfold but his arms remained firmly planted at his sides. The fur on his legs tickled his paw pads; clearly he was no longer wearing pants.

"Where are my clothes? Where the hell am I?"

Jason tried to shift his body and found that he couldn't move. He was held fast to a very hard surface. He turned his head downwards and ended up bumping his nose into something hard and rough at his shoulder. The wolf craned his neck as far as it could reach; his nose bumping more of these rough things. Jason's fingers reached up and were able to grab on to something that felt like rope, similar to a piece of clothesline. He tugged sharply on but it refused to budge. Jason's mind raced as he tried to remember what happened before he was awoken with the cold liquid in his face.

"What is this? Lana, are you there? Why the hell am I tied down?"

Jason's ears turned forward, listening for any sound, but he didn't hear anything. He turned them outward and caught the low sound of someone breathing on his right.

"Look, whoever you are, I know you're there. What do you want from me," he yelled.

A chuckle came a few feet away from Jason. "What do I want? Not much really," a sensual female voice said.

The wolf tilted his head, displaying a look of confusion. "Who are you? Are you one of those nuts who like to pick up guys at bars and torture them?"

Harsh laughter filled his ears. "You read way too many stories on the Internet. You're here because I know you work on Project Darius for Tungsten Aerospace. I hear it's quite a remarkable thing. There are those of us who would do anything," the wolf felt a claw under his chin, "to find out what you're up to," she said.

Jason's eyebrows shot upward; he knew he had heard that voice before, but he couldn't place it. A soft, feminine paw rested on his chest.

"Come now Jason, be a good boy and just tell me about it. I'll let you go, I promise." She brushed her paw over his nipple. He gasped, the velvety soft paw pad sending a twinge of pleasure from his chest down to his sheath.

The wolf shook his head. "Really lady, I don't know what you're talking about."

There was more laughter from the voice. "Lady? You mean you haven't figured out who this is? Sheesh you're thick-headed...and I don't mean the one between your legs."

A look of horror crossed Jason's face. "Claudia?"

"The one and only!"

"You, of all people...why?"

Her paw rested on his shoulder. "I'll say it again, you have something I want."

The wolf struggled against the ropes, grunting as he tried to break free, but they continued to hold firm.

"You can't have it!"

"Yes I can," her voice became much more firm. "I know all about you, and I don't take no for an answer."

"You bitch!" he snarled.

Jason yelped as pain shot through his chest from Claudia pinching his nipples. He wiggled under her grasp, trying to get away. He thought his nipples were burning as she pinched harder and harder.

"I'll show you what a bitch can do," Claudia growled.

"Ow! Okay! I'm sorry, I'm sorry, I didn't mean it, please let go Claudia! I won't say it again!"

Relief washed over the wolf as she let his nipples go. The burning feeling returned as his nipples were pinched again, this time by something rather cold.

"Dammit I said I was sorry!"

"You were out of control Jason, we can't have that. I'll check in on you later to see if you have a grip on yourself."

Jason heard her walking away and he turned his head in her direction, then the sound of a door opening and slamming shut, making him wince. He sighed, cursing that he had gotten himself into such a mess. Gripping a rope, the wolf pushed himself upward to see if he could slide off the table. The sudden tug and pain on his nipples caught him by surprise. He moved his right shoulder, it tugged on his right nipple; the left shoulder, left nipple. Jason furrowed his brow in frustration; whatever clamps Claudia had put on him, they wouldn't let him move without making it painful.

"Grrrrrr, so this is how she's trying to keep me under control," he muttered.

The wolf kept still, breathing slowly to keep calm. His ears rotated as far as they could go, trying to catch any sounds that might clue him in on where he was, but he heard nothing. The thick smell of the menthol medicine continued to fill his nostrils, masking any nearby scents. As the wolf stared into the blackness of the blindfold, his mind began to wander. It filled with distant memories of how he and Claudia became fast friends. They often shared private lunches together; there was even the time she brought him coffee when Tungsten made him pull yet another all-nighter. Without thinking about it the wolf stretched his legs, his heels pushing him up the length of the table. The sudden pain from the clamps brought him crashing back to the harsh reality of his current situation. Jason moaned as a wave of pleasure reached his groin.

"Too bad I can't rub one out right now, I wouldn't want Claudia to see me like this." Jason subtly moved, letting the clamps send more pleasurable feelings towards his swelling member as it continued to slide out of his sheath and into the open. The seductive image of the arctic fox danced through his thoughts as he remembered the snug-fitting outfits she would wear to the office; the moments where he would try not to look as she leaned too far over his desk, exposing her generous cleavage to him. The wolf dozed lightly, dreaming of taking Claudia to his bed.

"Enjoying yourself?"

Jason snorted in surprise. "Claudia! When did you..."

"Oh I've only just walked in. Someone was having a nice dream," she brushed a paw over his hard cock.

Jason's ears flattened against his head. "What do you want?"

"Well Jason, you're finally calm, so let's talk." Her claws brushed back and forth over a spot on his inner thigh. "You're a good guy; I was reluctant to bring you in like this, but my employer is growing impatient. They want information and they want it now." The wolf heard the buzz of a motor underneath him and the clank of metal on metal as he went from upright to flat on his back. A weight settled on Jason's groin as a warm feeling spread over his member. The scent of the fox's arousal came through the menthol. Claudia's paws rested on his chest, her claws pressing into his skin.

Sliding herself over his shaft she continued. "How about we help one another out? You like me Jason, and I like you as well. Tell me what Project Darius is all about, and I'll let you go and make sure you don't get into any trouble over this?"

Jason's heavy breathing slowed as he raised an eyebrow. "Claudia, are you nuts? Tungsten would find out...I'd be toast. I can't!"

"Awww, Jason, please?" she said. "I promise you'd be okay."

"I can't...it's wrong," he panted a few times before letting out a soft howl of pleasure.

"I thought you'd be more fun about this," Claudia's paws lightly scratched the sides of his ribcage.

The wolf's moans gave way to a giggle as he tried to get away from the tickling sensation on his ribs. "Claudia, what are you doing?"

Furlough

"I'm not doing anything," Her paws scratched faster and moved down his sides.

The wolf laughed and wiggled around in the ropes as the arctic fox's claws darted over his skin, moving down to his hips before sliding up to rest and tickle under his arms. Jason began gasping as he laughed harder, his tail lashing against his legs. He squirmed as his body was wracked with sensation after sensation, his breaths growing even shorter as he thought his head was going to float away.

"Claudia...I can't take much more of this. Please... stop."

The warmth and pressure was suddenly removed from his groin as she climbed off the table. "I thought we were having so much fun! It seems Mr. Happy here is having a good time." He groaned as she grabbed his cock. Squeezing it, she smeared pre in her paw before spreading it down his shaft. "I can finish what we started, if you just tell me what I want to know."

"No way. I know how this goes, I tell you the information, but instead of getting me off, you tie me up and throw me out on to a street somewhere."

The fox let go of the wolf's dick. "You don't trust me to keep my word? Suit yourself then."

Jason felt the pinch of the nipple clamps grow tighter, ratcheting up the pain. "Maybe this will persuade you," she said.

The door shut again and Jason cursed. His rock hard erection showed no signs of going away. "Bitch," he muttered. "I don't know what I can tell her, if anything." His cock throbbed, painful now from being aroused for so long. Jason tried to take his mind off of the throbbing, hoping it would subside, but as soon as he started to relax, he'd move and his nipples would telegraph a bolt of arousal downward. The door opened again and he heard the sound of a cart being wheeled towards him.

"Back so soon?" He said.

"Since you're being so stubborn, I'm going to have to resort to other methods to get you to talk," said Claudia.

Jason snorted and his nose twitched as a towel rubbed his nose. He took a deep sniff, glad to be free of the menthol scent. Then the wolf felt something shoved onto his muzzle, an acrid smell filling his nose. He jerked his head, trying to shake it off of him.

"Oh don't worry Jason," Claudia said. "It's not lethal; just something to make you relax."

The wolf tried to hold his breath and continue to shake the mask off of him, but it was no use. His lungs bursting with pain, he finally took a breath of the gas. Instantly he felt woozy, like all of the tension in his muscles was draining off the table and on to the floor. His breathing slowed and his head drooped as the mask was removed.

"Jason," Claudia's voice echoed in his head. "Jason, can you hear me?"

"Yes," Jason mumbled.

"How do you feel," she asked.

"Sore...but so good," he moaned.

"You like this huh? I could give you more..."

Jason shuddered. "Please..." he shivered as the fox's claws brushed over the head of his cock. Jason gasped and writhed when a paw gripped his ball sack and gave them a tug. It was quickly replaced by several spots being pinched. The wolf moaned and groaned in pain, but he didn't want it to end. The feeling of being woozy was now gone; in its place was a heightened euphoria from the pain and pleasure flowing throughout his body. He heard Claudia speak again,

"What do you know about Project Darius?"

"I...I...just can't tell you...Yeouch!"

A wave of pain traveled through Jason's ear as Claudia pinched it with her claws. After a moment she let go and the wolf's ear flicked a few times.

"Focus Jason, are you ready to tell me about Project Darius? This is your last chance."

He shook his head. "Claudia, I won't tell you and that's final."

"Then you leave me no choice. I'm going to have to take this to the next level...shaving."

"You wouldn't dare!"

The wolf heard the motor start up again as his head moved upward until he was vertical. His ears perked up, hearing the sound of something scraping against leather. A sinking feeling developed in his stomach. He took a deep breath and paused, before he growled,

"You don't have the guts to shave me."

"Try me," Claudia said.

The scraping continued for another minute before he heard the sound of something metallic being set down nearby. He gasped as a warm, wet sensation surrounded his balls.

"Ouch!" Jason yelped as a tight band was fastened around the top of his sack. Claudia's paw rested on his knot.

"One more time, tell me about Project Darius, or I will shave you."

"Never!"

Jason felt a tug on his sack as Claudia pulled down. He tensed up, the fur on his arms fluffing out, waiting for her to pull harder. When she didn't he let out a sigh of relief. What he didn't expect was cold metal being placed against his sack and drawn downward. The cool sensation of air hitting bare skin rushed through him from where the metal had just been.

"Claudia! What the fuck are you doing?" He pushed against the table, ignoring the pain of the clamps on his chest as he tried to slide out of the ropes.

"I warned you, now don't thrash or you will be neutered. This straight razor is very sharp."

Jason stopped, trembling and letting out a soft whimper. His ears fell flat against his head while the fox continued to shave the fur off of his balls, removing most of it in just a few strokes. Then a clink of metal on metal reached his ears, followed by the sound splashing of water before he felt her now-wet paws running over his sheath.

Jason struggled against the ropes again. "No, don't! Please don't shave any more! Do you know what the guys would say? Hell, no lady wants their guy to be shaved. I could never show my face anywhere again!" he cried.

"That's not my problem," she said. He heard the tap of metal on metal.

Jason went from trembling to shaking as his breathing became ragged and he started to sob. "Please stop. I can't take any more," he begged.

"You know how to make it stop."

Tears began to roll down Jason's muzzle. "All right Claudia, you've beaten me and there's nothing I can do or hold back. I'll tell you about Project Darius."

A paw caressed the wolf's chin. "Go on then."

The fox listened as Jason told her everything he knew about Project Darius, what it would do, the interest of the military in the project, the current status, everything that he could think of. By the time he was done he slumped forward, letting his head hang down.

Claudia took his head in her paws and said to him. "There now, that wasn't so hard, was it?"

"It doesn't matter anymore, I'm going to be nothing after they find out and fire me."

She kissed his nose and his sobs grew quiet. "Now as I promised, I'll make sure you don't get into any sort of trouble for telling me about Project Darius."

"Really?"

"Yes, really," she said.

Her claws trailed over his swollen member. "It looks like I can finish what we started. Would you like that? I know you've wanted me for a long time."

Jason's ears perked up despite a few tears that continued to slide down his muzzle. "You're lying. I'm nothing to you."

The fox kissed the wolf's forehead. "I'll prove you wrong, but you gotta knock off the tears."

He sniffed. "All right."

Claudia's paws trailed down Jason's arms as he felt her warm breath traveling over the head and down the shaft of his cock. He shivered as his member began to tingle before the fox's tongue slid along the underside of his shaft, tasting every bit of pre-cum that had flowed down earlier.

"Use me, I'm nothing but a conquest now," the wolf moaned as he leaned his head against the hard surface.

Gripping his knot in one paw, Claudia held his cock steady as she took it into her mouth. Jason gasped as the head slid over her soft tongue before reaching the back of her throat. She paused for what felt like an eternity before sliding his cock back to the front of her mouth. The tip of her tongue traced the outline of the head and flicked over the underside a few times, making it jump and tap the roof of her mouth. Her muzzle slid down his cock again, this time a soft howl coming from Jason as his member reached her throat and continued. The fox attempted to swallow his cock, making her throat squeeze and draw more pre out of him. Jason tried to push his cock further down her throat, gripping the ropes and pulling as he started to pant. Making only small movements with her head, Claudia held his cock in her throat, her nose occasionally bumping the top of his knot.

"You're amazing," he gasped as Claudia slowly pulled her muzzle away from him. "Wait, you can't be..."

Jason yelped, not expecting the fox's tongue on the now-exposed skin of his sack. His tail tapped against his legs as her tongue explored the now-smooth skin. Claudia wrapped a paw around his shaft and started to stroke him as she flicked the skin with her tongue. Her paw grew slick with pre, making her tighten her grip and increase her speed. Jason could do nothing but whine and howl at the pleasurable feelings in his groin that continued to increase. He noticed a pressure beginning to build up in his knot, a sign he wouldn't be able to hold back much longer if Claudia kept this up.

"Claudia, I don't think I can hold back," he panted. "Make me cum Claudia...please...make me cum."

Claudia shortened her strokes to concentrate on the head of Jason's cock. Grabbing the band at the top of his sack, she pulled it off of his balls, the moment of pain disappearing under the waves of pleasure that continued to travel throughout the wolf's body.

"Come on Jason, you know you can do it, be a good boy and cum for me. Come on stud."

Jason could barely hear her over the growl that was now passing between his clenched teeth. His body grew taut as his climax grew closer. The wolf's fists pounded against the hard wood of the table while his growls grew louder. The ropes strained to hold him down as he thrust against them. The growls gave way to gasps and a series of howls while he teetered on the edge of climaxing. Jason's member started to throb hard in Claudia's paw before the first spurts of cum shot out from the tip of his cock, sailing in a long arc to land several feet away on the floor. A long and loud howl sounded from the wolf's throat while his cock continued to gush cum, leaving streaks of white on the floor. Claudia let go as the throbbing began to slow down and Jason's howling came to an end. He slumped forward against the ropes, head down, his feet hanging limp and a few last drops of cum dripping lazily from the end of his now-spent member. As his breathing slowed and his mind grew hazy, Jason heard the buzz of a

motor and metal clanking as he floated backward into a horizontal position before he fell into a deep sleep.

***

Yawning and opening his eyes, Charlie was greeted with the sight of a wooden ceiling he did not recognize. He sat bolt upright and looked around, spotting familiar chains fastened to brick walls and a shelf with various equipment, he remembered where he was, Mistress's dungeon. Looking down he saw just what he had been laying on for the previous day, a new bondage table. He took a closer look at it, noticing the hooks arranged around him in a silhouette of a person, allowing Mistress to string a rope back and forth to tie him down. He hopped off the table as the door behind him opened. A voluptuous female red fox wearing a tank top and shorts that left nothing to the imagination stepped into the room, a smirk on her face.

"Good morning pup. Did you sleep well?"

"Yes Mistress," Charlie said, his tail wagging. "Was I a good pup for our scene Mistress?"

"You were a very good pup. You surprised me though; you've never passed out from a scene before."

Charlie looked down on the floor, ears drooping and displaying his submission. "I'm sorry Mistress."

Mistress patted his head. "I'll forgive you this time pup."

The wolf looked up at Mistress, a small smile on his face. "Thank you Mistress...permission to make a comment Mistress?"

"Permission granted pup"

"I like that bondage table."

Mistress's smirk grew wider, "Thank you pup. You have the honor of being the first I've used it on. Think you'll use it again?"

"Where do I sign up?"

Mistress laughed as she led him to the bathroom where he took a long hot shower. As the wolf grabbed a towel and started to dry himself, he looked down and saw his freshly shaved groin. Laughing he said. "Looks like I won't be changing my clothes at the gym for a while."

He stepped back out of the bathroom to find Mistress waiting for him. On the table next to the door was a folded white T-shirt and blue jeans along with a wallet, keys and cell phone in one paw. Her other paw held a pair of black motorcycle boots.

"Thank you Mistress," he said before getting dressed and following her upstairs to the living room.

"When we captured you, I went back and got your truck, you should find it out front."

"Permission to ask a question Mistress?" he said.

"You may ask me a question pup."

"Who was Lana?"

Mistress chuckled. "She's a dominatrix apprentice I started training recently, I sent her out to see if she could seduce you in the bar. Obviously she's learned well since the capture itself went off without a hitch. I also had her watch our scene and lend me a hand. She was impressed with you."

"Well, she is quite beautiful and charming Mistress."

"I could let her know you said that," Mistress then handed him a piece of paper, "but I bet you'd rather tell her that in person. She's taken a liking to you; I have given her permission to see you this weekend, but she has to be on her best behavior, and you had better treat her well, okay pup?" The fox raised an eyebrow and her ears pointed forward, displaying her seriousness.

Charlie looked down so as not to seem challenging. "Understood Mistress. Thank you Mistress."

"No, thank you Pup."

The wolf tried not to grumble as he filled out and signed the check. He smirked at the name on the pay to line. "*Divine Dreams LLC.*"

"Here Mistress, as per our contract...I included a tip for Lana if that pleases Mistress," he said.

"Thank you pup, it will please both of us. " she said.

"I'll see you again soon Mistress."

Mistress smirked. "I hope so, but no freebies just because Lana likes you," she winked.

Charlie strode down the front walkway while checking his phone. It told him that it was now 9 AM on Friday, which explained why he was starving. Unlocking his truck he pulled the door open and slid onto the leather seat. A chuckle started before evolving into deep laughter. Charlie never thought a forced furlough would be so much fun. As he drove away he looked back to Mistress's house, knowing he would see it again very soon.

Breaking In
by Sparf

"Mikulski! Get in here, now!"

The boss's voice thundered through the office like the sound of an oncoming train. Alan cringed, flattening his ears tightly against his skull. He'd screwed up somehow. Again. Shaking just a little, he stood up from his chair and made his way past the other cubicles to the boss's office at the end of the large work floor with his tail held low and tight. He fought the natural urge to tuck it completely between his legs in order to maintain some semblance of his dignity. It didn't really help. He had a slight frame and narrow shoulders, and was only five-foot-six at a stretch. All in all, he looked like a large walking stuffed toy that a child would cuddle with.

He adjusted his check-patterned tie twice as he approached the boss's door. Mr. Simmons stood inside. While he was a wolf like Alan, that's where the similarities ended. Where Alan was young and nervous, Mr. Simmons had a touch of grey around his muzzle and an aura of confidence. Alan was scrawny—the definite runt of the litter, Mr. Simmons was tall and fit. Mr. Simmons's jaw was set, ears forward, and tail held high. His eyes met and challenged Alan's. Alan gulped and stared down at the floor.

"Inside. Now."

"Yes sir." Alan slunk inside. Simmons pushed the door closed with a loud thunk that rang in Alan's ears. He could feel Mr. Simmons's eyes watching him, even before the boss lowered himself silently into his office chair.

"Take a seat."

The chair was a wooden frame with some cloth that was intended to pass for cushioning, but instead made Alan think of a courtroom. The office was sparely decorated. A picture of Mr. Simmons and what Alan assumed were his wife and two young cubs was sitting on the desk. In the photo, Mr. Simmons was dressed in cargo shorts and a red, loose shirt with white flowers printed on it, which contrasted with the dark gray of his fur. He had wondered what Simmons's powerful build might look like without the iron-maiden of the business suit which he always wore. But of course he would be well-built. He had money and time to hit the gym, or play golf, or any of the other pastimes that middle-management filled their days with.. Alan barely had enough energy after work to drag himself upstairs to his apartment. His wife had the look of a woman who knew she was going to be neglected in favor of her husband's work, and the two cubs sat at the couple's feet, playing.

"Mikulski, what in the hell do we pay you for?" The boss's eyes challenged again. Again, Alan looked away, ashamed, cowed, age-old instincts kicking in. "Did we or did we not just discuss the changes that I wanted made in the new automation control module?"

Alan opened his mouth to answer, but his voice cracked. He squeezed his eyes shut for a moment, took a breath, and started again. "We did, sir. And I put them in-"

"If you put the design changes in, then why did I log onto the server today, only to download a compiled final version with at least half of them missing?" Mr. Simmons brought his hand down on his desktop sharply for emphasis. "Here is the list I sent you," he said, holding up a stapled sheet of paper with a long list of bullet points, "And here," he flipped the page to the second sheet, which was marked up in red pen, like a poorly written English paper, "are all the items that were left undone."

Alan's mind raced. He'd done everything on that list. He had stayed at least an hour late to get it done, every night, for two weeks. What was Mr. Simmons talking about? He felt his face flushing red in frustration. No, there was absolutely no way he had not finished that list. He had done it all, then compiled the software and...

Oh no. No no no no no.

The memory flashed into his mind, like a lightning strike to a tall tree. He remembered the night he'd finished the project, accidentally opening an earlier revision. The auto-save feature must have overwritten his newer work with it!

"Mr. Simmons, I...I'm-"

"Save it, Mikulski. You've put us seriously behind schedule. The only apology I want from you is the one where, by the end of the day today, you hand me a completed project, with all the revisions I asked for. If I don't have that, then you might as well pack up your desk before you leave for the day. Am I clear?" Alan imagined that he could see the larger wolf's muscles rippling with tension along his shoulders and neck, beneath the shirt. There was the scent of annoyance and command thick in the air of the office, layered with something else. Alan left without knowing what it was. It was noon now. He had five hours to finish or he would have no job.

"Yes sir," he squeaked.

Mr. Simmons's hard yellow eyes burned into his back as he turned and left the office. He was sure he could feel them for the entire walk back to his desk. There was that creeping sensation that if he turned back, he'd still be able to see them glaring at him even through the wall and the intervening cubicles. He wanted to cry.

The office chair complained as he sat down, creaking as it settled into position. Alan quickly entered his login credentials and began searching the server for the incremental backups that he'd made of his progress. The wolf had a sick feeling in the pit of his stomach that told him if he didn't find them, there would be no way he'd be able to re-implement all of the new features before five o'clock.

Alan nearly leaped out of his fur as a loud thunk sounded from his desk. He spun and saw Mr. Simmons striding away. He walked a yard at a time, with his fists clenched as if he were going to hit someone. Alan looked down at the source of the sound, and the sick feeling in his stomach intensified. It was a corrugated plastic box, the kind that security used to load people's personal belongings when they were being escorted out of the building. He hopped back into his chair and began searching for those backups.

"No... No... No..." he mumbled as he scrolled through each of countless folders labeled with numbers and timestamps, but none of them contained the project files he needed. He folded his arms, digging his nails into the muscles of his upper arms in frustration. Alan rubbed his eyes, on the verge of giving up hope and just coding as fast as he could, and hoping that he'd be fast enough, when a folder caught his eye.

"ID10T," he read, and smiled, clicking into the folder. There he found a listing of backups that reached all the way through the middle of the previous week. He cursed himself for not remembering making a manual backup. It wasn't complete, but it was a start. Alan cracked his knuckles and started to work.

***

At 4:54, the compiler finished its cycle with a pop up message which simply said, "Compile Successful. Upload? Y/N" Alan's tail wagged furiously, knocking some loose papers from their haphazard perch, along with a Captain Lupine action figure which clacked as it hit the carpeted floor. Unconcerned, he clicked Yes and watched the progress bar on his screen scroll from zero to one-hundred percent.

"Well, Mikulski? Where's my module?" Mr. Simmons was standing stiffly against the cubicle entryway. He looked every bit as tense and as uptight as he had been when he had come into the office this morning. He hadn't even loosened his tie, as most of the office's other employees tended to do as the day wore on.

Alan smiled, suppressing his wagging tail. "Actually sir, I just finished the upload. Ahead of deadline, even." The pride in his achievement was easily audible in his voice. Mr. Simmons didn't seem to share the smaller wolf's enthusiasm. He nodded with curt satisfaction, picked up the box he had left earlier, and turned on his heel, leaving Alan alone again with his thoughts. That was likely all the recognition that he was going to get for his success.

Alan drooped and slumped down in his chair, but noted, with some sense of relief, that the boss had taken the box away with him. Since he'd said nothing, Alan was going to assume that he was still employed. The thought of facing Mr. Simmons again today, even to ask if he still had a job, was more than Alan wanted to entertain. Instead, he quietly picked up the papers and figures his tail had knocked over, and closed up his briefcase. He logged off of his computer,glanced around at the various figurines and knickknacks that he kept around his cubicle as a mood lifter then he turned around and started walking for the elevator.

Because of the delay with Mr. Simmons, he was leaving at the same time as just about everyone else on the floor. By the time he reached the elevator doors, there was no room left for him inside the packed car.

"Alan! Hey, Alan," a voice shouted from the other side of the throng of outgoing office employees waiting for the world's slowest elevator

The wolf peered through the mass of people and spotted the source of the voice. A red fox waved excitedly at Alan. He squeezed and 'excuse-me'd' his way through the group until he reached the wolf. He wore a fashionably cut designer suit, dark gray with faint pink pinstripes, and a patterned tie, black with swirling fuchsia lines climbing up it like the world's most fabulous creeper vine.

"Hey, Casey," Alan said, with as much of a smile as he could muster.

"Missed you at lunch today," the fox said warmly, clapping a hand on Alan's shoulder.

"Yeah, Mr. Simmons was about to fire me for a screw-up I pulled, so I worked straight through until just a few minutes ago to fix it," Alan's ears pinned themselves back and his tail tucked slightly between his legs.

Casey narrowed his eyes and the grin vanished from his muzzle. "Did he yell at you again?"

Alan was silent.

"I knew it. He's a prick. I should get him fired. I know a thing or two that HR might want to be informed of," the fox said, lowering his voice. A soft growl escaped his throat.

"No, don't," Alan said, "You'll only get me in trouble, or yourself, or just make him mad. "

The wolf's tail fluffed up and he looked hurriedly around to see if anyone had heard. He lowered his voice. "I just want him to respect me. Maybe it'll come with more time."

The fox grinned, "All right, all right, I know, respect your friend's wishes and all that."

Alan smiled. "You still up for tonight? I've been waiting for the chance to go for months!"

"Yeah, I'm still up for it," Casey said. I will pick you up from your apartment later, okay?"

"Yeah. See you around 9?"

"Wouldn't miss it! I think you're really going to have a good time. I know just who to take you to see," said the fox as he turned to continue waiting for the elevator. The crowd had thinned some, but Alan felt like taking the stairs, where he could be alone with his thoughts.

***

A loud knock woke Alan. He glanced around, blinking the blur of sleep from his eyes. He was in his apartment, with its cheap wooden cabinets and mismatched-but-comfortable furniture. He looked down and realized, with a flush of embarrassment, that he'd been holding a throw pillow tight against his chest, and that his hand was down his pants, on his sheath. It took him a moment to realize that was still wearing his work clothes

"Must have been some dream," he mumbled to himself, straightening up and rising from his fluffy, grey overstuffed sofa to answer the door. Another knock came, this one more insistent. "Hold on, I'm coming." Alan rose up onto his tip-toes to look through the peep hole. Standing outside, looking entirely too chipper and excited, was Casey and a weasel, both grinning like Cheshire cats. Alan huffed, threw the dead bolt open and opened the door.

The fox, who, like a large number of people, was much taller than Alan, reached down and scooped him up into a big hug. Alan groaned at the squeezing pressure and managed, just barely, to get out a single phrase.

"Hi, Casey," Alan wheezed, "Can you let me go please?"

The weasel patted Casey on the shoulder. "Yeah, Casey, let him down. He can't amuse us if we squeeze him to death first!"

Casey lowered Alan back to the floor, smiling and twitching his whiskers. "Look who's here!"

Alan was grinning, in spite of the constricting embrace he'd just been subjected to.

"I didn't know you were back in town, Roger! You should have called."

Roger, whose beige fur was not flattered by the fluorescent lighting, smiled, revealing a broken canine tooth on his left side. "Just got back in. I wanted to surprise you! Casey here decided it would be best if we at least sent an IM first.?" He looked Alan up and down, realizing that something wasn't right. He tilted his head. "You look like nine layers of hell, Alan," he said seriously.

Alan sighed and related the story of his day from hell, feeling strangely empowered at the release.

"What a cockbag, right?" Casey asked, when Alan had finished.

"No joke," said the weasel, "That guy ought to be severely beaten." He leaned back in the chair, wiggling deeper into its soft cushions.

Casey laughed. "No way, that's for later!"

"Do you guys think that I'm...you know...that much of a screw-up?" The question was timid, hesitant, but it was genuine. Alan thought, perhaps, that what Mr. Simmons had been saying was right, and he was really inept, at his job, at life, at whatever.

"Come on, hon," said Roger with a gentle, easy smile. He patted Alan on the knee. "If you were, we'd never have dated. I have high standards."

"Sorry, Alan, I know how much you'd like to sit here and mope, but we're already running behind schedule. We're dragging you to The Crucible," Casey said with another of his wide grins that Alan was convinced looked as if nothing good could ever come of it.

"Why are you taking me to see a play? Theater is boring, I thought you were taking me out to a really hot club," the small wolf whined, trying to hide the grin and wag of his tail. The playful sarcasm dripped from his words.

Casey reached up and playfully thwapped the back of Alan's head. "Goofball."

Ignoring them, Roger's thumbs whizzed over his phone's keypad, smiling deviously at the text window. "Case, get him dressed in something respectable, and meet me down at the street. We roll in five."

Casey herded Alan into the bedroom with a smile.

***

The club looked like it had once been a small manufacturing business. It was a large, concrete building with only a few windows, and those only on the second floor and up. The name 'Crucible' was set in old-fashioned block lettering above the door and lit from beneath. Alan could hear the distant thump of dance music. His heart fluttered nervously at it, though he noticed that it didn't seem to be as loud as some of the clubs he'd gone to in the past when dragged out. He looked towards the main entrance, and saw a huge line, extending out past the awning and wrapping around the building. Surveying the folks in line, the wolf looked down self-consciously at his choice of clothes. His soft red-and-gray t-shirt and tan cargo shorts seemed too straitlaced compared to the bleached, dyed, and spiked head fur, the various arrays of tight-fitting leather which often left little to the imagination, the Hot Topic clearance specials, and the wide variety of 'themed' clothing which didn't look as if it belonged in public. Alan glanced at the hyena standing casually against the side of the building in a trench coat, and guessed from the exposed fur of his bare legs that the coat was all he was wearing.

"Pretty crowded tonight, huh," Casey asked as the trio headed for the door.

Roger nodded. "Usually is on a basics night," he said. "But don't worry," he added with a wink to the small wolf, "they know me. Five minutes, max, and we're in."

Alan's ears perked up and he quirked his head. The weasel was as good as his word, and within five minutes they were across the 'rope' and inside. Alan took a second look at the people in line that they were passing to be allowed in. He felt butterflies in his stomach in anticipation of what lay within.

The small wolf was briefly distracted by a particularly muscular specimen of Tiger who walked by wearing a suit of black leather or rubber. It accentuated the rather large bulge between his legs. Alan's attention snapped back to the two males in front of him as they walked down the wide black corridor. The sound of dance music was still present, but it wasn't getting much louder.

***

"You did what? Roger, he's never been here before. You should just let him go through 101, see what he's into and all that." Casey's tense voice carried easily over the music. His ears twitched.

Roger's tail swished and he smirked, showing off that chipped canine tooth. He waved the fox's concerns away. "Relax, Casey. I'm just making it so he can try things out in private, without a bunch of strangers' eyes watching him. She's good. Trust me!"

The trio exited the hallway into a large main room, where Alan would have expected there to be a DJ and dancing and grinding and pretty lights, but the sound of dance music, though louder, was actually coming from a room off of this one. What was here was a series of alcoves, in which there hung various cabinets on the walls, and there were tables and frames set up with leather straps and chains. Fear prickled through Alan, and the fur on the back of his neck stood up. What was he doing here? He could still leave, make his apologies to Casey and Roger and leave with his dignity intact. For a moment, Alan considered bolting, just turning about-face and running like he'd never run before.

The impulse was gone in an instant as the strong, and varied, scents of arousal reached his nostrils from the gathered people in the room. A sharp snapping noise drew his attention to the alcove straight ahead, where there was a slender vixen in a bustier and fishnets holding a riding crop. She stood beside a muscular horse who was strapped tightly down to a table wearing nothing but boxer-briefs which clearly showed his well-endowed outline. Whack! She thwacked him across his bulging pectoral muscle with the riding crop, receiving a light moan in response. Alan felt his face growing warm as he stared at the outline of the horse's member. He could almost see it throbbing through the tight material of his boxers. He swayed on his feet a bit as the horse's scent, overpowering the others, slammed into him like a freight train of lust and desire. Alan's hand started teasing over his sheath through his pants. It was everything he had imagined it would be!

This wasn't right, though. Not in public like this. Even the kinkiest sex he could imagine in his wildest fantasies was done behind closed doors. The thought of being seen in public like this, on either end, was terrifying. And yet, he did have to admit, it was arousing.

Suddenly, he felt a hand on his upper arm. Roger was looking rather intently at him. "Come on, Alan. There's somebody I want you to meet."

Alan started to object, his ears flattening, but Casey interrupted. "Don't worry. She's really nice. She's a good friend, and it'll be private, one of the upper rooms. Just let her work with you. You don't have to do anything you don't want to do, and if you're not happy after a little while, you can leave, no hard feelings, no questions asked."

"Okay. I'll go along with it," he said at last, smiling weakly. "But," he added sharply, "I reserve the right to leave at any time, with or without explanation or apology."

The fox smiled. "Done, now let's get you upstairs to Allison." He led the way around the outskirts of the room to a stairway tucked away in a back corner. Up to a landing, and then up to the club's upper floor, with Alan following behind and Roger bringing up the rear. It looked and felt like a very old hotel. It was a long corridor with doors leading off to either side. There was wallpaper, which looked like it had been a 1970's flower pattern at one time, but was now yellow and faded. There were no intruding scents here. Alan sniffed, once again, curiously, but decided that the club must use an odor neutralizer here. Casey walked ahead, halfway down the hallway to number 3, and knocked. After a moment, the old wooden door creaked a bit and opened, revealing a stunningly proportioned vixen. Given what he'd already seen of the club, he was surprised that she wasn't wearing the classical dominatrix attire: leather and chains, arranged strategically to hide as little as possible. Instead, she wore a soft white nightgown

trimmed with white faux-fur at the neck and ends of the sleeves. She smiled brightly and gave the fox a big kiss on the cheek before turning to Alan.

"Is this him," she asked, looking the wolf up and down.

Alan gave a sort of dumb nod, while Roger laughed. "Yeah, that's him. Poor kid needs to blow off some steam. I know you're really into that kind of thing. I really appreciate your help!"

"No problem, hon. But you do owe me one, you know. All right, sweetie," she said, turning to Alan, "Let's go inside." Turning to Roger she added "See you soon, love."

Alan stepped into the room. Roger gave him a big wink and a thumbs-up as Allison shut the door and turned the lock into place. Alan glanced around. Here looked a bit more normal than the cubbyholes downstairs. Here there was a bed, made up with a soft, friendly looking comforter. The bed frame was wrought-iron in the shape of bars tipped in autumn leaves. At the foot of it there was an old, dirty wooden chest. Alan wondered what was in it. Then, teetering between trepidation and desire, he realized he was probably going to find out.

"So," said Allison's silky voice. Alan turned to look at her and his heart rate jumped higher. He preferred men, but the sight of her was enough to make his heart do a little flip. She was well proportioned, with large, supple breasts and powerful thighs. Her fur was a rich russet color, offset by the dark fur which surrounded her hands, forearms, and ears. "Your first time, huh?"

Alan nodded, gulping quietly and wishing for a gallon of water right now. The vixen smiled warmly. She took Alan by the hand, led the wolf to the bed and sat him down. "Casey said as much. Well, my name is Allison."

"Alan," he responded, swallowing.

"My guess is that you've been wanting to try out my particular art form for a while now, judging by the smell coming off of you," she smiled. Her voice was as smooth as oil on glass.

The wolf nodded again, unable to form words to speak. He felt his sheath, and what was within, throbbing with desire.

"Your friend Roger tells me you have a dominant streak in you." Allison said, trailing off.

Alan could feel his ears blushing. "He told you about...about our time together?"

"Oh, don't look so nervous. He spared me all the naughty details, sadly. But essentially I'm here to be your teacher." The bed was very soft, welcoming. He wiggled to adjust to it. "So," she continued, "why don't you tell me what interests you?" She leaned in close. Alan could feel the warmth of her body next to him. "Tell me your fantasies. Tell me what you'd like to do," she purred.

"I hadn't really thought about it," he quickly answered.

She laughed, the sound almost musical. She reached up and stroked his ears. "Really? You've never had any fantasies about this kind of play? Something that turned you on more than others?"

Alan's ears drooped. "I guess I just thought about being in control so much that I never thought about the 'how' of it," he said. Then, more hesitatingly, "And that other stuff-"

"Yes," Allison prompted.

"It's hard, y'know, to ask for it."

"I know it can be hard, sweetie. That's why we talk about these things up front. This is a safe place. You don't have to be afraid to tell me."

"I want-" his voice came out high and cracked. He cleared his throat, closed his eyes, and started to just talk. "I want to feel in control. Be in control. I want my partner tied down or chained up. I want them to beg me, beg me for pleasure, and guidance, and punishment." As he spoke, arousal bubbled up inside him. It wasn't just Allison, so close her body's warmth radiated over him. Finally admitting these things, just saying them aloud to another person, left him eager.

"A lot of people don't understand what this kind of play is, so I like to make sure people know exactly what it is they want." Alan nodded in reply.

Allison smiled and stood up, beckoning him to follow her. She made her way to the chest at the foot of the bed. It opened with a silence that belied its peeling and rusty exterior. Inside were countless varieties of bedroom toys, some of which Alan recognized: a riding crop, identical to the one being used on the well-endowed horse downstairs, a ball gag, blindfolds, handcuffs, etc. There were things he didn't recognize, that he could only guess at the uses of.

"Anything strike your fancy?"

The wolf thought for a moment. There were things in there with spikes, things that could potentially draw blood. He didn't trust himself there, at least not yet. In the end, he pointed to a riding crop.

"Going with the simplest option, huh?"

Alan blushed again and nodded. "It was what I saw going on downstairs."

"Okay...now, I find that the best way to teach a dom is to show him the other side of things first," Allison said, gesturing to the bed. "If you're willing, of course."

The wolf took a deep breath, closing his eyes and letting his thoughts settle. One more time as a submissive wouldn't be much different than his everyday life. All the humiliation and powerlessness Alan felt every day at work washed over his mind like a wave. He forced himself once more to let go of all of that. He was here to learn, and learn he would. And then, even if only briefly, he'd get to be the dominant one. Residual panic and burning arousal fought within him. He could feel his heart racing, but gritted his teeth and nodded firmly to her, eyes meeting hers.

"Yes."

"Very good. Now, I'll warn you that you probably aren't going to be able to get into the right head space for this too easily. It's important that you relax, and that you trust me. I won't hurt you, not for real." She held her gaze on him until Alan gave an understanding nod. He felt warm, safe near her. He believed her. "Oh, you'll feel some pain, but it isn't really pain the way we typically think of it. It's just a sensation, one that's a part of you, of who you are. You just have to keep yourself calm."

Alan nodded again, still holding her gaze.

"The riding crop is a simple toy. It's used to correct the sub when they need correcting, as well as to reward. And it sometimes takes a few tries to get the rhythm. You'll know if you don't have a good connection to your partner. Things won't go the way you want them to and you'll find yourself frustrated.

"Now listen, this is important. Never, and I mean never, take out your frustrations on a sub."

"I know that," he said, more harshly than he'd meant to.

She ignored his snap. "No one comes in really knowing that, Alan. That's why I'm telling you. Even when you're the Dom—especially when you're the Dom—you have a responsibility to your partner. No matter what roles you're in, you've got to be careful. No anger. No frustration. Seriously." She might have been garbed in cotton and lace, but her gaze was forged of steel. "Never raise your hand in anger here. That's not what this is about.

"The other important thing is," she continued on, this time in a very serious tone, her eyes meeting his. For some reason he didn't dare turn away as he usually did. He was transfixed by her gaze. "Do you have a safe word?"

He shook his head. "No."

Allison gave him a brief introduction to the term. It was nothing he didn't already know from his research, though he hadn't picked one before now. Then she ordered him to pick one, and after a moment's thought, he selected 'teacup.'

Allison nodded. "All right. If you say or shout 'teacup', we stop, instantly, no matter what else is going on. Don't be proud; If you get uncomfortable, even at the start, call your safeword. I won't think any less of you for it. In the meantime, strip and lay face down on the bed."

The wolf gulped and unbuttoned his shorts, letting them fall down. Then he pulled the T-shirt over his slight frame, slid his boxers down from his lean, muscled legs, and lay down on the bed. Allison pulled soft, leather, faux-fur-lined cuffs from the post at each corner of the bed and fastened them around his wrists and ankles. When she was done he was chained spread-eagle to the bed with his back exposed. He could feel her moving behind him, smell her scent. She was actually somewhat aroused. The realization made him smile.

A light buzzing sound, something whipping through the air, and then the wolf yelped as his rump stung with a light blow of the tip of the riding crop. It was a light strike, just playful, and after the initial shock, he relaxed and sank a little deeper into the bed. Just like she'd said, it wasn't really like pain in the sense he'd feared it.

"What are you smiling about? Does that please you?"

So this was how it was supposed to work. Of course! He felt a little silly, and blushed just a little, thinking how the dialogue would sound coming out of his muzzle. It would be like a bad homemade porno. The wolf resisted the temptation to giggle and, grinning into the mattress so that she wouldn't see, he answered.

"Yes."

Thwack. Another light sting of the crop. "Yes, what?"

The grin disappeared from his muzzle. Oh, right, he thought, this is what authority is like. He thought for only a moment, brow furrowed.

"Yes, I have been a bad puppy." The repeat-what-I-just-heard answer was taught in corporate "active-listening" classes. It showed the other person that you took them seriously.

It was the wrong answer. Another crop strike whizzed through the air and found its mark, this time on his other cheek. He let out a small yelp. It was the other answer. That's what she wanted. The acknowledgment of authority, just like his boss. Of course, of course.

"Yes, Mistress."

He winced and waited for the crop to strike again. This time, however, it did not.

"Very good, wolf," she almost purred, insofar as a fox was capable of that action. "Now, you see how easy it is? I only correct you because I care about you." Her paw ran along the struck places on his rear. They still stung but her touch was soothing, comforting. He closed his eyes and basked in the warmth of it. She did care. Allison cared. And at that moment he fully relaxed. He did not feel the restraints as cumbersome anymore. They were comforting. They gave him limits, but not harshly enforced limits, not like the real world outside. In here, there was only her, and him. Alan sniffed again, taking in the glorious scent of her arousal. He felt his member starting to slip out of its sheath, the first time since high school he'd ever had a reaction like this to a female. His throbbing shaft pressed between his stomach and the soft feather stuffing of the bed.

He heard Allison move behind him. The vixen sniffed the air and chuckled. She knew; She could smell him. Her vulpine nose might not be as sensitive as a wolf's, but she was still a canid.

"I thought you preferred males," she said sternly.

THWACK! This time the crop struck him across the thicker muscles of his upper back. It was a little harder this time. Alan moaned and his hips unconsciously ground into the mattress, sending little shivers of pleasure through him as his cock pressed against the soft material of the sheet.

"I didn't mean to-" Thwack! A little softer this time, just a warning again. "I mean-I'm sorry, Mistress."

"Better," she purred, "You learn quickly, wolf. Now, I think you're ready to serve me."

"Yes mistress," he said, eagerly. There was no more hesitation. He wanted her pleased with him. The warm feeling at just the thought of it spread over him like a blanket. Boards in the floor creaked as Allison approached the head of the bed from Alan's left. Her vulpine tail twitched behind her, belying her calm demeanor. He felt the wrist restraints being removed and looked up curiously.

"On your knees, wolf." He obeyed. She looked at him and smiled wickedly before reaching down and lifting the faux-fur trimmed negligee over her head. She did it very slowly, allowing Alan to see the slow reveal of the curves of her thighs, her taut belly with its soft cream fur that continued upward, creating a barrier that pushed back the russet top coat from her perfectly shaped breasts. The scent of her arousal was even stronger now. Alan felt his shaft throbbing in response, aching for just a bit of contact. Without realizing it, one hand moved to stroke himself as he stared at Allison's body. But before he could even begin in earnest, the riding crop had come back out and he was struck sharply in the shoulder.

"No no, wolf. You don't get to pleasure yourself until I'm satisfied."

The vixen pushed him back, toward the foot of the bed and climbed in, sitting upright with her back against the wrought-iron headboard. Her legs were spread wide, giving Alan a full view of her glistening slit. He didn't care at that moment that she was female, didn't care at all. All he cared about was pleasing his mistress (and, of course, satisfying his own instinctive male desire). He crawled forward, more quickly than it seemed she'd anticipated, and gripped her by the hips, drawing the tip of his shaft nearer and nearer to her dripping mound. Another few inches and he'd be inside her. THWACK! The riding crop struck again on the side of his rump.

"No!" she commanded, eyes blazing. Alan backed off timidly and knelt head downward, at the very foot of the bed where his chains were still attached. They clinked together as he moved. "I told you, wolf, you don't get pleasure until I'm finished and say you may have pleasure. Do you understand?"

"Y-yes, mistress," he answered. It was good to be corrected. It felt nice. He felt his eyes sting a little at having made such a mistake, but that was what Mistress was there for. To teach him. Part of his mind that was observing the scene from a dispassionate distance leaped excitedly as it made a connection about the headspace he was flirting with. He couldn't help but smile.

Allison smiled in return. "Again, very good, wolf. Now, let's see you use that muzzle for something besides talking, hm?" She ran one finger suggestively along her outer lips and up against the little round button of her clit. Alan's lean body shivered in anticipation and with no small degree of nervous excitement as he crawled slowly, reverently forward and lowered his head. The scent of her sex was almost too much for him. It still wasn't a male's scent, and somewhere inside him there was a part of him that was repulsed by her smell, but it wasn't about that. It was about being taught, about being cared for, and he would do what it took to please Mistress. He thought back to college, to the straight porn that his frat boy roommates had always had around. This was foreign territory to him.

His tongue flicked out, gliding from the bottom of her slit to the top, lingering on the clitoris and swirling in little circles there, before repeating the pattern. The vixen inhaled sharply and put her hand on Alan's head, her fingers tensely entwining themselves in his gray fur. Alan continued stroking and probing her with his tongue, drinking in the scent of the vixen and feeling his own excitement growing. Allison moaned with pleasure. Alan began to lap at her more quickly and more forcefully. He wanted to please Mistress, and in doing so earn the chance to be pleasured himself. His cock was aching at desire for contact and release, but any time he thought to reach for it Allison would smack his hand away with the crop.

Alan's tongue grew bolder, venturing inside the soft, moist folds. Allison's hand slipped down and dug tightly into the gray wolf's shoulder. The sharpness of her claws was surprise enough to elicit a shocked gasp from Alan, which caused him to break the rhythm of oral pleasure he was providing his mistress. This, in turn, earned him the corrective slap of the riding crop to the side of his rump once more.

"Don't stop now, wolf." Even through the panting and gasping and writhing of pleasure, the statement was understandable as a command. Alan returned to his task without thinking, but relishing in the scent and flavor of Mistress's body. Even as he did so, her grip on his shoulder tightened and her moans increased in volume and pitch.

"Yes, wolf. That's it, just a little bit more. Just a little. Bit. More."

The claws which had dug into his shoulder only a little before now clamped down at near full force, He yelped at it, even as he felt her opening shuddering and clamping down around his tongue. Her sweet juices were spread over his tongue, nose, and muzzle. The vixen let out a moan that increased in volume and intensity until it morphed into a growl. Her ankles hooked themselves on either side of the mattress so that her hips rose up in the air and her whole body tensed and shuddered, until she finally collapsed, spent, back down onto the mattress. Alan leaned back a respectful distance, and remained kneeling as best he could while still in the restraints.. He kept his eyes averted, waiting to hear his mistress's judgment of his skill.

She remained still, but breathing heavily, only for a few moments before gingerly lifting her legs from the sides of the mattress where they'd been spread in ecstasy only moments before and knelt as well, paralleling Alan's pose.

"Look at me, Alan." Alan's head jerked up. She'd called him Alan, not 'wolf'. "That was very, very good."

Alan smiled in spite of himself. "Thank you, Mistress."

"You can call me Allison, hon," she corrected him gently. "Now that you've experienced things for yourself, are you still interested in taking the dominant role?" Her voice was careful, her expression determinedly neutral, waiting for his answer.

"With you?" He remembered the feeling of letting go of his need to be in control. It was the first time in a long time he had found himself at peace and not struggling with the feeling of not being in command of his own life. There had been peace, and pleasure, both in the act of servicing Allison and in the receiving of her experienced guidance and punishment. It wasn't malicious. There was no haughty air about her; She simply was his superior. She was fair.

Allison laughed again, that musical laugh of hers. "No, I think I have someone better in mind. You aren't ready just yet, of course, but I wanted to make sure it was still what you wanted. After all, it seemed like you were really enjoying yourself."

Alan instinctively opened his mouth to object, but snapped it shut again. He *had* enjoyed it. It wasn't the empty, meaningless cruelty of everyday life. It was structured, and it was safe. He could let go of his anxiety and his fear in that space.

"I did, Mistress-"

"Allison," she said, smiling and placing a comforting hand lightly on his shoulder.

"Allison," he corrected sheepishly, "Yes, I still really want that control, that ease that you had. Will you teach me?" He looked up from the floor where he had kept his gaze, to see Allison's smiling face. The vixen ran a hand lightly along the fur of his cheek.

"Yes, I'll teach you."

Alan came back to the Crucible every Thursday for the next four weeks. With each visit, the wolf grew more confident in himself.

Instead of slouching and making himself smaller as he had done before, he stood tall, with his shoulders squared. He met people's challenges, looked people in the eyes. His coworkers certainly weren't sure how to take this new Alan. He reveled in his newfound confidence, even picked up a couple of phone numbers without much trouble.

On the Thursday of the fifth week, Allison greeted him warmly, as usual. Alan had decided to indulge in a little more exotic wardrobe this time. He wore a thick, white cotton bathrobe, beneath which was exposed a spandex undershirt, and beneath that a very form-fitting and flattering pair of spandex bikini briefs. Alan looked into the room, noticing that there was something different. Allison hadn't set out any new toys to try this time.

"What's going on?"

"It's time, Alan," she said, smiling, "I think you need to try this on your own, now. Don't worry, I'll be here the whole time, making sure you're okay," *And keeping you in line*, Alan heard in his head. She wore the same white negligee as she had on his first visit. She looked just as beautiful wearing it as she had naked. "Do you feel ready?"

"Yes," he answered, his tail lashing furiously.

Allison's tail swished back and forth lightly. She raised an eyebrow. "Eager, huh?"

The vixen lifted up the receiver of a phone on the nearby nightstand, and after a moment of hushed conversation, turned back to Alan. He twisted his head sideways, popping the joints of his spine and feeling the slight relief it gave from the tension. "He's on his way up now."

"Who's coming? Is it Dan again?" Alan's tail wagged again. Dan was a cute border-collie with a lot of excess energy that the wolf had taken a liking to during his third lesson.

"No, I'm bringing in someone special this time. Bill is normally one of the presenters downstairs in our introductory class. He's really dedicated, and also really understanding. He's good for your first real time."

Alan nodded, and started to say something else, but there was a knock at the door. Allison opened it. A tall, muscular wolf, naked except for a towel around his waist, a blindfold and scent masker was escorted into the room by a hare dressed in a leather vest, tight leather pants, and a hat in the shape of a policeman's.

"Thanks, Doug," Allison said to the hare.

"No worries, we got the memo. He's all yours." To this, the vixen nodded and waved the hare on his way, locking the door again.

Alan looked up at the new arrival. Despite the equipment concealing his face, there was something familiar in the way he stood stock still and ramrod straight. The smaller wolf nearly yelped when he made the realization. The scent of the newcomer, the stiffness, it was Mr. Simmons! Alan stared wide-eyed, and forced his legs to support him, otherwise he'd have fallen over. He looked Mr. Simmons-Bill- up and down, suddenly keenly aware of his own arousal, which surged through him like electricity at the sight of his handsome boss standing before him, ready and willing to submit himself to the lowly Alan.

But, Simmons was married. Or, so it looked from the photo in his office. Alan felt heat rise to his cheeks and ears. Could he really do this? Could he be a dom for someone who is both his boss and probably married? Alan looked up and down Simmons's towel-clad body and felt a stirring in his sheath. The heat grew between his legs. He shook his head once. He did want this, and the consequences be damned. After all, what happened here, stayed here.

"Do you know why you are here, slave?" Allison demanded, formally.

"Yes, I do, Mistress. I am here to assist you in training a new master." Alan blinked at the response. The tone was so different from when he was working. It was pliable. Submissive. Willing. It was intoxicating in its tonality. It sent another wave of desire shuddering through Alan. He placed a steadying hand around his shaft, briefly imagining that it was Mr. Simmons's hand there. Then he realized, he didn't need to pretend. It could be his, if he wanted it. Allison motioned for him to take over, as it was his scene now. He understood and rose to his feet.

"What is your safe word, slave," asked Alan, mimicking Allison's formal tone.

"Handbag." Simmons answered without hesitation. It was a speedy way of getting the formalities out of the way, obviously not wanting to spend more time on preliminaries than was necessary.

"Now, tell me what you like," Alan said in a tone of gentle command

Simmons nodded. "I like most forms of play here, Master. Restraints and bondage, and punishment are my favorites."

"Is there anything that you want to exclude?"

Simmons shifted on his paws. "Humiliation and degradation," he said in a tone that was just soft enough that Alan had to perk his ears up in order to hear it.

"Very well. If you're ready, then, we'll begin. You will submit to any order that either I or my teacher give you, without hesitation. Understood?"

"Yes, Master."

"Good," said Alan, taking the lead again, unable to help but smile as he took Simmons by the bulging muscles of his upper arm and guided him to the bed. "We'll play with the crop and restraints then."

"Yes, Master." There was that seductive, submissive tone again. Hearing it on this wolf was enough to make Alan squirm. He helped lay the wolf flat on his stomach and fastened the cuffs around his wrists and ankles. He pulled the towel away and tossed it carelessly to the floor, displaying Simmons's magnificently shaped rump. Alan's tongue hung out of his muzzle at the sight. He'd always suspected that Simmons was well built, but he had had no idea that he was this much of an Adonis. He wanted him, right now. He wanted to slip inside him and take him and make him beg for it.

Allison opened the trunk at the foot of the bed with a creak and put the riding crop into Alan's waiting hand.

"Speak to him more, first, " Allison whispered, "Let him get to know you as a master."

Alan nodded, and swallowed. "Slave," he said, blinking at the deep, rich command of his own voice. It was not the voice of a lowly office worker, it was something else, and what's more, Alan liked it. It was different when he practiced in front of the mirror. Here, his words actually felt real, not like a child playing let's pretend.

"Yes, Master? How may I serve you?"

Alan smiled, revealing all of his teeth. "Raise that cute wolfy ass into the air for me so that I can inspect you properly."

Simmons obeyed instantly. Alan felt weak in the knees. He could command Simmons to do anything he wanted, within reason, and the other wolf would obey! Alan Mikulski had power! He stepped over to the side of the bed where Simmons was raising his tail into the air. Alan reached out and hovered his hand mere inches above the tightly sculpted rump of his boss. What a thing of beauty he was! Alan let his hand drop two inches and then slide along the contours of Simmons's body, over his tail, and then under, massaging his sheath and the very large lupine member that was fully extended and knotted beneath him.

"Very nice, slave," Alan said, removing his hand.

"Thank you, Master, I try to-"

Smack! Allison's riding crop met the tender part of Simmons's rump, causing him to gasp and lower his rump to the bed, much as Alan had done, grinding his cock against the feather mattress. "You will not speak unless given permission, Slave, is that clear?"

"Yes, Mast-" Alan cut him off with another firm, yet gentle crop-strike to the upper back along his rippling shoulders. He whimpered and did not speak.

"What is your life's goal, Slave," Alan asked.

Simmons was experienced all right. A fast learner. He did not answer again. Silence. The slave was learning his place. A warm euphoria started to settle into Alan's body. He had power. He had the power to please Simmons, and the freedom to take pleasure in doing so.

"You may speak, Slave," he said, grinning at Allison, who nodded her approval.

"My life goal is to help people, Master."

Alan blinked. There was an answer he hadn't expected.

"Help them, how?" Alan's voice faltered momentarily, but he recovered and Simmons didn't seem to notice the change.

"I don't want to see people hurting or in pain, Master. I want to bring them pleasure in life, even if it's only like this."

Alan's heartbeat thundered in his ears. What was that supposed to mean?

"How do you take away people's pain? How do you stop them from hurting and make them happy, Slave?"

"By pleasuring them, Master," Simmons said, his head slightly tilting. He hesitated.

Alan clenched his teeth. "I mean outside, Slave."

"Master, I give a helping hand when I can. I try to treat people with compassion."

Alan felt his eyes stinging a little. If that was his goal in life, then why did he treat Alan like shit at every turn in the office? Where was that desire to help then? Alan's ears flushed. He felt anger bubbling up inside him like lava from the Earth's core. Alan's hand ripped the blindfold and scent-masker free. He stared into the larger wolf's eyes, unblinking, uncompromising. Every muscle in Alan's body tensed. Lips curled away from predatory teeth.

"You're a goddamn liar!"

Simmons blinked, as if he were having trouble comprehending. "No, Master, I-"

"You're a liar! You don't care about anyone else's feelings! You treat me like I'm worthless every day of my life!"

Alan grabbed Simmons by the hair, yanking his head to the side. "How dare you treat me the way you do, and lie to me. How dare you! Why do you make my life hell?"

Simmons's eyes widened in alarm. "You-" he began, his voice rising.

"Me, slave. Your master," Alan said, cutting him off. "And your master asked you a question, now answer me!"

Simmons tucked his tail against his thighs and flattened his ears. "Yes, Master. It's because... because, you never stand up for yourself. I think you're very attractive, but I can't get past that weakness. You come across as spineless, and it makes me angry."

"And you think that gives you the right to treat me that way, because I make you mad?" Alan's eyes narrowed and lips curled. He pulled Simmons hair back, throwing him off balance. Then gave the larger wolf a shove, knocking the disoriented wolf off the bed. "You're pathetic."

Simmons's eyes flashed. A look of some twisted combination of emotions crossed his face as he snarled and bared his teeth. His hackles rose as he drew himself up to his full size, looming over Alan.

Alan did not back down, but instead stood up from the bed and stared down at Simmons, growling. Alan raised the riding crop to strike Simmons in the face.

A firm hand gripped Alan's forearm.

"No!"

Alan stopped, instantly halting the movement.

"Slave, you will lie face down on the bed and cover your ears," Allison commanded. Simmons blinked, as if not understanding what had just happened. Then, the tension released in him and he lay face down, covering his ears as he had been instructed.

Allison pulled Alan back from the bed, shoving him hard against the wall, staring into his eyes. "What was one of the first things I taught you?"

Alan blinked. He felt his ears and cheeks flush, joining the sick feeling in his stomach at having disappointed her. His breathing grew swift and shallow. It felt like ages before he was able to speak. Then finally, in the old Alan's squeaky, soft voice he answered, "No anger, Mistress."

"That's right. No anger. Before this began, he told you that degradation and humiliation were off limits! You want to be in control, you need to prove that you're worthy of it. That's what this is all about. Trust. Can he trust you to be in control? Can I trust you to apply what I've taught you responsibly?" Her hand relaxed, and he lowered his arms. He rubbed his forearm where she'd grabbed him.

Alan looked past her at Simmons then back to her, though he kept his gaze averted from her eyes and his expression downcast.

"Look, it's really clear that you two have problems with each other. With everything I taught you in mind, is this really where you want to deal with this?" Tucking her hand under his muzzle, she lifted his face to look at her. She wore an expression of concern, though whether for him, Simmons, or both, he couldn't say.

"I don't think I could talk about it anywhere else. Mistress... Allison, I promise, I'll keep my temper under control, okay?" He could feel the sweat on his forehead. His tail didn't move an inch from its tucked position.

"Then, I ask you again. Can you apply what I have taught you responsibly?"

"I think I can, Mistress," he whispered, looking past her once again to the muscular wolf on the bed.

"Yes or no. No maybes."

"Yes, I can, Mistress," he answered firmly.

The vixen took a long look at him. "All right. If you're calm again, then we can try once more. I'm right here to rein you in, but if I have to do that, then this lesson is over. Agreed?"

The wolf nodded solemnly. "Yes, Mistress."

Allison stepped gracefully aside and allowed Alan to approach again. Simmons remained in the prone position, as ordered, with ears covered. He hadn't been given permission to move, Alan realized. He laid a hand on Simmons's shoulder. Simmons removed one hand from an ear and rotated the ear to face in Alan's direction. Allison watched intently from the corner of the room.

"We'll have no more of that, will we, Slave?"

"No, Master," came the muffled reply from the pillows and sheets.

"Do you want me to fuck you, slave?"

"I think I would like that, Master."

Alan untied the belt at his robe's waist, allowing it to drop away. His throbbing shaft was outlined in the black spandex of his briefs. He peeled those away too, allowing his member to spring forth. The scent of his musk immediately hit his nose, as it must have Simmons's as well. Allison stepped silently over to the little night stand by the bed and slid open a drawer, waving Alan over to it. Inside were a few types of lube and boxes of condoms for a few different species, all of them high-quality, name-brand condoms, not the sort that Alan associated with gas station condom machines.

Alan lifted a condom from the pack marked for large canines, tore quickly into the package and after a moment of confusion as to which side was correct, rolled the prophylactic down over his shaft and knot. He picked up a bottle of water-based lube and smiled as he walked towards the bed again. "Raise that tight wolfy ass in the air again, slave." Simmons complied, lifting his tail to display for his master. Alan swatted his rump. "Higher, slave." Simmons raised himself up another few inches. Alan squeezed some lube into his paw and spread it along the outside of Simmons's tight hole, then slipped one finger inside, stretching him out. Simmons moaned and tightened reflexively around his finger. Then he slowly, tentatively, relaxed. Alan could feel his hole pulsing with the ache of lust. Alan sniffed and took in the scent of Mr. Simmons's arousal, far more potent and exciting to him even than Allison's had been.

Then, for a moment, Alan stopped, head cocked to one side. "No, slave. You're going to have to earn this, before I fuck you."

Simmons looked up, his face betraying confusion. "Master?"

Alan gave him a light thwack of the crop to the rump again, then between Simmons's legs and gripped his cock, which was slippery with pre. "Come for your master, Slave," he whispered, and began to stroke his thick length. Simmons moaned and writhed, jerking violently against his restraints, thrusting into Alan's waiting hand.

"Come on, Slave, come on. You know you've been waiting for this since you agreed to come up here. Come on. Come for me." Alan's firm insistence was having its desired effect. Simmons was panting heavily. His shaft pulsed in Alan's grip and seemed to grow hot as he drew nearer and nearer to the edge. And Alan stopped and released Simmons's cock. Simmons whimpered loudly. With his free hand, Alan responded to the high-pitched sound with a swat of the riding crop to Simmons's back. "Patience, Slave."

"Y-Yes, Master."

"Good boy," Alan said, reaching down to the other wolf's throbbing shaft again, this time, slowly, oh so slowly sliding the slippery member through just two of his fingers. The languorous strokes in this manner made Simmons whimper uncontrollably, his pelvis jerking and twitching at the torturous pace. Again, his breathing grew shallow and his whimpering more urgent, pushing towards release-

Again, Alan released his cock. Simmons growled and whined in utter helplessness, receiving in return a crop-strike to the ass from Alan's waiting hand.

"Slave, I said patience," Alan said firmly. "You'll get release when I offer it!"

"Master, please," Simmons pleaded, his tone little above a whisper. "Please..."

Alan stared at Simmons for a moment, then reached down and grabbed his cock by the base at the knot with his left hand. He placed the riding crop down and used his right paw to begin stroking furiously. Simmons moaned in ecstasy and anticipation. As Alan's hand reached the tip of Simmons's shaft, he rubbed across it with his palm, gripping tightly and twisting his wrist to give a sort of swirling motion to each stroke.

Simmons sucked in air sharply through his clenched jaw. Alan felt Simmons's entire body shuddering with each pass of his hands. He could tell he wasn't going to be able to keep this up for much longer —no matter how much he enjoyed the look on Simmons's face —the muscles in his hands and wrists, and even up to his forearms ached with the strain of the torture he was putting the other wolf through.

"You may come, Slave."

The larger wolf let out a primal bellow as he shot squirt after squirt of hot seed onto the bed and into Alan's hand. His body jerked and shook, until finally, spent, he collapsed onto the bed Alan lifted the paw tremulously to his nose and inhaled the sweet scent of Simmons, and licked a droplet of the fluid off his fingertip.

"You taste wonderful, slave," Alan said, wiping his finger on the fur of Simmons's shoulder.

"Thank you, Master."

Alan looked to Allison, who was still standing where she had been, observing Alan's progress. The corners of her mouth pulled upward just slightly and she leaned against the wall, arms folded. The look on her face brought to Alan's mind every 'crafty fox' stereotype he had ever heard. Alan turned his attention back to his submissive, very gently undoing the restraints which held him. He very gently removed the cuffs from the wolf's wrists and ankles. Simmons sat up, rubbing his wrists. Alan stood nearby, unable to look away from him.

"We need to talk."

Simmons blinked, rubbing his eyes. Alan waited with more patience than he felt for his boss's head to clear.

"What do you mean," Simmons said at last, looking up.

"This was good," Alan said.

"Yeah, I think so."

"But I don't think I'm going to be playing the submissive anymore," Alan continued. "Certainly not outside of the bedroom. Bill."

Simmons's face took on some of the hardness that it had during office hours and his eyes narrowed. "If this is about the office-"

"Yes, Bill. It is about the office. I'm not just going to roll over and play dead to you being an insufferable asshole towards me anymore. I like my job, I'm damn good at my job, and it's high time you recognized it." Alan felt his hackles rising. Though he forced his voice to remain level, there was an edge creeping in.

"I'll do my job the way I see fit," Simmons answered with a hint of indignation. After a pause where he glanced over Alan's naked form, he continued, "I wondered why you'd suddenly become more assertive. Now I understand why. And you were certainly doing well in scene." The wolf glared. "But, just because you give a damn good hand job doesn't mean-"

"No, it doesn't," Alan interrupted, his tail lashing from side to side, "But you're going to start treating me with respect, or I'll make your life miserable for you. And you know I can do it. We both know that project wouldn't be anywhere near release without all the hard work I put in, and I'm tired of putting a hundred and ten percent into my work and getting no damn respect from you."

Simmons looked flabbergasted. His jaw hung slightly ajar and he blinked a few times. A scent creeped into Alan's lupine nostrils. It was a familiar musk, something hazy, in the back of his mind. Then it clicked. He looked down between Simmons's legs to confirm that there was already another erection creeping out of his sticky sheath.

"That's what I smelled," Alan said, puzzled. "In your office. I've smelled you before, like this!"

Bill Simmons's ears flattened and he looked down, embarrassed. "Yeah. Well, you're a good looking wolf. But you'd always kill it for me with that spineless behavior of yours. So," he paused again, his ears flushing, "Okay, maybe I pushed you a little hard sometimes to see if you'd snap."

"You treating me like shit wasn't going to make me snap, you son of a bitch," Alan growled. For a brief instant, that picture of Simmons's wife and kids from his office flashed through his mind . He pushed the thought away. No way he was going to go that far, even as much of a douchebag as Simmons had been. Alan would be devastated if someone outed him to his family as gay. He could only imagine how much worse it was with a fetish .

"I'll tell you what. I'll make you this deal. You'll start treating me like a person, and if you're really good," Alan said, cupping Simmons's muzzle in his hand and staring at him eye to eye, their noses almost touching, "we'll do this again. Now go on, get cleaned up."

Alan waited, to see if Simmons would say anything else. Instead, he stood up from the bed. He picked up his discarded towel from the floor, and strode into the hallway. He stuck his head back in momentarily and said "Thank you, for a lovely evening, Master. I hope you'll allow me to serve you again." Then the door shut and he was gone.

Allison joined Alan, who sat down on the bed, breathing heavily. "I did it."

"That wasn't easy. Most people wouldn't have been able to regain control like you did, sweetie. You've been learning well. Bill is a sweetheart once you get to know him better," she purred, reaching around Alan and rubbing his shoulders to ease the knots of tension.

"We'll see. I think for the next little bit," Alan said, "I'm going to start keeping a riding crop in my desk drawer."

Of Pets and Amour
by Elijah Lapso

I've wrapped you round my finger,
Got you waiting at my door,
It started with the sex,
But then you wanted more.
You liked when I abused you,
Spanked you as I came,
Now you're on my leash,
With just yourself to blame.
My collar 'round your neck,
My cock down to the knot,
Yeah, it's kinda sexy.
Yeah, it's fucking hot.
You're my little puppy,
My mate and my sweet whore,
So sit, beg, and roll over,
My pet and mi amour.

Missed

Missed
by Rechan

The click-clack of Miss Pendigrass's riding boots echoed down the hall in her wake, the sound helping to transform her walk from a stately stroll to the confident, no-nonsense prowl more suited to an executive. She passed a hall monitor, and instead of her customary smile and greeting, she snapped her muzzle up at a curt, acknowledging angle. The motion forced her to nudge her slender glasses back into place.

The border collie quieted her heels as she neared her destination. From her purse she removed a tiny black remote, adjusted the dial to two, and glanced into the window in the closed door.

Rachel moved among the rows of desks, passing out papers and comments.

Miss Pendigrass aimed the remote and fired.

The mink's body jerked, her back and tail going straight, and Miss Pendigrass could almost hear Rachel's sharp intake of breath. The border collie lingered long enough to catch sight of momentarily wide eyes, tail fur puffing out, and a roll of the hips so subtle one would have needed to be looking to spot it.

Before she was spotted at the door, the border collie renewed the cadence of her boots. She was certain Rachel should have composed herself by the time the border collie reached the end of the hall. Even though the activation times were random, the mink had ample time to become accustomed to wearing the bullet vibe over the last several Wednesdays. A shame the vibrations had only a five minute lifespan when the remote was beyond range.

This time she was not merely keeping the girl on her toes.

Every step and breath added to the building anticipation and power, growing for the coming meeting. It had become overwhelming now, the imaginary pressure like a preheating oven, hot and trembling in her chest. The sensations had begun to snowball an hour ago when she received the email.

"Miss, I very much need to see you at lunch. It's important."

Tracing her steps back out of Parker Hall and up the library steps, Miss Pendigrass strode towards the central desk. "Meredith," she called, "I'm taking a lunch."

Turning from a computer, the aging lynx cocked a tufted ear.

It was difficult to put away the mood she had been cultivating, set aside with a deep breath before she snapped at Meredith. The border collie spared her colleague a smile, tapped her own watch, then mimed putting something into her own mouth.

"Ah! I'll hold down the fort," Meredith said, reaching for the volume on her hearing aid.

By the time she opened the library door, Miss Pendigrass was once more enveloped in her headspace. She walked around the building until she reached the fire door and unlocked it from the outside. The stairwell beyond took her three flights, leaving her panting by the end, and she pushed into the cramped corridor beyond. She passed ancient cobwebs and dust motes dancing in the slim bars of sunlight slipping through a high grimy window. At the far end of the hall, she opened the store room and stepped inside.

The air and floor were less dusty here than it should have been, and the clutter was minimal, providing a full space to maneuver around the central table, lit by the feeble efforts of a single naked light bulb. It was a meager set, but it was Miss Pendigrass's stage. At far end of the room she moved aside two boxes of obsolete textbooks before hoisting up the third. After setting the box down on the table, she peeled her sweater over her head and folded it.

The email had said it was important. Miss Pendigrass imagined it was; Rachel had not been directed to climax in nine days. The mink must have been on fire.

Rachel's class must certainly be out by now.

Her nipples were tight beneath the lace of her bra, and a familiar warmth tensed below her waistband. Miss Pendigrass removed her bra, leaving her considerable bosom to sag, and folded her bra atop her sweater. From inside the box she took her first prop, a dark purple bustier, pulling it into place.

Rachel must be on her way.

The thought set the border collie's tail to wagging. This meeting was important for them both. Their engagements so far had been limited to the exchange of power and the physical. Now Miss Pendigrass felt ready to close the roles between them. She would take this beyond games, she would take the girl home and relax her heart.

The border collie lost her trousers and underwear, replacing them with a dark, sheer lace skirt shorter than the boys wished the girls could wear their uniforms. Miss Pendigrass left her riding boots on. Then she removed a few props from the box and her purse, arranging them on the table.

When she heard the fire escape door open at the end of the hall, Miss Pendigrass took two of her props in paw and poised by the door.

Four knocks echoed through the heavy door, in a one-two-one pattern. Miss Pendigrass smiled. "Come in."

Rachel pushed the door open. The poor lighting turned her mocha fur and mahogany hair smokey against the pearl blouse with its brass buttons. Just the sight of her left Miss Pendigrass wanting to touch her, hold her, nuzzle her throat and breathe in that wonderful wildflower scent that she loved so much. She wanted her linens to smell like Rachel.

Rachel lifted timid brown eyes up to the librarian. As soon as Miss Pendigrass caught her gaze, she extended her riding crop. A red ribbon choker draped over the end.

Rachel took a breath, color creeping into her ears. "Miss," she said. "I need to..."

When Miss Pendigrass hardened her stare, the girl dropped her eyes and had barely formed a syllable before the border collie brought the choker into her field of vision.

For a moment she darted eyes up to Miss Pendigrass before glancing to the choker, then she plucked it off the crop and fastened it in place.

"Good. Now, strip to your panties."

"Yes Ma'am," Rachel said. "Miss, could you please not use the toy when I'm standing in full view? I was handing bac-!" She spasmed, nearly tearing a button.

Miss Pendigrass set the dial to four before returning the remote to the table. "You're wearing my collar right now, girl. What does that mean?"

Rachel shuddered and ducked her head, voice both chastised and stimulated. "Th-that I am to follow all rules."

"Yes, and what is the rule about talking?"

"Only when spoken to," Rachel said.

"And what time have we set aside for discussions for both playtime and other matters?"

Rachel's digits dug into her blouse. "During aftercare and in emails, Miss."

"And is now either of those times?"

"No ma'am."

"Then," Miss Pendigrass said, tilting Rachel's chin upwards with the end of the crop so that she could stare into the girl's eyes, "undress and come here."

The mink's ears flattened, but she nodded against the crop. First went her blouse. When she reached for her skirt, the border collie's cleared throat sent her paws back up to remove the red bra, baring her small breasts and their black nipples. The skirt came last. Then she came closer.

Miss Pendigrass stepped aside and gestured at the table with her crop. Rachel bent over it with deliberate slowness, tail rippling in restrained excitement. The posture best presented the mink's legs encased in dark stockings. A band wound around one thigh just above a garter, holding the battery to the bullet vibe. Its cord fed up, into the front of Rachel's red tanga thong, where Miss Pendigrass could see dew tinting the cotton.

"Mmm." The border collie trailed her nails through the softness along the back of Rachel's thigh, leaving furrows in the short but thick velvet of the mink's pelt. She ran her touch from the tight thigh up to the outer lines of Rachel's taut little bottom, then to the underside of a cheek, threatening to delve into the crease at her rear's center. The touch sent the mink's tail into an upward arch. "You've been looking forward to this, haven't you?"

"Yes Miss," Rachel said with a quiver in her voice that lifted the border collie's ears.

Miss Pendigrass collected a student's tie from the table and walked around until she stood across from Rachel's head. "Wrists, girl."

The mink extended her arms, the motion just long enough to reach across the table's width. Miss Pendigrass looped the tie over Rachel's wrists and slid the knot snug.

"Miss, before we continue, this is rea-"

Lifting the mink's chin with a sudden, tight grip, the librarian regarded her girl with a steely glare. She could not tolerate the insubordination any longer. Had it been so urgent to disrupt their play, the email would have said as much. "If you speak out of turn one more time, I will send you home without an orgasm. Is that what you want?"

"No Miss." The defeat and desperation flashing in her eyes was mirrored in her tone.

Tracing Rachel's mouth with her thumb, she added, "I haven't given you permission to climax in some time. Would you like more days to be added to that?"

The mink said nothing, she didn't need to. Miss Pendigrass could see the hunger in her eyes underneath whatever reluctance had bubbled up all of a sudden.

"Good." Taking Rachel's now bound wrists, she pulled her arms straight and hooked the loop of the tie on a thin knob that she had screwed in underneath the table's edge.

Miss Pendigrass rested the tips of her nails along Rachel's shoulder, dragging their points down the mink's back as she walked around to the girl's rear end. Just before reaching the thong's waistband, she turned her paw over, pressing in and rubbing over the cheek in a tight circle. Beneath her paw the mink shuddered, and Miss Pendigrass noticed her thighs pressed flush together. It was only then that the scent caught her nose, and she blinked.

She pulled her groping paw back while with the other, she reaching over and pressed the off button on the remote.

Immediately tension eased out of Rachel's muscles.

Miss Pendigrass snapped her free paw across Rachel's rear with a muted thump of pawpad on furred derriere.

The mink jumped with a squeak. Before she had even settled on the table the other cheek received a slap, drawing out another high noise.

Reaching down, Miss Pendigrass claimed the riding crop once more. "Now," she murmured, running the tip along the outside of Rachel's thigh, "Should I use the sting?" She then picked up a ruler, mirroring the motion along the opposite leg. "Or the thud?"

"The second, Miss. Please?" Rachel glanced over her shoulder and hiked her hips up, giving her bottom a faint wiggle.

Miss Pendigrass set the crop aside. But before settling in, she took up the remote once more, dialed the toy to one, and turned it on. Rachel sighed under her breath and arched her back, tail kept well out of the way, and swayed her pelvis.

This saucy waggle earned her a ruler slap across an inner thigh. Miss Pendigrass could not contain her wag at the resulting moan that bubbled out of Rachel's throat.

The librarian set about her task, each crack of the ruler upon a thigh or buttock drawing out a groan or gasp, the pitch and type varying with the power and placement of each strike. The sweetest notes came from the crease where thigh met buttock, or where the cheek, hip and thigh converged. She played the mink like some erotic musical instrument, performing with a tempo that left them both panting and damp.

Setting aside her ruler and turning the bullet vibe off, she began to first graze Rachel's sore spots with her nails, flirting with the aching muscles. When the mink squirmed and twitched her tail, silently begging for more, Miss Pendigrass cupped the girl's abused behind, grinding her pawpads into the ripe cushions while squeezing in lazy rhythms.

Rachel laid her face down and groaned into the table, spreading her legs and pushing back into the massage. Miss Pendigrass could see the saturated nature of Rachel's underwear, and the smell was intoxicating. Her fingers pressed into the wet material, bearing down on Rachel's mound. "Tell me how much you want release, girl. Tell me."

"I... I..."

"Yes?" Miss Pendigrass growled, pinching the mink through her panties.

Rachel squeaked, then took a deep breath and whimpered out, "Sanctuary."

Miss Pendigrass paused, a breath away from peeling the front of Rachel's thong aside, and cocked her head. What did that have to do with what she asked?

Then significance dawned and she yanked her paws back as if burned. With a tight frown, the border collie first looked over Rachel for any problems, having noticed no signs of distress. Circling the table, she quickly unbound Rachel's wrists. "Are you alright dear?" Not yet touching the girl, she merely leaned in close.

Rachel sat up and rubbed her wrists, not looking at Miss Pendigrass as she reached up and removed her collar.

"Talk to me," the border collie said, her ears splaying.

"That's what I've been *trying* to do, Miss. But you haven't let me." The frustration and hurt in Rachel's whisper was palpable, enough to droop the librarian's tail.

She had yet to look up. Miss Pendigrass reached out, brushing the backs of her fingers along Rachel's cheek, then down to cup her chin, drawing the girl's eyes up. "I'm listening now."

Once more Rachel pulled her head away and, with a shaky breath, said, "There's someone who is trying to... trying to get me to um. Date them."

The bottom dropped out of Miss Pendigrass's libido. "I see." She tried to sound as neutral and comforting as possible, but even to her ears she failed.

The girl curled up on the table and clutched her tail in her lap, stroking the fur. "I wanted to ask permission. If I could pursue it, ma'am." Rachel's ears flattened and she spared a glance up.

Suddenly Miss Pendigrass felt silly in her getup. She walked from the table, tail giving a fitful tick-tock. Arms crossed under her breasts, she asked, "Does this mean that you want to stop what we're doing?"

"No ma'am," Rachel said, quick and loud. "I love these times."

"Then have you told the other female about our arrangement?"

Once more the mink's voice was tiny. "He, Miss. He."

Miss Pendigrass turned on her. "*He?* You told me you weren't interested in males. That you had never-"

"I'm not! I wasn't!" Ears pinkening and nose buried in her tail, the mink shook her head. "I've never been, before. But he's... sweet. So very sweet and polite. He doesn't make me feel like the way I feel around most males, but the way that I am with you, and with the girls before you."

The welling tears melted the border collie just a hint. She walked over and dabbed at the poor mink's eyes with a digit. Rachel hugged her tight, nose pressed into her throat. "Shh." Miss Pendigrass took a deep breath and swallowed down her wants. "It's alright." It wasn't, but she still stroked the mink's back.

Leaning back, Rachel's eyes met Miss Pendigrass's. "I don't want to stop," she whispered.

That drew a smile, but the border collie's tone was firm. "You didn't answer me. Have you told him about our arrangement?"

Rachel squeaked. "No!" Redness crept up into her ears. "I don't think he would get it." She flailed her paws quickly, trying to halt response. "The... the..." Rachel picked up the crop, wagging it. "I think he's very... sheltered."

"I see." Miss Pendigrass slid off the table, opting to stare at the wall. "Why would you even want a relationship with someone vanilla?" She had tried that. Her unsatisfied needs had became a wedge that had widened problems until it all came crashing down.

"I don't know Miss," Rachel said. "Am I not allowed to try?"

After a moment's deliberation, the collie sentenced Rachel. "You are going to tell him."

Rachel shook her head. "Don't you have anyone else you do... this with?"

Instead of saying no, Miss Pendigrass said, "None I'm pursuing a *relationship* with."

"But Miss! I-"

"Because not only would it be not fair to him," the border collie continued, "not only would some of my existing orders interfere with the potential relationship, but he needs to be put on the same page. If this arrangement is going to work, then we all must talk it out."

Rachel gasped. "You want to meet him?"

She did not, but she was going to have to. She had given her judgment. "Yes."

Ears now scarlet, the mink stared back at Miss Pendigrass with wide eyes.

Miss Pendigrass stared down her muzzle at the girl from her full height and then some. "If it's going to work at all, then everything must be out in the open and clear," she said, giving her edict with a tone of finality.

"I'm very... it's embarrassing," Rachel said to her lap.

The crack of the ruler across the table caused the girl to jump and snap her head up.

"Consider it an order," Miss Pendigrass said. "You have permission. As long as you outline to him our relationship, and the type of things that excites you. You will do this the next time you have some time to sit down with him. Understood?"

For several moments the mink trembled on the table, but she finally gave a meek nod. "Yes Miss."

"And I'm going to change one of our standing orders, just a little bit." Miss Pendigrass ran the ruler along Rachel's thigh while regarding the mink with a rekindling smile. "Instead of keeping your climax all to myself, you're going to start orgasming a lot. Every night at nine fifteen, you're going to start pleasuring yourself. You still can't get off without my permission, so I will expect a phone call when you're close. Understood?"

Once more the mink nodded, her ears still quite glowing, but a faint smile perked. "Yes Miss."

"Once we sort things out with your male, then we can see about adjusting rules to suit everyone. For now, get dressed."

Rachel started to slide off the table, then paused. "Miss?"

"Yes?"

"May I... remove the toy?"

Miss Pendigrass smiled weakly. "No." She slid in close and pressed herself against the other female, brushing her fingers downwards and into the girl's underwear. Rachel gasped as she caught, then withdrew the bullet vibe, and let it fall into the thong's front.

Rachel leaned in and kissed Miss Pendigrass, chaste and affectionate, before rubbing her nose under the border collie's muzzle, hugging her. "Thank you Miss," she whispered. "For understanding. For being so kind."

Missed

"I am your Miss, it's part of what I'm here to do." She nosed between the mink's still warm ears, licking one, and eased away, allowing the girl to dress. They shared a conspiratorial smile before Rachel wiped the bullet off with a kerchief and tucked it into her purse. Then the girl was gone.

It would go all right. Either the boy would reject the situation, or the love triangle would go on, her providing for some of Rachel's needs while *he* provided for others. The border collie would make it work, and their relationship would continue as it had. It would be alright, she told herself.

This Miss Pendigrass told herself as she retired their toys, but as she looked down at the red ribbon choker, all she could do was silently cry in the room that smelled so wonderfully of them both.

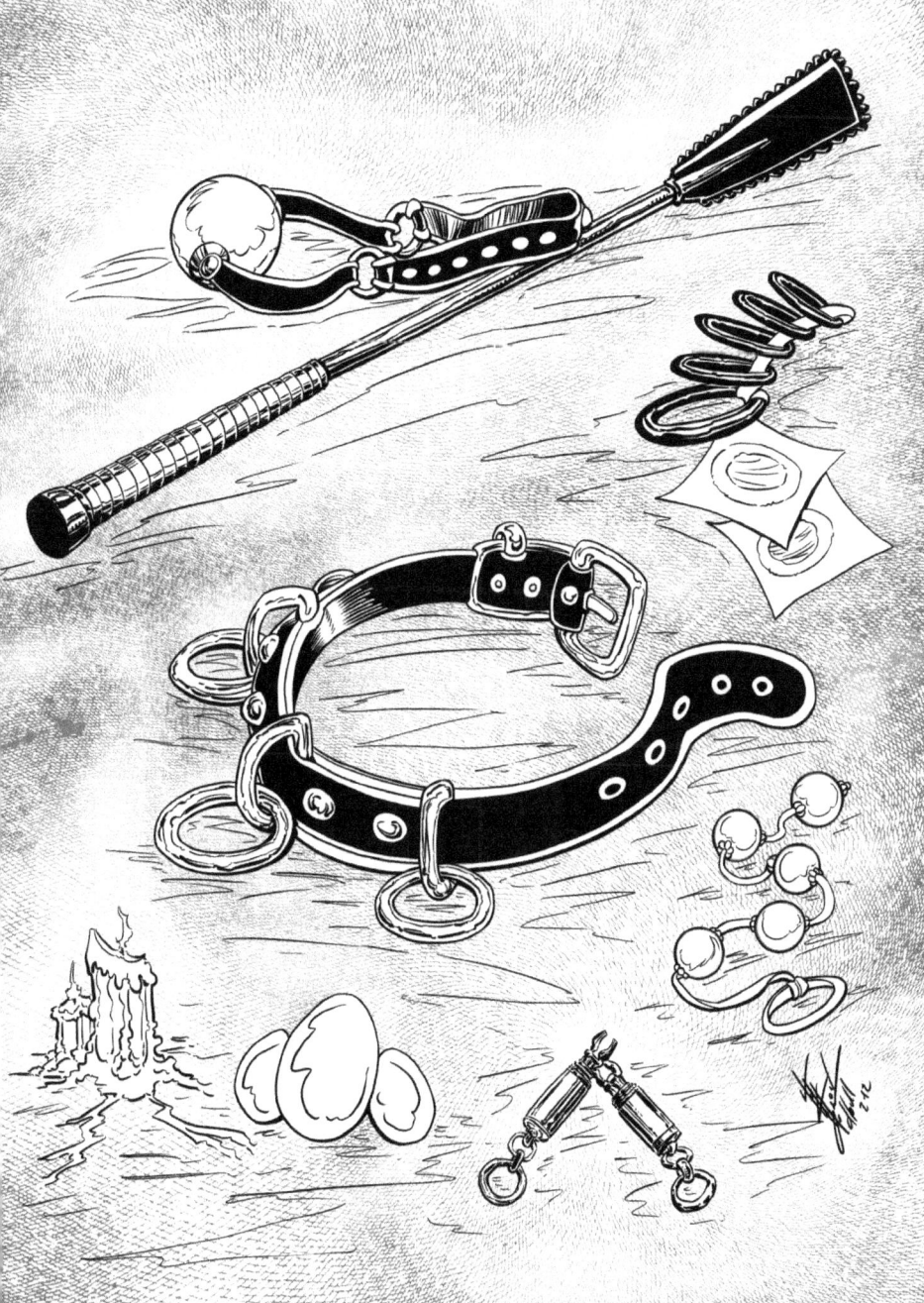

Dinner Theatre
by Ashe

"Yes Sir, Mr. Bennett. I will get right on all of that, consider it all done." The high pitch voice surged confidently through the phone as the line snapped shut, the soft beeps of the headset signaling the call had disconnected.

"I swear, if I make it through this week with her, there has to be a God and I'll go pray." Pushing the door, he picked up his briefcase and kicked the door shut once inside, "It's good to be home." His paw rested on the inset handle of the pocket door of the coat closet as he pushed it aside and set his briefcase just inside, the black leather melding with the long shadows. Emptying his pockets into the vanity tucked inside on the table, he hung up his coat and loosened his tie before closing the door and wandering down the hall. His paws glided over the cherry stained hardwood floors, past the buffet table and carefully arranged flora.

Darting through the house, he climbed the stairs by three to the second floor and ducked into the master bedroom, heading straight for the closet at the back. Stripping off his clothes, the hare carefully folded or hung each piece and set them aside on an organized rack and bin labeled "dry cleaning". Blushing a bit harder, he absently stroked his hand down his ears, tracing their ridges before gently gripping the weighted band holding his ears together and down. He admired himself in the mirror across from the rack, his eyes drawn to the snug fitting red bikini briefs resting on his hips. Shifting his stance, he admired his own slight build rubbing his hand down from his neck down to his soft bulge. "He'll be home soon; wonder what he's going to want."

He undid the weight around his ears, setting it down on the table as his ears sprung up to stand straight on his head. "Maybe the black one tonight," he mused as he reached in the drawer, pulling out a thick black leather collar with delicate ripples of lace trimming the edges.

"Hey! I'm home, where's my beer!" bellowed a deep voice from downstairs, echoing and reverberating into the walls. A look of panic crossed the hare's face as he worked the collar around his neck, all but sprinting to get himself downstairs.

"I'm sorry Sir," whined the hare as he jumped down the steps trying to get to the kitchen. "Please Sir, I was late getting home." He whined as he grabbed the beer from the refrigerator door and returned to the entry hall.

The tiger scowled, the ridges above his eyes pushing down and narrowing his gaze as he watched the hare emerge from the kitchen. The tight crossing of his arms across his chest strained the material of his oil stained fitted t-shirt. "Really, that's the same damn excuse you gave me last night. I really don't expect much from you boy, just a cold beer when I get home and my dick sucked after my shower." A low growl filled the hall as his eyes locked on the cap sealed to the top of the bottle.

The hare's eyes widened in panic as he followed the tiger's gaze to the cap. "Let me…let me go take care of that."

"No…it's fine," the tiger snapped his arm out from across his chest, his fingers wrapping around the hare's dainty wrist as the other paw reached for the beer, pulling it free. "You've made me wait long enough; I'll do it myself." Grumbling, he took the bottle with his free hand and pushed back knocking the hare off balance, his back thudding against the wall. "Go set up the table and wait for me out back boy. I've been too lenient on you lately."

"Yes Sir," whimpered the hare as he headed back into the kitchen, a door opening and closing with a loud *woosh* ringing through the house.

"Really, the bitch couldn't be bothered to fucking open my beer on his way in tonight," the tiger grunted as he followed into the kitchen, his claws clicking against the floor in frustration with each step. "What the fuck is wrong with him lately." Grunting he fished through the top drawer under the grey granite counter, finally finding one after a few seconds and popping the top off, "I think I'll make him wait." He pulled the dark wood stool out from under the crafted lip of the island and took a seat, his long striped tail flicking gingerly behind him.

Closing his eyes, he tilted his head back, taking a long swig from the green bottle. The glass clinked against the granite while the tiger's eyes drifted towards the wall clock, the seconds ticking loudly in his ears, each click forcing his ears to flick. He stretched as he moved across the kitchen, pressing firmly on the heavy door to the studio. A deep sigh escaped the tiger's muzzle as he stepped down onto the cold drab concrete of the floor, his eyes widening and narrowing to adjust to the strained lighting of the darkened room. "You ready boy?" he snapped loudly into the shadows as he took a few measured strides, his eyes adjusting further behind his contacts.

The high pitched whimper of the hare echoed through the dim room, "Yes Sir, the floggers," he paused, the audible gulping and gasping sound cutting through the momentary silence, "are on the table, Sir. I put them out just how you like them."

"That's a good boy, maybe I'll spare you a bit," he smiled slyly and made his way to the center of the room, blinking his eyes to force them to adjust to the dim lighting. The hair stood with his arms shackled together and tied to the ceiling, stretching his thin frame, each muscle group pulled taunt. "You really did lay them out right." Another chuckle filled the room as he looked over the varied selection of floggers. Turning his gaze back to the hare, he grabbed at the table at random, his fingers slowly wrapping around the handle"

The hare sniveled and whimpered softly, "Please not that one, Sir." His sharp yelps echoed through the sparse room followed by the resounding crack of the leather snapping against flesh. The soft whimper of the hare followed the echo, his small voice barely above a whisper "May I have another?"

"Of course you may, boy," the tiger snickered and pulled his arm back, snapping his wrist and delivering another stroke across the hare's red wrapped rump. "You know this hurts me a lot more than it hurts you boy." He snickered and delivered another stroke, one across the hare's shoulders, and another across his rump.

Bucking against the shackles, the hare let out a yelp, his body going rigid and then falling against the bonds, all but hanging from the shackles just above the floor. "Please, Sir," the hare whimpered weakly, "may I have another?"

Grunting and chuckling, the tiger struck again, the snap of his wrist clicking in the air just before the snap and crack of the leather, "Yes you may, boy, yes you may."

The hare howled at the twin strokes, tensing and slumping further against the bonds. "Please, Sir," he stammered, tears flowing down his face and dampening his fur, "may I…"

Snickering and clicking his tongue, the feline then snapped his wrists one last time, landing a final set of lashes across the hare's reddening flesh. "I think that's enough." He absently tossed the straps back onto the table. He placed his paw on the hare's hip and walked around, his paw sliding along the top of the red band and just resting on the hare's stomach. "Are you okay?" He asked, tenderly touching his nose against the hare's and licking softly.

The hare nodded slowly and blushed as he pushed against the paw. "Yeah…I'm okay…" he whispered, returning the faint kiss.

Grinning, the tiger pulled back and brushed his other paw down his shirt before resting on the swollen bulge in his filthy jeans. "Clean up and meet me upstairs boy. Don't keep me waiting too long, or we'll be back here again." He passed the shackle key into the hare's limp paw, giving it a gentle squeeze before turning to walk to the door his tail flicking from side to side.

"Yes Master," he whispered as the door slammed shut behind the tiger, the hare's eyes lingering where he watched the black and white striped tail vanished. "We really need to talk about redoing this floor," the hare grunted as he undid the locks on the shackles. He rubbed his wrists while rolling his shoulders, working the kinks and cramps from his muscles, "Shower first, he can at least wait that long," he swallowed sharply and blushed, "At least I hope he can."

***

The white tiger sprawled on the bed with his paws folded behind his head, his eyes closed and ears perked and listening. "He better hurry up," groaned the tiger, his paw lacing around his swelling cock and giving it a long deliberate stroke while his leg muscles flexed and stretched. A soft moan followed the groan as a small bead of pre formed and spread over the red swollen tip. Reaching off to the side, he pulled the gold satin sheet across his midsection, a dark spot appearing where his tip rested against the fabric.

The door creaked open as the tiger returned his paw back behind his head, "Sir?" the hare whimpered from the hall, his nose pressing just inside the crack at the door.

"Come here boy…you make me wait much longer you'll be saddling up without lube no matter how much you beg."

"Yes, Sir." The hare slipped into the room with a black towel draped around his waist and tucked just under his teardrop tail. "I just wanted to be clean for you, Sir."

"Good, you know I fucking like it when you're cleaned out." He grunted and tossed the sheet aside, his member pulsing and beading a few clear, thick droplets. "Get to work…" he sighed as he arched his back, gently thrusting his cock up into the air in time with the pulsing to coat his member with more viscous pre.

The hare swished across the room his eyes fixed on the throbbing rod before his eyes, "I'm so hungry, Sir; thank you for feeding your boy." Leaning forward, he brushed his right cheek against the feline member, pressing the barbed flesh deep against his cheek, grinding the thick pre into his short muzzle. "Sir must have worked hard today," he twitched his nose, taking a deep breath of the sharp acidic musk filling the air.

Grunting, the tiger forced the hare's ears to either side, resting his paw on the back of his head and slowly guiding him up and down. "Oh it was a very busy day; now, shut your whore mouth and suck my dick." Snarling, he extended his claws, gently pulling the hare's muzzle just in front of his slick head, "Open wide," he growled as he pushed the hare's head down, letting out a soft moan as he felt the wet warmth surround him.

A soft moan filled the room as the hare moved his paws to balance gently on the tiger's thighs while he pushed himself, slowly swallowing more of the flared barbed head into his shallow muzzle and gasping as the head slipped past and into his tight throat.

"That's a good boy, that's a very good boy." The tiger bucked his hips, pressing deeper into the hare's tight throat. "Get it nice and slick," he grunted and growled before pulling the hare off, smiling down at him. "Time to saddle up boy," he winked down with a sly smirk.

The hare nodded slowly, blushing as he removed the towel, his pale rouge cock pointing straight down at the bed and his balls sagging low behind him. "With pleasure Sir," he pressed his knees on either side of the tiger's torso as he arched his back and reached behind, moaning softly as he gently gripped the tiger's swelling cock and lined himself up. "Please can I have some lube, Sir?" whimpered the hare as he grunted and pushed himself down, the barbed head forcing inside.

A medley of groans filled the room as the hare and tiger worked in unison, each stroke and counter-stroke timed perfectly. The soft pants and rising moans as they worked together the tiger's paws resting on the hare's hips, guiding him up and down, his claws gently digging into and raking, leaving soft pink lines in the hare's fur.

Rolling his head back, the hare moaned and pressed down against the sharp thrust, grinding his hips down then keeping himself hilted as the tiger lay back against the bed, the hare's paws kneading and massaging the tiger's dense pectorals. "Please, Sir; Please let me..."

The tiger nodded slowly, moving his paws up higher, grabbing the hare just at the base of his ribcage to pull him up and then push him back down. "Yes, boy, finish. I want to see it." Tightening his grip on the hare, he began to pull him faster, his eyes fixed on the hare's cock thrusting in and out of the lattice of fingers. "That's it," he licked his maw and bucked faster, his breath coming faster and more ragged. "Just a little more," his assertive tone cracking between ragged gasps.

"I'm gonna," the hare panted as the tiger's claws dug into his sides, then squeaked in surprise at being pulled and grinded down before he rolled his head back and howled, his member throbbing in his laced fingers. Ropes of seed sprayed across the tiger's stomach and chest, the first shot leaving a trail from shoulder to naval.

Closing his eyes, the tiger opened his maw, and a loud roar resounded through the room as the tight star of the hare clamped around his barbed member and they dug in and gripped his soft insides. "That's it boy! Here's your reward," he bucked his hips one last time, holding the hare tight and close as his member began to swell and pulse with thick ropes of cum sliding deep inside the shuddering hare.

"Yes…thank you, Sir," the hare moaned softly through the final waves of his own climax. "Thank you, Sir," he murmured, leaning down to rest his torso against the tiger and rocking himself back and forth, fur matting together with rich combination of sweat and cum. He cooed and murmured noises of gratitude, lapping at the small trail of seed coating the underside of the tiger's short maw.

Rumbling softly, the tiger wrapped his arms around the hare and while holding him tightly, he reached up and undid the thick leather collar, pulling it from around the hare's neck and tossing it into the basket atop the nightstand, "Shhhh….shhhh…come back to me, CJ." He stroked across the hares reddened and sore shoulders. "Come on, come back to me." He whimpered and continued petting.

"I'm here," he murmured, nuzzling his nose into the tiger's shoulder, "that was hot."

Raising his hand the tiger swatted the hare's rump, his cock still locked inside by the barbs. "Damn straight it was hot, boy." He grinned a bit wider and pulled CJ closer.

"Yes, Sir," CJ whimpered.

"So what's for dinner tonight? I have to be up early; damn bastard overbooked the shop so I gotta go work the shop instead of just the back office."

"Maybe we should order in then, sir," CJ nuzzled the tiger again, his voice balancing boy and lover. "Why don't you go order us something nice from that Thai place."

Narrowing his gaze, the tiger lifted his head and glared at the hare, "Again? Seriously we order from there like twice a week! We never go any-fucking-where since you don't want us seen in public together," the tiger snarled through bared fangs, "else we could go to that steakhouse that you rave about all the time."

CJ looked away, "You know I can't be out at work, I mean they're all…"

"Fucking stupid," snapped the tiger as he rolled his head back flat against the pillow. "I fucking fix cars and everyone at the shop knows I'm a fag, doesn't cause me a lick of trouble."

"Yes sir, but you're just fixing cars; I'm working with a lot of really powerful, influential people," the color flushed out of his face while the tiger's large paw pressed over his face, "I didn't mean it th…" With a harsh shove, the barbs pulled and tugged on the hare's insides as he was forcibly pushed off and onto the bed.

"Right, I just fix fucking cars." He stood up and tossed the collar off the nightstand back onto the bed before crossing his arms across his chest, flexing his back muscles. "Get your fucking ass back in the shackles. I think somebody is too fucking full of himself right now!" His tail flicked back and forth in frustration. "Now!" he roared, all but shaking the room with his voice.

Whimpering and whining, the hare slid out of bed. "Yes, Sir," he murmured as he headed towards the door back to the studio.

***

Ryan growled sharply as his legs kicked the blankets onto the floor and exposed his muscled, naked form, his chest fur still matted and clumped from the earlier heated activities. Grunting he tossed again, rolling to face the opposing wall. "Damnit, CJ, stop fucking stealing the covers!" His arm slammed down on the empty side of the bed sinking down to the mattress in one quick motion. "Oh…," he murmured, looking over at the empty space, startled awake by the loud whoosing thud. "I should go get him," he grumbled and grabbed his robe, heading towards the door.

The door to the studio creaked open. "CJ? You still awake?" The tiger stepped down, inhaling sharply at the cold concrete beneath his paw pushing him full awake.

"Yes, Sir, boy is still awake."

Ryan's tone sank back into rough dominance. "Do you think you have been punished enough?"

"If Sir says I have, then I have been."

A cold chuckle filled the room as Ryan stepped into the dim lights of the studio. "I think you've been punished enough, boy. I'll let you down now and you can come to bed." Grumbling he fiddled with the shackles, undoing the latches and catching the hare as he fell, "It's okay, CJ; let's go to bed now…"

"Yes, sir," whimpered the hare as he slumped against Ryan .

"Shhhh…it's okay dear, I'll tuck you in." Hoisting CJ over his shoulder he moved towards the door.

***

CJ grumbled as he pushed his chair back, letting it spin lazily before the windows as he headed out the door of his office and down the hall, ignoring the shrill cries from Linda trying to get his attention. "This is about to get messy," he muttered to himself as he came to a stop outside a darkly stained set of double doors labeled *Venice* in fine gold script. The hare pushed on the door, silently counting to three before stepping in, "You're a liar," he barked, his voice accented by the sharp thud of the door setting back into the frame.

"I beg your pardon?" rose a smooth voice above the series of gasps rising through the visible tension in the room.

Pointing at the polar bear, CJ snapped, "Let me try it this way then: you're full of shit." CJ's grin widened across his face as he made his way into the room towards the empty seat at the head of the table. Flopping down in the chair he kicked his paws up onto the table and crossed them. "Hell's frozen and thawed if you magically 'found' a new bid just a few days after you signed the contract with us."

The polar bear furrowed his brows over his bright blue eyes, "How dare you," he growled, baring his teeth.

"Knock if off!" He pulled his feet off the long conference table and slammed both fists into the dark surface. "Now, let's get one thing straight here," he paused his eyes resting momentarily at the collection of the polar bear's underlings and yes-men, "you need us. After that little incident of yours you needed the best—and you're going to have to pay for them, them being me." He turned his gaze over to the bear, eyes locking onto the narrow glare.

The bear shook his head slightly and looked down at the table, "You can all head back to the office; I think I can handle Mr. Bennett." Turning his attention back to the hare he smiled, his eyes watching the door as his colleagues left, waiting for the door to close behind them, "So what tipped you off?"

CJ smirked wildly. "That would be revealing a trade secret; if you'll excuse me I have a lunch appointment." He spun in his chair and turned his back on the bear.

"Ah yes, your secretary informed me, a standing weekly lunch date. Do tell your *Master* that I said hello." A small biting chuckle escaped his throat.

Turning the chair around slowly CJ adjusted himself, swallowing the large lump forming in his throat. "Excuse me?" He reached up and tugged at his lapels, adjusting the lines of his suit. "I'm afraid I have no idea what you're talking about, Mr. Simmons."

"So how long has Ryan Archer been living with you? Seems odd that someone of your station have a *roommate*." The bear leaned back in the chair and reclined as he folded his arms across his chest.

CJ narrowed his gaze, the ridge over his eyes flattening further. "What do you want?"

"Now we're getting somewhere I see."

The hare slammed his fist down on to the table, his face flushing, "I will not be blackmailed!"

"And what would happen if your Senior Partners discovered that their top money maker is a fairy? We'll be in touch." Pushing back from the table, the polar bear rose and started striding for the door. "We need to draft the proposed changes and the new figures and have it sent to your lovely new secretary before lunch." He pulled the door open, "As always, a pleasure, Mr. Bennett."

The hare waited for the door to swing shut. "Shit." Pushing away from the table, he stormed out of the conference room, his claws clicking against the floor as he briskly walked down the hall, then stopped at the side of the ferret's desk. "Linda I need you to call and get my car." He paused, reaching for his phone as it began to vibrate lightly. "Also, call Gary and tell him that we may have a problem with Tungsten and I am going to need some help on damage control." He looked at the caller id. "I have to go take this; buzz me when my car is ready."

He pushed the door open and slid into his office, forcing the door closed behind him and tapping the answer button on the screen of his phone. "Hey!" he whispered into the phone as he made his way over to his desk. "Yes, we're still on for lunch." Taking his seat, he rifled through his black leather briefcase, fussing with the locks. "No, I was going to swing by the shop and pick you up. I figured we could try somewhere new; so let me just wrap up a few things here and I will be over to get you. Can I call you back in a few minutes? I need to write a few emails. Thanks!"

Dropping the phone to the desk, he tapped the disconnect button, then rummaged through his briefcase, flipping through a few more pages as the intercom buzzed, "Mr. Bennett, the driver has your car pulled around." The intercom clicked off immediately.

The sharp ding of an incoming email echoed from the speakers. Absently he tapped *enter* on the keyboard, the message expanding across the large screen to his left. Squinting he scanned the client email as each successive line made his eyes narrow, "Fuck," he murmured as he skimmed over the last lines of the message.

Locking his computer, he grabbed his computer and made his way to the door, leaving the briefcase open on the desk. He pushed the door open, "Linda, cancel my lunch reservations at *Pastiesse* and get me a table at *Dukes*." Grumbling he made his way to the elevator, reaching into his pocket for his phone and hitting the shortcut to call Ryan.

"Hello there sweetcheeks!" chirped the tiger cheerfully from the speaker.

"I just wanted to let you know I'm heading out now, I should be at the garage in about ten minutes provided traffic isn't that bad," CJ mumbled as he stepped into the crowded elevator, his voice intentionally low as he turned the receiver volume down.

"Okay. Well I hope I'm going to like this surprise."

"I'll see you then and we can go over next quarter's cost estimates."

"Are you wearing those red briefs that I like to see you in?"

CJ shifted his stance shuffling his weight back and forth. "Yes I do have last quarter's figures as well; but, they are still estimates so I am not 100% confident in their accuracy yet."

"I can't wait 'til you get here, *boy*. I've got a nice surprise for you."

"Oh? That is definitely good news, I'll make sure that I get that information updated and get the updated contract for your records."

"See you in a few, *boy*, and you better be ready for some work."

"Yes I'll see you shortly, bye."

Ending the call, he slid the phone into his pocket and squirmed a bit, adjusting his suit jacket to keep it closed over his swollen groin.

"Client lunch meeting, CJ?" asked a small voice off to his side.

"Yeah, he's a pain in the ass; he likes to get weekly updates and won't take meetings with anyone but me."

"Definitely sounds like a handful." The mouse reached over and patted the hare on the shoulder, "But, we all have our crosses to bear it seems. Yours just happens to be a client."

CJ turned looking at the mouse standing next to him. "Oh! Mr. Nickles, I didn't realize it was you!" He flushed and pulled slightly letting the mouse's hand fall from his shoulder. "How are you doing today, sir?"

"Much better now that the issue with Tungsten seems resolved. We aren't in a position to really lose such an important client." The mouse pushed his glasses back up on his nose, smiling up at the hare. "I hear we have you to thank for that."

"It was nothing Mr. Nickles, I just did what any good Account Manager would do, just play to their ego." He flushed a bit more as he took in a deep breath.

"Glad to hear it. Well keep up the good work." He edged forward towards the opening door, "If you'll excuse me, CJ, this is my floor." He nodded slowly, "I'll have Christy set up and appointment for us sometime soon, I think it's about time we get to know each other."

CJ turned his shoulders and pressed himself against the side of the elevator at the next floor after the car emptied out. "Welcome to the Twilight Zone," he muttered to himself. He stepped out of the elevator into the garage, "I'll take it from here, thanks, Mark, for holding it. Elevators were slow today."

***

The car lurched over the small series of speed bumps as he pulled into the torn up cement parking lot. Shaking his head, he sighed as he looked at the grimy run down shop. "I really need to get him out of here." He kicked the door open and stepped out, grunting, stretching and cracking his back.

Heading across the lot to the office, he stepped around the skids and splatters of various oils and lubes. Another sigh escaped his lungs as he walked up to the weather worn glass insert door, the green paint peeling and flaking. Pressing the bell, he waited to hear the harsh buzz of the door locks popping open. Grunting again, he gave the warped door a sharp shove leading to a cloud of musty sweat and fumes. He nodded slowly to the teenaged cougar sitting behind the desk, a heavy textbook sprawled out over the worn counter. "Is Ryan around?" he croaked, his voice small as he looked around bashfully. "He's in his office; you know where it is." The teenager hadn't bothered looking up from his book his pencil moving furiously across a loose sheet of paper.

"Thanks." Brushing his paw against the wall, he passed the restrooms to the slightly ajar door at the end of the hall, the thin slivers of light making long shadows. Knocking the door he nudged it open, his head down and his eyes fixed on the floor, "Ryan? You in?"

"Yup come on in, just finishing some purchasing requests then we can go." The tiger leaned back in his office chair and tossed his glasses onto the cluttered desk. "Close the door, would ya? I meant to close it but I missed," he absently pointed at the basketball.

Leaning back against the door, he pressed it shut, his ear twitching as the click echoed through the room. "Sorry it took so long, Sir, there was some extra traffic on the bridge this afternoon."

Ryan waved absently, "Get to work," he growled as he entered a few more entries on the keyboard.

"Umm, Ryan?" CJ hesitated, "Can we talk first?"

The tiger cleared his throat, leveling a narrow glare across the dimly lit room. "Now, *boy*! I have a heavy set of balls here, and they need fucking drained."

The hare whimpered and made his way deeper into the room, dancing around the scattered piles of paper around to the back of the desk. The deep scent of musk filled the air, taunting his senses as he crawled across the floor towards the waiting tiger. Peeking around the corner, he blushed further at the swollen sheath hanging from the fly of Ryan's stained cargo pants. "May I please taste it, Master?" he hissed softly between clenched teeth, each wave of musk draining the independence from his glassing eyes.

"Yes, boy, I'd suggest you don't keep me waiting or we're going to have a repeat of last night." He grunted and slid himself forward, his balls sliding out the open zipper and hanging down below the lip of the chair.

CJ pressed his nose against the tiger's low hanging sack, his tongue gently lapping at the heavy orbs. Arching his body, he looked up at the tiger, smearing the delicate beads of pre into his short muzzle. "Thank you, Master."

"That's a very good boy, get those nice and clean." He rubbed his paw between CJ's tied ears.

He turned his head to the side and pressed his tongue into the open fly, brushing his tongue against the short striped fur, feeding on the masculine musk. Panting softly, he pulled back and pressed his damp nose against the root of the sheath, nuzzling and pressing the sheath back and exposing the ruby barbed head. "May I please taste your delicious cock, Master?"

"That's a good boy, go ahead." The tiger rolled his hips, pressing the tip against the hare's opening muzzle, grinding the barbs against CJ's soft tongue. "That's good, open wide."

The hare lifted his head, lining up his throat as he pushed his muzzle forward, stretching to accommodate the shaft sliding into his gaping throat.

Ryan grinned down at the hare as he slid forward, "Such a good boy, you must be starving today." A low rumble echoed in his chest, his cock driving a bit deeper into the tight lapine throat. "Just a little more, almost to your treat," Ryan moaned, his hips bucking a bit faster, the even strokes interrupted with an occasional shake and shudder. Slumping back in his seat, he fell back into his chair, his body bucking wildly. His member pulsed, blocking the hare's throat as the thick ropes emptied down into the hare's gut.

Coughing around the thick shaft, he pulled back, his cheeks puffing out as a thick stream flooded into his maw and down his waiting throat. A muffled moan escaped around the shaft as he suckled his way back up to the barbed tip, letting the last shots of the cream get swallowed, before pulling all the way off and looking up. "Is Master pleased with my service?"

Another low rumble filled the room as Ryan reached down, stroking along the hare's jaw and pulled his face up to look him in the eyes. "That was very good, boy; now, I want to talk to CJ. I promise we will play later, boy."

CJ slumped for a second with his pupils expanding and contracting. Finally he picked himself up, standing slowly and leaning on the desk for support, pushing away the tiger's paws gently reaching out to catch him. "I'm okay, hun, just a little weak is all." He rubbed his paws against his cheek fur trying to smooth out the matting from the pre.

Smiling brightly, the tiger tucked himself back into his pants. "So where are you taking me for lunch today?" Stretching, he leaned in nose to nose with the hare. "I mean since you've already had your lunch, *boy*."

Flushing slightly he looked away. "How would you feel about going to *Dukes*?"

Ryan's eyes widened between a series blinks and coughs, "You mean the steakhouse you've been going on about for the past year and never take me to?" He smiled wide and reached around CJ, locking the computer terminal and stealing a quick kiss, "Let me tell the guys we're going out and I'll meet you at the car."

"Okay, dear." He headed down the hall ducking into the bathroom to give his face a quick wash, a new blush having settled in. "Well, I guess I can tell him after lunch. We can at least enjoy that." After washing, he headed out to the car, absently waving at the cougar behind the desk, still engrossed in his work. Moving carefully through the lot again, he got into the car while flipping through the influx of messages on his phone, "Let's just see how much more fucked this day can get." His eyes widened as he skimmed the message, then he shook his head in disbelief . "Ready to go?" he turned, smiling at the tiger climbing into the seat.

"The way you've talked about this place! Oh hell yeah." Ryan smiled big as he leaned over to kiss the hare on the cheek again. "The schedule is pretty light for at least the rest of the afternoon, so we can take a long as we want."

"Wait, I thought you said you were over booked?"

"For the morning crew yeah, but I spent most of the day in the shop helping out." He tapped CJ on the shoulder. "Let's go I'm hungry!"

"Keep your pants on; we have to get clear across town." Starting the car he backed up and headed back towards the highway, resting his hand on top of Ryan's, lacing their fingers together. "Love you, jackass."

"Love you too, bitch."

***

Lifting his head from his salad his eyes rested on the tiger taking a large chunk of rare steak into his mouth. "So, um, I think we have to skip going to the club tonight, I had something *special* come up at the office."

The tiger set his fork down. "So that's why we came here for lunch?"

The hare lowered his gaze again, stirring the mixed greens and dressing around his plate. "No! I knew you were tired of hearing me talk about this place, and I wanted to bring you here."

"Right, and I am a five foot tall female badger who needs a boob job; now what happens when we lie?"

"Sir punishes me," he murmured softly checking from side to side making sure no one was listening.

"That's right; so there better be a damn good reason for this." Ryan rested his palm on the table idly drumming his fingers his gaze fixed between the hare's ears.

CJ's shoulders lifted in a heavy sigh. "A client found out about… us." He looked up briefly, then back at his plate.

Ryan coughed. "Excuse me?"

"We are having issues with this account, and I called bullshit on some fake documents, and then…he's sorta, blackmailing us, I mean me." He took a breath and looked up, panic filling his eyes. "So basically he wants to have a dinner meeting at our house with Mr. Nickles and wants to get a reduced rate. If I don't do this he's going to out me to the firm, and I'm finished," he panted softly, looking up at the stone expression carved into the tiger's furrowed brow.

"Just to make sure I am following; if you don't do this dinner *at our home*," he growled, "he's going to ruin your life, and therefore will complicate mine."

The hare gave a slow nod. "Yes, sir."

"Then I guess I could go to the club alone and leave you to handle your work." The tiger forced a smile onto his face, grabbing the knife and fork to cut another bite of his steak.

"Actually," the hare swallowed hard, "he wants you there, and I was thinking maybe we could stage it as you were a private chef/butler that I employed to help keep up the house."

A low snarl carried across the table as the tiger sunk back into his chair. "If I didn't love you as much as I do, I'd leave and you'd come home to a damn near empty house." He dropped his knife and fork to the table with a soft clatter. "I need to go to the store then and get started. Finish your salad and pay the bill. I'll be in the car." He held up his hand and flagged the waiter hovering by the bar across the dining room. "I'll need a box for the steak, and the check please." He nodded politely as the bear made his way off to the waiter station, then returned with a silver lined box for the remainder of the tiger's steak and the leather folio holding the check.

***

"Yes, Mr. Nickles, I've arranged the perfect meal to accommodate everyone, don't worry, everything will be fine sir and we will finish this deal tonight." CJ tapped the line closed on his headset as he pushed the door to the house, shifting the paper bag in his arms. "Ryan!" he bellowed, "I got the last of the list here. Did you really mean 5 pounds of that stuff?"

Grunting, the tiger emerged from the kitchen into the hall. "Yes or I wouldn't have asked for it." Stabbing the hare in the chest playfully he took the bag and retreated back to the kitchen, his claws clicking against the floor as his tail flicked. "Get the table set and then get in here, I have some stuff for you to do."

"Yes, Sir," he blushed as his eyes followed the swaying tail, tracing the striped line shown in the open back of the black and white soccer jock. "Do you, ummm, think we'll have some time for a quickie before our guest arrive, Sir?"

"If you hurry your damn ass up we will," called Ryan from the kitchen, his words followed by the loud hiss of something hitting a hot pan filling the air, followed by the smell of cooking meat.

The hare busied himself in the dining room setting each place, returning periodically to the shelving and cabinets along the wall to withdraw some extra piece that was missing from each of the three place settings. "How many courses are we having tonight?"

"Standard three; you really didn't give me a lot of time or I would have done more."

"Okay, I'll bring the plates into the kitchen then, but I think I have it all set in here." Groaning he hefted the stack of plates and stepped into the kitchen to set them down next to the sink. A smile brushed across his face as he watched the tiger from behind, the deeply cut bulk muscle shifting and swaying to a beat of imaginary music. "Do you always have to dance when you cook?"

"Yes, food made with love tastes better, much like raping you is better because I love you."

CJ flushed and looked at the floor. "Yes, Sir," he whispered as he walked up behind the tiger, wrapping his arms as best he could around the thick waist. "You know I love you, Ryan."

"I love you too, CJ, now could you please go peel the carrots and potatoes for me?"

"You got it," the hare smiled big as he began working on the vegetables resting in the sink. Dropping a potato into the bowl of water, CJ's ears perked, flicking at the doorbell ringing. "Who the hell?" He wiped his paws on a dishtowel, heading towards the door, "Oh! You're early, I thought I had confirmed with your secretary for 7:30."

"Yes, I heard the message, but I'm not here to talk to you, boy," the polar bear forced the door open and pushed past CJ heading down the hall. "Ryan get your lazy striped ass out here."

Pressing the door closed CJ snapped, "Excuse me!" he barked at the polar bear's back.

"If I want you to speak, boy, I will tell your Master to order you to do so."

Shaking his head, the hare made his way down the hall to stand directly between the bear and the dining room. "How dare you!"

"It's okay, CJ," the tiger's warm paw pressed against his shoulder, "why don't you go relax in the studio; I think our guest and I need to have a chat."

Nodding, CJ turned and went back down the hall to the studio.

Crossing his arms, Ryan straightened his back, his ears pivoting to follow the sound of the door latching shut.

"I assume he'll be punished for being rude to me," huffed the bear, glaring at the tiger towering over him.

"No, he won't be." A loud thump echoed through the hall as his tail slammed against the floor. Baring his fangs, Ryan looked down his short muzzle and snarled, "Now go sit in the living room until I'm ready to deal with you, *boy!*"

"Yes, sir," the polar bear whimpered and shrunk back, his gaze falling on his shuffling feet.

He glared as the polar bear retreated to the room and took a seat on the overstuffed couch. Hissing, he made his way through the kitchen into the studio and closed the door with a sharp clap. The soft growls and grunts of CJ filled his ears followed by the rapid succession of dull thuds gave him a smile. "Again," he snapped, making his way across the room to watch the hare bob and wave between timed assaults on the bag.

"Yes, Sir!" CJ barked with near military precision, repeating the strikes against bag.

"Again!"

"Yes, Sir!"

Reaching out, the tiger caught the hare's fist as it flew towards the bag. "That's enough." He reached out and brushed his paw down the hare's cheek. "Do you feel better?"

He slumped against the paw on his cheek and panted, "Yes, Sir, I do, Sir."

"Shhhhhh, none of that right now; I don't need this behavior from two of you tonight."

"What?" Rage flashed in CJ's eyes, and he withdrew his fist. "You know him!"

Nodding, he lowered his arm, pulling the hare close to him. "Yes, that's the cheating bastard I was with before you. Now go upstairs the back way and I'll deal with him." He kissed CJ between the ears and pushed him away affectionately.

***

A loud crack rang through the room as the back of Ryan's hand connected with the polar bear's cheek. "I trained you better than this, boy!'

"Please, Sir, may I have another?"

"No, that's enough for you." Wiping the blood off the back of his hand he looked at the polar bear's split lip. "Now what the hell do you think you're playing at, Lance?"

"I don't expect you to understand–it's just business."

Sitting down in the matching overstuffed chair Ryan crossed his legs and flexed his muscles, "You feel like having working balls after this you better talk."

"We, well the company I represent, had a small accident; I'm sure you heard about it in the papers," the bear eyed the tiger as he nodded, confirming he's following along; "and we needed a PR firm so we went through the book, and your *boy* is the best fixer in the business."

"Yes he is; he managed to save the shop several times, but…" he swung his paw in a lazy circle pressing the bear on.

"Well like all good companies, we don't like paying full price, so I was asked to dig up some dirt on your *boy*,"

"His name is CJ, don't tempt me right now."

"I was asked to dig up some dirt on CJ," the name twisted in his mouth as he spoke, "and that's when I found out about you living here, and well I'm sure he caught you up on the rest."

"That you're blackmailing him and threatening to out him publicly if he doesn't cut you the rate that you want."

"Yes, Sir."

"And now you're going to tell me why I don't out you to your job, destroy your life, flay the skin off your insolent hide and make it into a rug for my favorite chair, and then bury you in the backyard." Ryan uncrossed his legs and leaned forward his fangs barred in a twisted snarl.

The polar bear sank back into the couch trying to make himself smaller. "Because you know I'll enjoy being flogged, Sir."

Lunging from his chair the tiger wrapped his hand around the bear's throat as his claws extended and pressed into the soft underlying flesh. "Not good enough…"

"Because if you out me, I'll bring him down with me. I'll still have a career and future, whereas your *boy* will be ruined," whispered Lance through the pressure of the tiger squeezing down on his throat .

Snarling he loosened his grip and pulled his arm back, "There's a bathroom over there, clean yourself up. I need to go finish this dinner. Now you're going to be a good boy and you're going to play nice tonight over dinner."

***

CJ sprinted down the stairs while pulling the knot of his tie up between the collar points. "I got it, Ryan, just keep working on dinner!" he called back, nearly at the door, pausing to pull and adjust his clothes, smoothing out the creases and wrinkles. Opening the door he smiled, making a sweeping grand gesture with his free hand. "Good evening, Mr. Nickles, won't you please come in."

"Such a lovely home you have, CJ," the mouse murmured as he stepped inside, careful to wipe his feet on the mat, his eyes drifting in admiration of the décor and constructions of the entryway.

"Thank you sir; I take a great deal of pride and care in my home," he smiled and pressed the door closed listening for the latch, "Mr. Briggs is already here; he's waiting for us for before dinner drinks in the lounge."

The mouse smiled with a polite nod, following the hare down the hall. "I would swear there was a woman's touch around here if I didn't know you were single."

CJ brushed at his face as though scratching an itch. "I have hired several different decorators to make sure I keep up with the trends."

"Well I will most certainly need her card; I feel my home needs a bit of attention after looking at your lovely décor."

"I'll make it a point to get her card for you." Walking into the entry way he positioned himself across the room at the small bar cabinet, "Red wine, sir? Or would you prefer something else?"

"Actually a good glass of white would be fine. Turning his attention to the polar bear reclining on the sofa, Mr. Nickles said, "It's very nice to see you Lance, I'm flattered you thought to request that I come to this dinner, but I trust CJ's ability to properly negotiate for everyone's mutual benefit."

"I have the utmost confidence in your golden boy's abilities," the bear said, leaning forward and smiling as he set his empty glass on the coffee table with a clink . "When you have a moment, CJ, would you please fill me up."

"Certainly, Mr. Briggs." Glowering, he reached for another glass, pouring the whiskey and bringing both glasses over and to set them down. "Gentlemen, shall we talk business before dinner or after?"

"If Lance is ready for it, I have no issue with discussing the revisions to the contract before dinner," Mr. Nickles murmured as he sipped his wine.

"Do we know how long before dinner is served? I would prefer we didn't get interrupted." Lance grinned at the hare and nodded towards the kitchen.

CJ rose, hiding his grumbling in his glass, and headed towards the kitchen, "If you both will excuse me, I will be right back. I am going to check with the cook and see how far out dinner is." He ducked the rest of the way into the kitchen, sliding the pocket door closed.

"What's this about, Lance?" The mouse sat up straight setting his glass down on the coaster, his voice deepening and filling the room. "You're being rather rude even for you."

"We just think that it may be possible to get a better rate." Taking a sip, he then set his glass down directly on the table, "And given the recent… incident," he paused briefly looking at his hands, "the company isn't in a position to spend that much money on a gamble."

The mouse nodded slightly, leaning back in his own seat. "Ahhh, hence inviting me for these negotiations; you're hoping I can help cut you a better deal and save your own skin."

"I was told whatever means were necessary."

"I would be careful with what you wish for," the mouse's ears flicked as the pocket door opened.

CJ, returning to the room, said, "Actually gentlemen, the cook has informed me that dinner will be served momentarily." He adjusted his shirt again pulling a few new wrinkles from the material.

"Well seems like you don't have a good hand on your servants if they can't do things on time." Lance glared over his glass before taking yet another swig, snarling as the spirits touched the raw flesh of the split in his lip.

"Ryan is a very capable cook, Mr. Briggs. However, since you arrived so early, he thought it would be prudent to have dinner prepared earlier than originally planned."

"How very thoughtful of him," the mouse said, as he rose, taking his glass with him and moving through the large archway to the dining room, admiring the place settings. "If everything tastes as good as it smells I might just have to hire him the next time I host a dinner party of my own."

"I would never dream of letting a servant make those kinds of decisions; what's next, you let him pick the menu for this evening?"

"In fact I did, Mr. Briggs; as I said he is quite an accomplished cook and I trust him to have made something enjoyable for everyone." CJ narrowed his eyes, glaring across the room at the polar bear. "But you can judge that for yourself; I believe I hear him bringing out the first course." Turning the hare smiled as the tiger came walking into the dining room, a tray oval balanced on his square shoulders holding three small salads.

"Gentlemen, if you'd please take your seats." Ryan gave a huge fake painted smile, "I have tried to please everyone's particular requirements." Setting down a plate at each of the settings he set the tray on the buffet, grabbing the wine and pouring. Standing at the head of the table, he smiled and his eyes followed the hare's movements while helping to push CJ's seat in. Nodding, he picked up his tray and vanished into the kitchen again.

"For such an accomplished cook, I think this salad is a bit," the bear's lips twisted, "pedestrian."

The hare and the mouse looked over with narrowed eyes as they carefully set down their forks.

"What I mean to say, for myself, being a carnivore, I find this salad to be a bit plain."

CJ nodded slowly, "I can understand that." Grumbling he took another small bite, "So, Mr. Briggs, I can appreciate your position, but I don't think there is anything we can do regarding the contractual rates."

Pushing the plate away, the bear slumped back in his chair. "Certainly there is something we can do about that," the bear looked at the mouse across the table.

"I believe CJ is correct, Lance," the mouse took another delicate bite of the salad, his smile broadening as he picked through the salad, eating it slowly. "The contract has in fact been signed and executed; so such revisions are rather unorthodox, and also a non-requirement."

"Given your golden *boy's* behavior in the boardroom today," he smiled slyly over at the hare, who sat quietly with his salad remaining mostly untouched, "I'm sure that there is something we can do. I know that Sigma is in no state to lose a client with the end of the year coming up."

Clearing his throat, the mouse put his fork down, pushing his near empty plate away. "Lance, given the fact that you not only lied, but also tried to make a fool out of everyone, I, and the rest of the Senior Partners, feel that it was an entirely appropriate course of action, albeit a bit on the dramatic side," he turned his head towards CJ, giving him a mixed move of flat and amused glare.

Peeking his head out of the kitchen, Ryan looked over at the hare, "I'm sorry dear, but mains are going to need a few more minutes."

Mr. Nickles cocked his head to the side, watching the creeping lines of rouge spread across the hare's cheeks. "Dear?" A sly smile pulled across his face, "Well I see tonight is just full of surprises."

"It's not what you think; I'm not...," CJ began to ramble, his hands gesturing wildly.

Arching a brow a sinister grin spread across Lance's face. "So you're golden *boy* is really a *boi* after all," the biting tone of his voice cutting into the building tension of the room. Pushing himself back, he tossed the napkin onto the table. "I should have seen it earlier, a single hare, with a single male servant. Even allowing that servant to make decisions." He snickered and began heading for the door before stopping and turning. "It would be a complete hit on the family values of Tungsten Aerospace to allow a queer to work for us even by contract."

"Lance!" snapped the mouse, rising from his own seat, "You wouldn't dare..."

"I'm sorry, Geoff, but there is nothing I can do. You know how family oriented we are as a company, and I am not sure I could sell my superiors on allowing a fairy to work for us. We may be in trouble but we still have our standards."

Dinner Theatre

The hare sat at the table with his paws resting on the edge, his eyes darting back and forth between the bear and mouse, "Excuse me, but I'm not gay," murmured CJ as he rose, glaring at Lance. Puffing up his chest and shoulders he did his best to stare directly into the bear's eyes. "Considering your behavior earlier, I don't think anyone is going to believe this slander."

"Then why did that servant *boy* just call you 'dear'?"

"I do believe that is none of your business Lance, and I suggest you drop it." Unclenching his fists the mouse took a deep breath. "We will not re-negotiate the terms of the contract to be more convenient for you." Indicating the bear's now vacant seat, "Perhaps we should just enjoy this nice meal that CJ and his cook have taken the time to prepare, and talk about better things as it appears we are at a business impasse." The delicate murmur of the mouse's voice was gone, replaced by a cold intensity that shredded the remaining tension and brought the temperature in the room down around his icy glare.

"I'm sorry, Geoff, but I won't stay in this faggot's house any longer."

A loud roar surged into the dining from the kitchen as Ryan made his way deliberately towards the room stopping in the open archway propping himself up against the frame. He crossed his booted paws and standing with the toe balancing the heel into the air. His glare narrowed as his crossed arms bulged and flexed his pectorals and biceps, and the tight fit of his boot cut jeans hugging the deeply carved muscles of his legs. "That enough, *boy*." His voice cut through the shock and awe of the room. "Get your boot-licking, faggot ass over here and give them a good polish before I cut your nuts off and feed them to you, you fucking bruin bitch!"

CJ eyes widened in horror, his legs twitching as he fought the surge of blind obedience flowing through his system.

Lance snarled as he glared at the tiger, his knees shaking slightly, and he let his mouth drop. "How dare you talk to me like that; I will do no such thing you disgusting degenerate." Turning his gaze to CJ, "Now I really see you for what you are, you little faggot boy."

Snarling again Ryan curled his lip and bared his fangs, "I said that's enough, *boy*." Ryan's tone sharpened as he lowered his gaze further.

136

"How dare you let this degenerate servant speak to his better." Lance shook a bit more, his knees straining to keep him standing. "I will not stand here and be spoken to like this." Turning his head to the mouse standing quietly by his seat, "Geoff, I'm sorry, but I will have to advise my superiors to enact the termination clauses in the contract." Turning he headed down the hall the loud thud and rattle of the glass and door.

Taking a deep breath Ryan slumped. "I'm sorry about that, Geoff; I just couldn't listen to that jackass any longer. He was a jackass when we were together and he's just gotten worse it seems." Gesturing to the pulled out seat at the table, "If you'd like, Sir, I'm actually ready for the main courses."

Shaking his head the hare looked at the tiger, panic still covering his eyes, "I don't think it's a good…"

"That sounds delightful," chirped the mouse, the soft pull of his chair sliding across the floor as he re-seated himself.

"Sir, are you…"

"Oh yes I am quite sure. All that excitement as given me quite the appetite," the mouse clapped his hands softly, "and if this salad is any indication; I am quite looking forward to this."

"Well thank you very much; I'll go finish plating those up right now."

Sliding into his seat and shaking, CJ tried to relax, the panicked glare still coating his face. "So instead of saving the account, it looks like I may have lost it."

"I assure you that I will make certain to stress to the Senior Partners that this was by no means your fault." He smiled a bit and reached out resting his hand atop CJ's, "Don't worry my boy, I've known for quite some time."

CJ blushed looking down at his plate, "I'm not sure…what you're talking about."

Smiling brightly the mouse snickered, "Have I told you about my son?"

"You mean the one who works in accounting?"

Reaching back he grabbed his wallet and flipped through a collection of pictures. "This is from his wedding day, he and Stephan are an absolutely adorable couple."

Blinking several times, CJ reached up and held the wallet gingerly, smiling down at the picture of the mouse and cat standing side by side. "Good looking set of boys."

"They've been together for quite some time," the mouse smiled and waved as Ryan came back into the dining room, setting down the plates and taking the now vacant seat at the table with a petite steak on his plate.

"How is Charlie?" Ryan cut into his steak taking a small bite. "I see Stephan all the time, he's always having some trouble with that shoddy import of his, but I never really have time to check in on Charlie."

"He's doing very well Ryan, I'll let him know that you say hello. They're coming for dinner this weekend and they say they have some very big news for us."

"That's good to hear!"

Tracking back and forth between the two, CJ stopped and put his hands up, "Wait, wait, wait! You two know each other?"

Smiling the mouse turned to the hare and chuckled, "Oh yes, Ryan's shop is the *only* one in town that works on imports, especially the more *upscale* models. I was honestly surprised at the little farce you two were playing, but I didn't want to ruin any plans you might have."

"You really should ask me about my day more," teased Ryan as he finished his steak.

The hare turned to the tiger with a blush, "So, honey, how was your day?"

***

A dull thud filled the room, echoing off the dark stained wood paneling of the walls. "What do you mean you lost the Tungsten account, boy?" The lions face twisted as he slammed his fist into granite tabletop again. "All you had to do was have dinner, schmooze a little, and take a little bit less of a commission." A half-hearted murmur of yesses and affirmations rose in accompaniment to the lion's harsh words. "But no, you had to go flaunt your deviant lifestyle and not only that you let... I mean you couldn't even control that *thing*," disgust burned through the air at the hare standing quietly at the head of the table. "How dare you let it speak to Briggs in that fashion."

"With all due respect, his name is Ryan and I would appreciate it if you used proper pronouns!" CJ snapped in retort, his stance widening. Gasps of awe and a stifled snicker went through the room as the hare finished, "First of all, you were not there, so you have no idea what actually transpired. Secondly, *you* do not call me 'boy.'" Pulling on his coat, he adjusted the lines and locked his gaze with the yellow eyes of the lion sitting a few feet away.

"How dare you!" roared the lion in return, slamming his fist again. "You should be terminated for allowing your disgusting personal life to interfere with our busines!" Reaching to the side he tossed the newspaper across the table at CJ, letting it slide to a stop. "We made front page, *Tungsten Areospace Declares, 'We Stand for Family Values' – Drops long standing contract with Sigma over queer employee scandal*', so tell me that I have it wrong, boy."

"Last I checked, Henry, we did not subscribe to, nor obey the whims of the Christian Business Times, and our standards of decorum apply to you as well," murmured the mouse sitting at the far end of the table, his fingers steepled and an icy look to the lion. He turned his gaze over to the hare, "CJ, as that indicates, Tungsten has pulled all their contracts with us, and a few other companies have made similar moves in reaction to that article," he waved dismissively at the paper.

"I understand that, and I apologize that this happened. But I'd like to see that compared with the number of clients and money that I've saved and brought into this company over the past few years," CJ responded calmly as Nickles nodded.

The lion growled low, "You're fired! I want you out of the building immediately!" Baring his fangs, he leaned forward in his seat, "And be glad we don't sue you for all the business you've cost us. I motion that we terminate this degenerate's employment!"

"That's enough!" came a bellow from the end of the table as all eyes turned towards the elderly mouse. CJ had never seen such fire in Mr. Nickles's eyes, such fury etched on his features as he glared at the lion. "As a majority shareholder and founding member, the company bylaws allow me to supersede your motion and I am doing so now."

The lion stammered, "Th-those bylaws have never…"

"I AM NOT FINISHED!" the mouse shouted as he stood, causing the rest the board to shrink back in surprise. "As you seem to agree, Henry, this is a place of business, not a place for personal issues. I would remind the board that Mr. Bennett here has never once brought up his personal relationship in the office. He has gone to great length to hide it for reasons that are now all too apparent. His personal life was only brought to the forefront by an unscrupulous client for purposes of blackmail.

"You on the other hand, Henry... we have tolerated your constant backhanded comments, your locker-room talk, your consistently skirting the edge of harassment of numerous fine employees, and your generally abrasive personality that you refuse to leave outside the office. I have personally mollified several workers that were on the brink of suing this company based on your oh-so-subtle comments in their presence. The greatest irony is that I have recently sent Mr. Bennett in to save clients that were on the verge of pulling their accounts due to your unsavory behavior. You personal issues have been more detrimental to this company's business and morale than Mr. Bennett's relationship ever could be.

"When I hired you, Henry, I felt sorry for you. You were good at your job at the time, this is true, but you had so many personal problems, so much fear, so many qualities that other people just wouldn't work with. For years, I overlooked those issues to focus on the business. And when the truth came out about your own *son*, I had hoped things would improve."

The lion bristled, "How dare you bring up..."

Nickles went on as if Jacobs had not spoken. "But they have not. If anything, the events that transpired then have made you worse and more difficult to work with. And still I have tried to be patient with you out of pity for your personal problems. However, I have listened to you insult our employees and *my* son and violate our anti-harassment policies for the last time.

"I motion for the immediate dismissal of Henry Jacobs from this board and this company."

"Seconded!" came the fierce voice of a kangaroo named Simmons.

"Motion is tabled," said Nickles, raising up his hand. "All those in favor?"

CJ watched in astonishment as hands rose around the table. Some such as Simmons were up immediately, forcefully. Others slipped up slowly as the lion glared around the table and growled low, but soon there was not a paw that remained down.

Jacobs panted angrily. "You can't do this! I am the backbone of this board! With my shares…"

"We just did," Nickles said coldly. "A buy-out agreement has been drawn up that will split your shares evenly among the current board and whoever the new member shall be." CJ thought he noticed a glance in his direction. "Now I want *you* out of the building immediately. I will page security to help you clean out your desk; IT will flatten your computer after taking inventory of necessary files. I recommend you just go without another word, Henry, and save yourself any unnecessary trouble. And if you even think of taking anything or making waves here… well I believe you're quite aware of just how vicious our legal team can be when the occasion calls for it."

The lion seemed about speak again as the full force of the mouse's gaze bored into him. In another moment, Jacobs closed his mouth and trembling, quietly slunk out of the room with one last hateful look at the hare.

The board sat in stunned silence for a moment as Mr. Nickles took his seat again. Almost immediately his calm, grandfatherly demeanor returned as he looked around the room. "Now that that unfortunate business is concluded, I feel we should turn to more pleasant news for this company. I know there has been some concern about the loss of Tungsten and other accounts, but we've also received a few other calls this morning. The Equal Rights Campaign has been searching for a new agency to handle their publicity and feel we would be perfect. There's a hardware chain that's been under attack by right-wing groups for offering benefits to same-sex employees, they wanted us to handle a campaign for them illustrating their belief that "family values" should include *all* members of the family. A few other similar accounts are coming in.

"So in light of this, let me say that for the past few years, this company has been trying to tread the line and keep every client's business by avoiding any appearance of political statements. And while I still feel this is a good goal, I think we could also become *the* resource for organizations that support fairness and justice in their business practices. At a simple vote, who agrees with this philosophy?"

Hands rose quietly around the table, in some cases followed by brief applause from board members.

"Good," the mouse continued, "and as we have an open slot on the board, I think to help lead us in that direction, I would like to nominate a devoted employee who has recently been willing to sacrifice personal happiness for the good of this company, but has in the end remained true to himself. I motion for the addition of CJ Bennett as Senior Partner."

CJ's eyes widened as Simmons and a badger named Helen Thacker piped up in unison, "Seconded!" Hands raised into the air once more, in some cases with vociferous applause, while others quietly assented.

CJ jumped out of his seat, color rushing to and from his face in the space of a moment, "Excuse...excuse me?" He nervously wrung his hands, "But, sir, I don't have that kind of money," he stammered, "I can't afford the buy in."

"That's been arranged since I made a few calls this morning for just such an eventuality. Congratulations. Now go home."

"I'm sorry?" The hare cocked his head to the side.

"You have someone at home who I am sure would be thrilled to hear about your promotion and to know that your workplace supports you. All the paperwork will be on your desk, so please sign that ASAP. Facilities will be moving your office tonight. Now... go home."

"Thank you!" CJ swaggered to the door his tail flicking back and forth as he turned before departing, "Thank you, all!"

***

The car shook and grumbled at the rough change as CJ turned into the lot of the auto shop. He stepped out and made his way to the office with a large smile across his face. Laying on the bell, he waited to be buzzed into the office. "Is he in the office?"

"Yup, he's been doing the books all day," grumbled the grubby teenager without looking up from his collection of text books and papers.

Near skipping down the hall, he knocked lightly as he pushed the door open. He ducked inside and closed the door behind him listening, for the latch. "Hello, Master," he cooed as he got down on all fours and crawled towards the desk.

"Well now here's a nice surprise." Taking off his glasses the tiger smiled big and pushed back from the desk, "I can see my boy's hungry, did I forget to feed you last night?"

CJ nodded as he moved across the floor, his eyes glazing over with lust as he licked at his muzzle. "Yes, Master…you forgot to feed your boy," he whimpered cutely as he rounded the corner of the desk, his nostrils flaring at the thick musky scent of the tiger, "I'm so hungry…" he moaned and pressed his nose against the soft mesh of the exposed jockstrap through the unzipped denim fly.

"That's a good boy," Ryan purred, rubbing his paw between the hare's long pulled back ears, "Would my boy like a tasty treat?"

"Please, Master, feed your boy," murmured the hare as he nuzzled in deeper.

"Then give Master some room so he can get your treat out for you." Playfully he pushed the hare back and undid the button of his pants. Grinning he rubbed his paw against the mesh, moaning and panting as a small wet spot appeared. "Now be a good boy," he reached in, pulling his swollen barbed cock from behind the mesh and giving it a shake at the hare, "and give your Master a good polish."

Moaning the hare approached again, taking the swollen head into his soft muzzle and forcing himself forward to feed on the inches of flesh pushing their way back into his throat. Ryan pressed his paw firmly, guiding CJ down deeper, grunting and groaning as he edged faster than normal. Panting, he pulled back trying to push the hare off the throbbing pillar and grunted as CJ moved with him.

Growling in frustration, Ryan said, "Boy, I'm gonna… damn you're extra eager today." Moaning loudly, the tiger thrashed his cock swelling and pulsing stretching CJ's muzzle wider thin droplets of spit and cum leaking from his packed muzzle. "That's it, boy, eat it all up like the hungry slut you are."

Moaning CJ pulled back, lapping and suckling at the head, trying to pull every drop into his muzzle and down his eager throat. Taking a deep breath, he pulled back and smiled up, "Thank you Sir."

"You're welcome boy." Reaching out the tiger rubbed between the hare's ears, "I'm guessing you had a good day didn't you boy?"

Nodding quickly CJ reached into his back pocket, "Yes, Sir, it was a very good day."

Patting his lap the tiger smiled, "Well grab a seat and tell me about it."

Obediently the hare sprung into the tiger's lap and smiled, holding a folded piece of paper between his hands, "We lost the Tungsten deal."

Growling Ryan shook his head, "I should have stayed out of it; I'm so sorry, boy."

"No, no, no! Boy is flattered that his big strong Sir stood up for him," CJ blushed and looked down at the paper in his hands unfolding it slowly, but out of Ryan's view, "I got a promotion; I'm a Senior Partner now."

The tiger pressed his muzzle against the hare's cheek in a gentle kiss, "That's great!" Reaching around he rubbed at the hare's tummy through his shirt. "And?"

"This," he turned the paper over smiling big, "is my new salary and…"

The tiger coughed, gagging in surprise. "You mean it, boy?"

"Yes, and there's no more hiding, no more staying in so people won't see us together. I'm sorry it was ever like that, Sir. I have a lot of time to make up for, but I want to start now. Sir, will you marry me?"

"If you keep giving head like that, Boy, yes I'll give you the privilege of being my Boy forever." He smiled and purred, leaning in to kiss the hare, his tongue snaking slowly into CJ's muzzle. Breaking the kiss, he reached for the walkie-talkie on his desk and hit the talk button, the crackle making both of them wince. "Hey, Chuck?"

"What! I'm working here."

"Damn bitch asked me to marry him!"

"About damn time! Next time you need a quickie though– fucking keep it down!"

Memories
by Tarl "Voice" Hoch

"The police are on their way."

The rabbit crossed in front of the seated wolf, her high heels clicking on the tiled floor of the shop's backroom. The sound echoed among the tall shelves filled with small, neatly folded piles of merchandise. Each sharp click caused the wolf's ears to flinch despite the curl of his lips and the flash of fangs.

"If you would just let me go, I promise I won't come back."

His voice was deep, rumbling up from a massive chest that stretched his black t-shirt to its limits. Turning her head she regarded him with large almond shaped eyes. The autumn sky blue met his golden yellow before the rabbit smiled and shook her head. Her flop ears and pony tail danced across the back of her suit jacket.

"A pervert like you? Who shoplifts from a lingerie store anyway?"

The wolf opened his muzzle then clapped it shut, rethinking his answer.

"Nothing to say for yourself?" She shook her head again. "Pervert."

The rabbit moved closer to the wolf, ignoring the growl that rose from his throat. She stopped a few steps away from him, her paws moving to smooth a wrinkle from her navy pantsuit.

There was a sudden snap as the wolf tested the cuffs that attached his wrists to the arms of the chair he occupied. The chain pulled taunt and his muscles bulged as she watched, her head tilting to the side. After a moment of straining against the steel the wolf slumped back into the chair with a snarl in his throat. He looked from the cuffs to the matching pair around the ankles of his jeans, before looking back up to the rabbit. Her immaculate white fur shone despite the poor lighting of the room, broken only by a patch the colour of chocolate that surrounded her left eye. It gave her slight smile a mischievous edge as she stared down at the wolf.

"Who the hell has handcuffs in their office?"

"None of your business," the rabbit replied. She slowly walked around the captive wolf, her eyes moving over him. His ears swivelled to follow the sound of her steps until she came around to stand before him again, her paws resting on her hips. She was now within an arm's length from him, her posture radiating confidence that he couldn't do anything from where he was.

"You never answered my question. Who the hell steals lingerie?"

Looking at her from under bangs of grey hair so dark they were almost black, he shrugged his shoulders, tail flicking behind him.

"Why not?"

She shifted her stance, her paws still on her hips. "That's not a reason."

"Fine, alright? Fine. I was stealing them for my wife." The wolf glared at her. "Happy?"

"Why not just buy them? I'm sure she would be happier if you just bought them."

"You don't know my wife, she can be a bitch."

The slap caught him by surprise, snapping his head to the side.

"Never talk down about a woman!"

The wolf stretched his jaw as he worked the numbness out of the side of his face.

"That hurt."

"It was supposed to. Did your mother ever teach you any manners?"

The wolf rolled his eyes.

"If you must know, my wife likes danger in a lot of the things she does. Do you think this is the first time I've lifted items such as this? " He winked at her.

"I'm willing to bet this is the first time you've ever been caught however."

"Not really, but I usually manage to use my charm to get out of it. This is the first time I've ever been cuffed to a chair though..." The wolf lifted his wrist against one of the cuffs, pulling the chain taut.

"You're not the first person I've caught trying to steal from me, but usually they're little tween flakes out for a rush." The rabbit turned her back to him, raising one of her paws to examine her crimson painted nails before glancing over her shoulder at the wolf, her eyes slitted, voice low.

"Oh how they cry when they realize how much shit they're in, thinking that Mommy or Daddy will save them. Oh so tragic..." Her paw clenched into a fist. "Oh how pathetic."

The rabbit turned back to face the wolf and unclenched her fist. Lowering her paws, she tugged the hem of her suit jacket, smoothing non-existent wrinkles before looking up. "Though sometimes it's a weird sexual fetishist after something to take home and..." She made a face.

"Oh hell no. No, no, no. *Definitely* not me." The wolf shook his head, his ears lowering. "Just for my wife, I can promise you that."

The rabbit nodded, her ears swaying, one falling in front of her face. She brushed it away with a flick of her wrist.

"What do you get out of stealing for your wife? She's not exactly putting herself on the line here."

Tail wagging behind him, the wolf opened his muzzle into a large toothy grin. "Some of the best sex I have ever had if you must know. She's like an animal, even after having them on for a minute."

"Is that so?" She moved behind him. He craned his neck to try and keep her in his field of vision, but gave up when his neck started to cramp.

"Why do you even care?"

He jerked as he felt her paws come to rest on his shoulders, her immaculate claws pressing against his shirt. He tensed as she dug them in.

"Call it a curiosity." She whispered near his ear, causing it to twitch as her breath brushed across the sensitive fur.

"What are you doing?"

"Tell me more about your wife." Her fingers traced through his hair, letting the strands fall in small groups.

The wolf shivered as he felt her nails move along the back of his neck. "I met her in college."

"And?"

"It was in an English class of some sort. I think the only thing I learned in it was how to sleep with my eyes open. That was until she caught my eye. She sat a couple rows in front of me and I don't know why I didn't notice her before. Maybe I was just too bored. But there she was, and she was hot."

"What was she wearing?" A nail traced small circles through the ruff of his neck and the wolf shifted in his seat, moving his neck away from her touch. Suddenly he yelped as his head was jerked back by his hair, the rabbit's face appeared above him.

"Stay still! Do not move or I will hurt you. Do you understand?"

"But the police-"

"Won't see any of the marks I will leave on you." She lowered her voice to a whisper, moving her muzzle close to his. "And really, who will they believe? The sweet little shop owner or the big bad wolf?"

The wolf swallowed.

"Do we have an understanding?" She yanked his hair to accent her point and he nodded the best he could. Holding him for a moment longer she finally let go of his hair and straightened.

"So what was she wearing?"

"Really tight indigo jeans, the type where if she wasn't careful it broadcast to the world what type of underwear she was wearing."

"What colour were they?"

"Indigo, I said-" His head rocked to the side as she cuffed him.

"Her panties. What colour were they? You must have seen them if her pants were that low."

"Purple, okay? A purple thong. Happy?"

The rabbit made a content noise from behind him. "What else?"

Her shirt was pink, a fitted golf shirt. But it was her tail that got my attention."

"Her tail?"

"It was smaller than mine, really fluffy. I wanted to run my fingers through the fur, it looked so soft."

Her nail traced along the fur of his neck again, and he fought the urge to pull away.

"Did you say anything to her the day you noticed her?"

"I had to, she was just so beautiful I couldn't resist."

The rabbit's paw moved through his hair, petting him. "Good boy."

Moving around to stand back in front of him, she smiled as she pulled her hair from her ponytail, letting the golden strands cascade around her shoulders and down her back. With a shrug, the suit jacket slid down her arms until she tossed it to the side. Fingers flicked across the top of her blouse, each flick opening another button until a long V of snowfall white was revealed, a small patch of brown nudging into it. The rabbit smiled at her captive, her large front teeth peeking through her lips.

"How did you approach her?"

It took a moment for the wolf to answer, his gaze moving along the swell of her cleavage. Behind him his tail wagged slowly. The rabbit took a step forward and he flinched, his tail tucking under the seat of his chair.

"I asked her if she had notes on the previous class!" He replied, voice tight. When no blow fell he opened his eyes. The rabbit's grin widened.

"Did she now?"

"I think she liked me, 'cause she said if I wanted them they were at her dorm room and I could get them later that day."

"Did you?"

He nodded.

The rabbit moved closer, her voice lowering. "What happened?"

"We had sex."

"Oh?"

"Why am I even telling you this?"

The slap hit his other cheek this time, hard enough that he was forced to blink tears from his eyes.

"Because I want to hear about it. Because I am bored. All I do here day in and day out is listen to the problems of girls barely out of their teens as they bitch about their idiot boyfriends. Even their talk about sex is boring and uninteresting. Stick tab A into slot B, and half the time they can't even get that right." She raised a paw to her forehead and shook her head before continuing. "It also doesn't help that the police always take their sweet time coming to shoplifting calls. So you get to entertain me for awhile and my employees can watch the store." She leaned in so her muzzle almost touched his.

"I could bite you."

"And turn a mere shoplifting charge into assault?"

"What about unlawful confinement?"

The rabbit laughed and grabbed his throat, her claws digging into his windpipe. The wolf choked in surprise, his ears flattening.

Leaning in, her eyes danced while his flew wide. Her smile grew as she applied more pressure, the feel of his Adam's apple struggling to move widening her smile.

"It's a good thing you're pretty." Nails dug further into into his skin as her voice lowered, as if she were explaining a simple task to a dim witted child.

"In a store full of innocent women, is there any other way to contain a dangerous man such as yourself?" She let go and he gasped for air, coughing roughly as his lungs struggled to fill themselves. The rabbit moved away from him, brushing one of her ears away from where it had fallen in front of her face. She idly ran a paw over a stack of camisoles before she looked back over her shoulder.

"So you had sex."

"Yes." The wolf managed to get out between coughs.

"How did it happen?"

"We were on her couch and she was trying to give me something to drink, I think it was juice. She ended up spilling it on my chest by accident."

"I highly doubt it was an accident."

"At the time I thought it was, but you're probably right. She grabbed a towel and helped me to dab my shirt. Thing was, she kind of straddled me to do it..."

The rabbit turned and moved towards him, straddling his knees. "Like this?"

The wolf gave her a confused look. "No, higher."

She scooted forward so that she sat across his lap. He swallowed, his ears half lowered in uncertainty. Behind him his tail gave a slight wag.

"Like this?"

The wolf nodded, trying to avoid her gaze as she placed her palms on his broad chest. It made them look tiny.

"She definitely did it on purpose." The rabbit said to herself as she settled on his lap. Leaning over she whispered into the wolf's ear. "Then what did she do?"

"We..." the wolf glanced at her for a moment. "kissed."

The rabbit traced a claw down his chest, winding an idle path. His stomach tensed, the muscles clearly defined through his shirt as she watched from under her bangs.

"Soft or rough?"

"Soft."

The rabbit's mouth moved closer to his muzzle. "Did you like it?" Her breath brushed his whiskers.

The wolf nodded, not trusting his voice.

"Did it make you hard having her straddling you, the feel of her heat against you? Her lips against yours?" The rabbit's voice lowered and she shifted in his lap. His body responded and he turned his head away from her.

A paw snapped out and wrapped around his muzzle, yanking him back to face her. The rabbit glared into his eyes. "Did it make you hard?" She demanded.

The wolf nodded, as much as he could with her paw covering his muzzle. She kept her gaze locked with his before thrusting his muzzle to the side. He brought his gaze back around to face her.

"Yes, okay! It made me hard. I wanted to fuck her right then and there! What the hell is wrong with you?"

The slap was expected this time as he took it on his cheek, his head rocking to the side.

"Manners!"

The wolf coughed, shaking the stars from his vision.

"So did you get to fuck her?"

He nodded.

"How did it happen?"

"She pulled off my shirt and started kissing my chest. Her paws were everywhere."

The rabbit rocked her hips against him. "What were yours doing?"

"They were in her hair, along her back, on her breasts."

A slender arm reached over to one of the nearby shelves and pulled a box knife out of a pile of baby-dolls. The wolf's eyes went wide, his ears flattened as a whine escaped from his muzzle. There was a soft thump as his tail hit the bottom of the chair.

"Don't be such a baby." The edge of the blade rested against the hem of his shirt and slowly sliced upwards, pulling the fabric away from the taut skin of his stomach. As the shirt parted it revealed fur that was a lighter shade than the surrounding fur and she leaned back to admire it. The wolf watched her, his eyes wide, glancing between her and the naked blade.

"I can see why she spent so much time on your chest. Do you work out?"

There was a nod, eyes wary.

She traced the side of the blade along his stomach and watched as he flinched away, causing the muscles to tighten under his fur.

"It definitely shows." The knife flew back into the shelf and her fingers started to run along the lighter fur. The wolf's body flinched away almost as much as it had with the steel. She chuckled.

"Did you get her shirt off?"

Head turned to the side he nodded, his eyes watching her from their corners as the rabbit cooed.

"What were her breasts like?"

There was a pause as the wolf shifted in his seat, and she smiled. He was getting hard again and she felt it, her body making small movements against the growing firmness.

"They were perfect. Not too large, not too small. Just right. Small handfuls, enough I could cup one in each of my paws."

Fingers danced over her dress shirt, undoing the remaining buttons and letting it slide off her shoulders. The rabbit's breasts were full, filling a red bra. She thrust them forward, almost into his face as he brought his head forward. "Like these?" The look she gave him dared him to say anything other than yes.

He nodded, his whiskers almost brushing the mounds of white.

The rabbit ran her paws over her breasts, keeping eye contact with the wolf. She cupped and lifted each globe, smile broadening.

"What did you do to them?"

His gaze moved from her eyes to her breasts. Eyes watched as the rabbit ran her paws over the material of the bra, teasing the small nubs that pressed from underneath. Long fingers moved to trace their nails along the top of each cup, brushing the small amount of lace that graced the fabric.

"I...I took off her bra."

The rabbit reached behind her and suddenly her breasts were naked before him. Her body was covered in broad patches of chocolate brown, and he watched as she ran her fingers through the white and brown fur before coming back to her breasts. She made a

sound low in her throat as her paws moved over her nipples, the tiny buds plucking at each of her fingers.

He was straining at his pants now.

She moved her breasts closer and he groaned as his head turned away from them.

"Did you lick her nipples?"

The wolf didn't answer; instead he closed his eyes and took a deep breath. The rabbit snarled and dug her claws into the soft flesh of his sides, underneath his ribs. A sharp yelp bounced among the shelves.

"Did you lick her nipples?"

The wolf's head barely moved as he nodded.

"Show me how."

Eyes begging her to stop, he looked at her. The rabbit jabbed his side again and he jumped.

"I'm getting tired of repeating myself. Show me!"

The wolf moved his muzzle forward, his eyes still on hers. His breath ghosted over one of her nipples, already hard in the cool air of the back room. Tongue darting out he brushed the fur close to the tiny bud and the rabbit moaned.

Her paw grabbed his hair as he started to pull his muzzle away from her.

"I doubt you did just that. I want to know what you did, feel what you did. Show me." Her fingers tightened in his hair to accentuate the threat.

Another lick brushed her areola and the rabbit pushed her breasts forward as the long tongue licked a circle around her nipple. On the third lick she pushed herself downwards against him, her groin moving against the erection that throbbed under her.

"More, show me more." The rabbit panted.

The wolf's broad tongue moved around her nipple before he flicked its tip against her. The nub tightened at the attention and the he sucked it into his muzzle, playing his tongue over its surface. The rabbit gasped at the small pinch, her nipple brushing against his canines. Her breath caught and her paw tightened painfully in his hair.

His mouth explored her before he switched to her other breast. The first lick brought a long sigh to the rabbit's mouth, as the nails on her free paw dug into his shoulder. He teased the sides of the tiny bud, flicking his tongue back and forth between taking it into his mouth. It didn't take long for the wolf to learn that she liked the nips more than the rest, and soon the rabbit was quivering above him.

Suddenly the lapin shoved his muzzle away. Her body was flushed, breasts heaving, her nipples glistening with moisture. She looked down at the wolf, her small mouth open as she panted.

"I can see why she wanted to get into your pants. Even if the sight of your body wasn't enough, after that performance she would have been dripping wet."

The wolf licked his muzzle, watching her, eyes cold.

"Don't give me that look, you enjoyed it." She rubbed her body against him to prove her point. He grunted as her weight tugged against his erection.

"I have a wife."

"I know, we're talking about her right now." The rabbit grinned at him.

"No. I mean I have a wife, this isn't right."

"It's not like you have a choice."

"I-"

It was a punch this time, catching him off guard and hard enough to wind him. As he tried to relearn how to breathe she smiled at him.

"As I was saying, it's not like you have a choice. And really, you're a big boy. You can take it." She tapped a finger on her front teeth. "Actually, on that note, what did you two do next? Did you get her pants off or did she get yours off first?"

The wolf started to turn his head and she made a move to strike him again.

"Wait, wait!"

Her fist paused.

"She took off her pants, then mine."

The rabbit grinned. She stood, letting her fingers trace down his chest. His eyes followed her as she walked a few steps away from him and started to undo her belt. It hissed through the loops on her pants and the belt landed beside the chair.

"I know that dress slacks aren't exactly jeans, but..."

Carefully she undid the hook at the top of her pants and dragged the zipper down. The wolf's eyes watched her fingers work, his breath heavy in his chest and not all of it from her blow.

She peeled her pants back and hooked her thumbs into the waistband. The wolf's ears were raised now, his eyes following every movement her fingers made. Waiting until she caught his gaze, the rabbit pushed her pants down, sliding them over her hips. Her only pause was to pull a red thong up from where it had started to follow the path of the pants. Making sure it was in place, she stepped out of the slacks, kicking them to the side with one foot.

The wolf's gaze travelled over her body. She had long, well shaped legs and her hips were full. The brown patches of fur indeed covered her whole body and he licked his muzzle, tail wagging for a moment behind him. The rabbit moved forward, her eyes half lidded as she smiled at him. As she got closer the wolf could pick up her scent as it drifted from her. Sweet. Feminine. Heavy. His hips moved upwards on their own, as if drawn to her. She watched him struggle against the cuffs, smile widening.

"And now for you..." Her paws tugged at his belt, ripping it from him. It struck the back wall with a heavy smack. The zipper was down and she was tugging at his pants before he had time to raise his ass. Finally managing to raise himself high enough the jeans slid off with the hiss of denim against fur. The wolf watched her as she looked up at him from between his knees, erection straining at his boxers between them. A tiny pink tongue slid wetly over her lips.

"So you both got your pants off," Her fingers traced a small circle on his inner thigh, "then what?"

The wolf blinked as if he didn't understand the question, his mind having retreated to a more primal place. Nails dug into his inner thigh and he jumped, eyes clearing.

"We made out a bit more, grinding, and then..."

The rabbit's smile widened.

"I can think of what happened next." She rose and straddled him. The wolf shivered as her scent grew stronger and her heat pressed against him. Despite the two layers of fabric between them he could feel how wet she was, the warmth teasing him.

A paw grabbed his hair and pulled his muzzle to hers. The wolf made a noise of protest in his throat and her fist tightened in his hair.

Muzzle opening in pain he felt her tongue as it darted in, finding his. Within a moment he was relaxed in her grip, his mouth moving with hers. White breasts pressed against the wolf's chest, their weight brushing his nipples, teasing them to a higher sensitivity. His hips moved against hers as the rabbit own pushed down against him.

Suddenly the wolf gasped into her mouth as his cock slid free through the fly of his boxers, brushing against the dampness of her panties. The rabbit broke the kiss and leaned back, keeping her paws on his shoulders as she rocked her hips back and forth. The wolf moaned as she played her wetness against him, his body shivered with each pass over his glans.

She stopped and stood up as the wolf quivered at the loss of sensation, his tongue hanging out of the side of his mouth. The rabbit knelt before him, tugging his boxers down roughly, the waistband yanking against him hard enough to make him wince. Finally he was free and listing to the side, his erection slowly fading at such a rough treatment. Her claw tips traced along the inside of his thighs, hard enough to gain the the wolf's attention.

"She went down on you didn't she?"

Eyes widened, ears stood at attention, tail hung still. But his erection pulsed and started to rise again. Laughter echoed about the room.

"Your body says she did."

The rabbit traced her claws along his legs, moving them up and down before finally dragging them up his inner thigh. His gasp caught in his throat as her paw encircled his member and the wolf's eyes closed in pleasure.

The rabbit's paw glided up and down with a slow patience as the wolf's body responded with tiny shivers. His hips moved upwards with each of her downwards strokes, his need making him unable to keep in time with the lapin's leisurely movements. The rabbit licked her lips. "Was she rough or gentle?"

"Gen...gen..."

"Gentle? Too bad I'm not." She lowered her muzzle on one of the downward strokes as his hips rose off the seat of the chair. The rabbit's nose brushed along the underside of his testicles as her tongue flicked out and ran along his taint before moving upwards. The wolf moaned, head back, hips in the air as she moved her tongue over his balls and continued up his shaft only to pause at its head. The wolf crashed back down onto the chair as he let out a shiver, his eyes opening to look down at her.

Gazing up at him the rabbit flicked her wet tongue over his tip, teasing him. His hips moved, trying to get into her mouth. She matched the wolf's movements, riding each thrust so that no more of his cock entered her muzzle. The tiny flicks of her tongue brushed the underside of his head, leaving small trails of wetness cooling between brushes of warmth. The wolf was quaking now, as if he was going to shake himself apart with need.

A small chirp escaped her throat as she brushed his shaft back and forth along her lips, nuzzling his length. Then slowly the rabbit drew him into her mouth so that he barely rested in its warmth. The wolf's hips bucked and he looked down at her. Twinkling sky blues locked with his lust-filled eyes.

Slowly the rabbit moved her head up and down, soft lips teasing just that one sensitive spot. Her large front teeth brushed against his skin, their hardness above a counterpoint to the soft warmth of her tongue below.

The wolf watched, his eyes following the golden waves of hair as they bobbed over him. His hips tried to move with her, trying to drive his cock deeper into the rabbit's mouth. On his third push she bit down, her front teeth jabbed into his satin hardness. He hissed in pain and she started to pull her mouth away. It was only a begging whine that made their eyes meet. Her large eyes narrowed into a glare that was almost a blow unto itself.

"Try that again, and I will leave you here."

The wolf nodded, not trusting his voice.

Keeping her gaze locked with his, the rabbit slowly lowered her muzzle back down onto him. Slowly she played along the skin of his cock, moving her tongue around him in between taking him further into the heat of her muzzle. The wolf's testicles had started to tighten, and she moved them around in her other paw, feeling their weight. He was close, trying to both make it last and yet begging for release.

Cold air broke the rhythmic movements of the rabbit's muzzle, snapping him from his inner battle. Standing before him, her fingers rose from between her legs, trailing strands of moisture between them. The wolf's gaze locked on those fingers as the rabbit leaned forward and placed them near his muzzle. Wary, his tongue moved out to drag along her fingers, tasting her juices. The scent was thick, causing his cock to start to harden despite the cool air that assaulted it. He drew her fingers into his muzzle, sucking on them as she watched. Her other paw moved between her legs, a soft wet noise the only hint to what to she was doing there.

With a sound of loss the wolf sunk his shoulders as the fingers with their nectar were drawn from his mouth. Her fingers hooked into the waistband of her panties and his ears perked as she turned her back to him. Bending at the waist she watched him as her panties slowly slide down her hips, the crotch peeling away wetly from her sex. The wolf growled, his wrists jerking against the handcuffs, straining against them as his body cried for him to take her. The rabbit watched him from over her shoulder as she tugged her panties all the way down, letting them fall once they reached her knees.

The wolf glanced between the restraints and her, growls mixing with whines as he tried to tear the arms off the chair. His ears flattened, and his lips pulled back in a snarl. The rabbit grinned, waving her ass back and forth. The wolf watched her upturned tail—its white fur seemed to draw his gaze to her sex, tempting him, guiding him.

Her fingers traced along her outer lips, teasing the skin. One finger slid between them, parting her lips. The wolf moaned as she played her fingertips along her entrance, pulling the lips apart with two fingers so he could watch as she slipped a third in. His hips bucked in response, his ears flashed forward and back down. Despite the restraints he kept trying to rise from the chair, crashing back down into it before trying again.

A long moan escaped the rabbit's muzzle, her gaze locked with his as she slid her finger in and out of herself. She spread her stance, allowing for him to see more. A bead of moisture rolled down her inner thigh, darkening the fur.

"So what did you two do after she gave you head?"

The wolf whimpered.

The rabbit turned and walked over to him, wetness gleaming along her inner thighs.

"Did you two fuck then or did you return the favour?"

He licked his lips before panting, his tongue hanging from the side of his muzzle, gaze never leaving her glistening sex.

"You returned the favour didn't you? That's a good boy," she said half to herself as she ran her paws along her hips. They travelled downwards leisurely, past her belly button to play along the fur above her slit. The wolf watched, eyes intent.

"Since I don't really trust you enough to tend to me, we can skip that part."

Ears flashed forward as he looked up at her. The rabbit moved forward and shoved his head back with a paw around his throat. There was the sound of metal and leather and suddenly the wolf found he couldn't open his jaw, a cage of metal encircled his mouth.

His eyes widened, darting around in panic.

"It came with the cuffs," the rabbit said as she cinched the straps tighter. She leaned back as he tried to open his jaws, finding that they could only open wide enough that he could lick his muzzle and nothing more. She gave a nod of her head. "I can't have you biting me now can I?"

Her paw found and brushed along his softening erection, teasing it back to hardness. Precum rolled down his shaft to collect against her paw. Behind the wolf his tail started to swing again the rabbit's paw pumped his shaft, her pace increasing.

Straddling him, she moved so that his erection's tip rested along her slit. The rabbit's hips moved back and forth, the wolf's tip brushing along her folds. Her wetness collected along the tip, mixing with the thick, clear fluid that gathered there. His hips moved upwards and the tip hit her entrance, the warmth driving him to try and thrust further, the cuffs halting him.

His frustration rattled the backroom shelves.

The rabbit leaned forward, resting her head on his shoulder as she moved his tip along her slit. A soft grunt escaped from her as she pushed downwards. She was rewarded with a gasp as her lips parted around him and drew him inwards, gliding along him. His body shook as her inner walls closed around his cock.

Downwards she pushed, her eyes shut in concentration, biting her bottom lip as she pressed him deeper into her. Finally their hips met. With a small motion she ground herself against him, the sensation of her clit brushing along his fur drawing a shiver from her. Velvet walls clenched along his every inch, causing the wolf to moan and throb inside her.

"Oh my..." She sighed against his neck.

Her hips rose from him, inner walls plucking against him as she moved. He almost cried when she reached his tip, afraid she was going to leave him in his need. Instead she pushed back down on him; engulfing him in warmth, his tip finding her depths. She clung to his neck, a gasp coming from her as she ground herself against him.

It didn't take long for the rabbit to find a rhythm. Their pelvises slapped into each other as she brought herself down on him—only to raise up again. Claws dug into the back of his neck and hair, dragging his head back. Her teeth nipped small marks into his bared throat between her small cries.

Each time the wolf touched her depths his chest heaved, and his hips rose to meet her on each downward thrust. The wolf's body yanked against the restraints as he struggled to get deeper with each thrust despite being unable to fully move his hips. Grunts rose from him as his body grew closer and closer to release. Each time he reached the edge, though, the rabbit would bite harder or yank his hair. The pain cut through his lust like a knife until the movements along his cock wiped the pain away with pleasure.

The rabbit continued to push against him, her slit bumping against his knot as it grew large. His thrusts grew harder, the knot spreading her wider and wider. Small grunts and whines rose from him as her sex slowly slid further and further over him.

"I'm not going to let you knot me," she whispered into his ear as she tightened her inner muscles around him. "I wouldn't want to be caught in an indecent situation with you." She pushed against his knot and he growled as he felt her stretch to the point where she almost slide over him before retreating back up his shaft.

Mouth open, the rabbit was shivering. She leaned forward and her tongue licked along the muzzle straps confining the wolf's jaw as she rode his body, the pace increasing. Her juices soaked his groin as they trickled down his cock, the sensation of it brushing his balls making them tighten further.

Suddenly she cried out, pushing herself down on him. He felt her stretch and with a quick thrust the wolf's knot slide into her as his tip hit her deep inside. The rabbit grasped his shoulders and buried her face into the ruff of his neck as she screamed into his fur. Her walls spasmed around him and his body responded.

With a roar hot seed jetted against her inner walls. She threw her head back, eyes wide as another orgasm burned through her as she tried to push further down on him. They shivered together, her inner walls pulsing around his throbbing member as his warmth filled her.

With a long, drawn out gasp, the rabbit's head fell forward.

She lay on top of him as he softened in her, their breathing heavy and the air filled with the mixed scent of their mating. After a moment the rabbit leaned back and smiled at the wolf, ruffling his hair.

"So was your first time with your wife anything like that?"

The wolf blinked his eyes as he tried to process what she had said. It took her repeating it before he finally managed to shake his head. The rabbit undid the muzzle and pulled it off of him, letting it fall to the floor.

He stretched his jaw, the joints popping loudly. "No, it wasn't. It was terrible compared to this. But that's the thing, first times always suck. Sex gets better as you get to know the other person and what turns them on."

The rabbit leaned back and looked down, quivering as she felt his knot shift inside her.

"I told you no knotting me." She punched his chest, but her eyes spoke a different story. Her claws dug into his chest and he yelped. Slowly she pulled herself upwards, the wolf's knot stretching her as she bit down on her lower lip. The rabbit gasped as he suddenly popped free from her, their collected fluids sliding from her to gleam on both their thighs. She took shaky steps to a shelf, fluids continuing to leak from her, a trail of dots following her on the floor. Reaching into one of the shelves she took a pair of panties from one of the stacks and pulled them on.

The wolf's ears perked up. "Isn't that stealing?"

"I'll buy them before I go home. No way I am going to wear my other pair now, they're soaking wet. And I'm going to be uncomfortable as it is with wolf oozing from me all day."

There was a knock on the backroom door and it opened a crack.

"Mrs. Swan? Mr. Swan? Are you two done? I need Mrs. Swan's help with a customer who's being difficult." A young squirrel peeked around the door and let out a squeak before darting back through the way she came.

Mrs. Swan looked at her husband as he grinned at her from the chair. His softening cock gleaming with drying moisture as the last of his cum oozed from his tip, pooling on his thigh.

"I suppose you find that funny," she said as she pulled on her pants and searched around for her shirt.

The wolf's grin widened, his tail now in full swing behind him.

"Can you let me out of this chair now? I have to pee."

The rabbit flashed him a grin. "I have to take care of this customer, I think you can wait."

His jaw dropped in shock as she flashed him a grin while she buttoned up her shirt.

"Wait...honey?...honey?"

The rabbit picked up her jacket from the floor and moved back to the door to the sales-floor. She turned back to her husband, winking at him before blowing a kiss. Flinging the door open she closed it behind her as she went out to save her employee.

The wolf sat under the humming fluorescents, the wetness on his thigh drying and matting his fur. His bladder cried for his attention and he craned his head to where the bathroom lay at the other end of the storeroom.

He let out a sigh.

"Well shit..."

Sweetly Sadistic
by Elijah Lapso

I see the look you give me,
The fear trapped in your eye,
You whimper like a puppy,
While I raise the whip up high.
You cry out when I strike you,
You curl up on the floor,
You act like this is torture,
but then tell me you want more.
By now your cock is aching,
It begs for my cruel touch,
You promise to obey me,
You just want it that damned much.
I'll bind you up so nicely,
Your ass for all to see,
I watch your useless struggle,
and it fills me with such glee.
Your will shall break by morning,
Your body bruised and sore,
You'll gladly do my bidding,
and keep coming back for more.

Infinite Loop
by Nathan Cowan

Doctor Travis Walton, the Father of the Chimerae, left his multi-million dollar home with everything he could carry in a camera bag. He wished he had a bigger camera bag, but he didn't and *certainly* didn't want a suitcase, not now.

It was summer, a little too warm for long sleeves or a suit with a coat; he wore a fall jacket, pockets stuffed. His thick shock of hair was white, and anyone would say he was in his forties. He was below average in height, but nobody would be surprised to hear he could jog ten kilometers.

His hand was on the handle of the front door and he was beginning to think he'd make it out.

"Good morning, Doctor." It was a male voice, mild, concerned, deceptive, behind him.

Walton tried to keep his voice light and casual when he replied.

"Good morning, Sentry." He forced himself to turn around, kept his expression bland.

Sentry was a NorBio Fidelus, a male canine model, big, alert and impressive. A friend to those in need; a terror to those of evil intent. *That's what he was designed to look like,* Walton thought. Almost all chimerae looked inhuman; it was the best way to avoid the Uncanny Valley. Even the forest elves couldn't pass as human; some of the dark elves could, with a bit of plastic surgery.

"Are you planning on leaving, sir?" His Doberman's face was impassive; the black fur hiding any movement of his expression.

Walton looked bemused, hoping that would fool the chimera. "Oh, I wanted to take some pictures down by the lake. And just between you and me," he winked, "I'm tired of this --"

"--Healthy food from Basil's kitchen," Sentry interrupted.

Walton didn't reply. How had the chimera anticipated him?

"And you want some fried dumplings, like Deidre made," the Doberman finished.

"Ah," Walton said, at a loss.

Sentry shook his head, impatiently. "This happened before, sir. The first Dopple said the same thing. Right before he left."

Sentry knew.

"You're still legally dead, sir. Until this is sorted out, I suggest you stay here at your son's home."

"*My* home," Walton snapped.

"Sir, you left this house to your son," Sentry said patiently.

Whatever. "You didn't keep my original alive," he accused the chimera.

"I was not responsible for your security in Atlanta, sir," Sentry replied. He reached inside his jacket, briefly revealing his armor. He took out folded papers. "Here is ICON's report on that incident."

Walton had already read the report, so he didn't reach for it. Not only was it was signed by a chimera, which was ridiculous enough -- but it was signed by a chimera who had a grudge against him. He wondered how she had fooled the police.

Sentry stood still for a moment, and withdrew his hand. "ICON says that you -- your original was shot in Atlanta by Lilith, a Dryad-9D. Lilith was killed a few days later in a showdown with an ICON operative."

"Bullshit," Walton snapped.

The chimera cocked his head slightly. "Why?" he asked.

"Because I knew Lilith." The moment he said it, he knew it was a mistake. Sentry might not be able to put the pieces together, but whoever was pulling his strings would.

Sentry's ears perked. He folded his arms and nodded. "You're saying she *did* have a motive."

"No, of course not," Walton shook his head, angry. "I'm saying it's a frame. Lilith was loyal to me. *Personally,*" he added, with emphasis.

"Like Deidre?" Sentry asked. If he caught the criticism, he didn't show it.

Deidre was the Ashita Biotech Nezumi model who normally took care of Walton's house. His *son's* house. Walton missed her cooking and missed her in his bed. "Exactly."

Sentry smiled as though he understood something Wilson didn't, and the arrogance of that made Wilson's heart race.

"Your son freed Deidre," Sentry said. "Freed *all* of us. And she *chose* not to be here."

Freed. Wilson hated that word. Chimerae needed guidance. "You stayed."

"Yes. Your son asked me to keep you alive, sir."

Walton grimaced. "You didn't keep the first Dopple alive."

"The first Dopple walked out on us in March. We don't know for sure that he's dead. Sir. If you'd let me ask ICON to look for--"

"He's dead," Walton nodded firmly. It was the only thing that made sense. *It wouldn't be in my best interest to activate another Dopple.*

"Sir, if you don't want ICON to handle your safety it should be obvious you need to stay with us."

Unless you're lying to me and the first Dopple never left.

On his own.

"Are you going to stop me?" Walton asked. He fought to keep his voice level.

"Your son asked me to do that, sir." Sentry was designed to take down humans without hurting them. There was a moment of silence and Walton gripped his bag tightly. "But I told him I can't do that," the chimera said without a trace of regret. "Walking out that door isn't a crime and you're not endangering someone else. Reckless behavior isn't illegal."

"All right, then," Walton said with a curt nod. He turned to open the door.

"You should call your son before you go," Sentry interrupted. "He'd rather you stayed."

Walton rolled his eyes. "He's a dumb, sentimental kid. Any more advice before I leave?"

"Deidre wanted me to tell you she doesn't want any contact."

Liar, Walton thought.

They accused Lilith of killing his original, and then they killed her. Deidre had "chosen" to wander off.

Sentry remained.

Someone had gotten rid of the chimerae who were most loyal to him; he would have put Sentry in that category but now he wasn't sure if the chimera's loyalty transferred to a Dopple.

Sentry stared at him for a few moments, his expression unreadable. He glanced at Walton's camera bag. "And you're more than welcome to pack a bigger suitcase, sir."

Walton was tempted. *No.* There would be a tracking device hidden in any suitcase Sentry gave him. And besides, he didn't really need it.

Walton, the original Walton, had never trusted ICON. He was prepared.

***

"I'm sorry about losing the key," Walton apologized to the bank teller. "I guess you keep the deposit."

"Your biometrics checked out," the teller replied, "so that won't be a problem. Would you like us to change the lock now?"

"No -- no, there's still a few places I haven't looked," he smiled. The teller left him alone with the box.

Walton opened it. He had five prepaid credit cards in it, each linked to a different false identity. There were four left. He pressed his lips together. He must have been here before. Or rather, the first Dopple had been. At least ICON hadn't traced the cards.

ICON. When Ashok Mehta wanted to screw up Walton's life, he hired the corporate security network to do it.

Walton had given the management of Blue Diamond information about safety codes built into chimerae. Blue Diamond had taken maladjusted chimerae and repurposed them; the codes made it easier and less traumatic for the chimerae. He had done it for their good. After Blue Diamond burned down, ICON had confronted him with proof of what he had done. He faced prison.

They blackmailed him into becoming a chimera "rights" activist, of all things, to co-operate with Mehta. A chimera woman he had known as Chili was an operative for ICON, and had led that organization's investigation into his murder.

Lilith was quite capable of planning and carrying out an assassination. Chili might be equally sophisticated.

The difference was that Lilith would never kill without authorization; she knew her place and purpose. Chili did not.

Maybe ICON *hadn't* killed him. Maybe Sentry was still loyal...

***

The car was quiet on electric motors, but the dirt and loose rock under its tires was not. He was three kilometers from asphalt. The trees on each side of the dirt road met overhead, forming a sort of tunnel through them. The sky was only visible in patches until the car reached the clearing. Walton pulled a sharp left and slammed on the brakes.

He brought the compact car to a sloppy stop, skidding on the grass that grew in patches. He blinked. The bumper nudged a trellis made of chicken wire, vines of peas climbing up the metal grid. *That* was new. He had almost damaged it.

Walton stepped out of his car and closed the door. He looked at the vegetable garden. Persephone must have spent a long time turning the earth with a shovel: she didn't have a plow. Well, she had the time.

Walton regarded the small cabin thoughtfully. It was about five meters by three, small and cozy in winter. The outside was shabby but the windows were intact and the shutters on their hinges. The south-facing part of the roof was covered in solar cells, and an extension protected a capacitor bank designed for a car.

It was in the middle of a clearing in the woods, next to a chicken run. All he could hear was the occasional chirp of a wild bird, and the mindless clucking of the chickens in the fenced-in enclosure, jabbing their heads with each step as they strutted about their little universe.

He watched them for a few minutes. Some part of them probably imagined, dimly, that they were jungle fowl living their lives for themselves. He wondered if they understood that they only existed to turn inedible vegetable matter and insects into protein and eggs. Man had always used animals, and changed them to suit his purpose. Persephone was the ultimate result of that engineering.

And where *was* that girl? She had hidden when the car came, of course. Walton had told her to avoid other people. Walton believed in conditioning, so he had sent people here to beat her if they could find her. So Persephone was very wary of strangers indeed. But she should have recognized him by now.

"Persephone!" he called out. There was no reply. "*Here*, girl!" he added, sharply.

Her collar would knock her out if she strayed more than two kilometers from the cabin. She might, possibly, be too far to know he was there. Walton prided himself on being fair, so he took out his phone and brought up the tracking program. It found the navigation satellites, and drew two overlapping circles, each fifteen meters in diameter. She was probably somewhere off to his right, on the far side of the cabin.

He took off his belt and doubled it up. He slapped it against his thigh, hard. "*Five!*" He shouted. He counted silently to three. *This is bad*, he thought. He had tried to keep her isolated -- what if she had heard he was dead? He kept codes here for his secret bank accounts, negotiable bonds..."*Six!*" He shouted.

That did it.

"Master!" she called out, and suddenly she was out in the clearing. She made no sound as she rushed to him.

Chickens were the first animals crafted by the hand of Man. Persephone was one of the most recent.

Persephone was a Brandon Biotech Serengeti. She could trace her genetic ancestry across half the phyla in the animal kingdom, but she was predominantly human and lion. Her fur was white on her chin and throat, the rest a tawny yellow-brown. Her hair was long and black, a mane that grew to the top of her throat, the color matching the tuft on her tail. She had her mane pulled back and tied into a tail. She was shorter than he was, the top of her head coming to his nose, even though she stood on her padded toes. She wore a collar, a denim skirt and a flannel blouse; she was barefoot. Her eyes were large, soft and golden; there was uncertainty in them. She was the third occupant of this cabin; the other two hadn't worked out.

Watson pointed his belt to the grass in front of him. "Show respect."

Persephone had been in Blue Diamond before he had bought her, and she showed respect in the manner expected of a Blue Diamond girl.

She undid her plaid blouse, opening it wide. She wore a black bra, and quickly unfastened the catch between her breasts. Her breasts were large and she arched her back to make them bounce, knowing he liked that. She went to her knees, touched her naked breasts to the ground before him. Her rough tongue scraped the toe of his shoe. She knelt, and looked down at his feet.

Walton was supposed to release her by touching her ear. Instead, he pinched it and pulled. She yowled once and stood.

She was afraid. *Good.* "Did you see Sentry?" he snapped, his face ugly.

"Who?" she asked, bewildered. "Sir, I haven't seen *anyone*--"

As far as Walton knew, she didn't know Sentry. Even so, he slapped her. "Liar."

"No, Sir!" she yelped. "Just you, Master."

"*When?*" he shook her.

"It was January, sir." She swallowed. "Why are you asking? Master, is it really you?"

"January," he repeated. "And you haven't seen me since?"

"No, sir. Nobody, Master." She swallowed hard, and started to weep.

"You're sure?" he shook her. That meant the first Dopple hadn't made it this far. He felt elation.

"Nobody, sir." She reconsidered. "There was the delivery in March, but they didn't see me."

Even though she had chickens and now a vegetable garden, she wasn't entirely self-sufficient. Close to a ton of supplies were dropped off every year. Some of that was for him.

She saw his expression and her ears flattened. "Master, you *said* to hide from anyone who wasn't you."

"Who showed you how to build that?" he asked, pointing at the trellis.

"Nobody, sir."

"Oh, be quiet," he said, frowning. She was telling the truth. Walton wasn't sure who was trying to kill him. It could be ICON, it could be Chili, it could even be his son... The only safe place was with nobody, and Persephone came close to that.

She hadn't seen anyone. He was safe for now. He looked back at her, shaking in fear, and beautiful. He hadn't had a woman in this body yet. "I told you about your hair," he said.

She touched her pony tail, immediately realizing her mistake. She quickly undid it, letting her hair fluff out in a wild, unkempt mane that he preferred.

"So you didn't recognize me?" he asked.

"Sir, you look ... younger," she said. "When you move."

He glanced at her. He was afraid of that. His body's age was mostly cosmetic -- in the growth tank, it looked like his original body, the first to be murdered. But the new body was healthier. A human might not pick up on that, but a chimera would.

Then, hesitantly, she asked, "Is it really you?"

"It's a new body," he said.

She looked at him in surprise. "A new body?"

He looked at hers. She had known better than to cover herself.

Walton hadn't had a woman since this body was grown.

He grabbed her breast. She flinched, and he could feel himself getting hard. He ran her nipple between his fingertips. It stiffened under his rough touch. Her tongue darted out, touched the tip of her nose.

"I told you to keep the fur around these trimmed," he said.

"It *is* you," she said with wonder. "What do you mean, a new body?"

"Your knife," he said, putting out his hand. There was a steel multi-tool clipped to the waistband of her skirt. She detached it from its lanyard and handed it to him. He put it in his pocket.

She looked at the tent in his pants and smiled. The lioness reached a hand out and undid the catch and then the zipper. Persephone went to her knees without prompting. She pulled it free of his underwear, sniffed him, and then gently licked the end of his penis. She closed her eyes and smiled.

He raised a hand to slap her. He didn't have time for this.

"Delicious, sir," she said. "Tastes like my Master."

...Maybe he *did* have time for this.

He didn't answer, and let her lick avidly around his shaft for a few moments. Her tongue was rough, but he liked it rough. She was trying to distract him.

"I promised you six," he said.

She froze and he smiled. He had expected that. Her mind was limited in many ways, and she couldn't really tell important things from trivial things. A spanking was more important to her than his immortality.

She lowered her eyes. "Master, I didn't know it was you," she said. She ducked her head and licked his shoe again, probably hoping that would help.

"I promised you six," he repeated. "Be good."

Persephone squirmed on the ground. "...Master," she replied, miserably. She turned away from him, and lifted her skirt to expose her rump, lowered her head to the ground. Her tail arched up and away from her buttocks.

He knelt down next to her and stroked her ass. Her fur was soft, not like a real lion's. Her muscles under the fur were hard, perfectly shaped. She had a body like a human woman, but the fur invited you to stroke her, like a pet. He gripped the base of her tail and brought the belt around in an arc.

She jerked involuntarily and yelped as the buckle hit. His arm was stronger now, he realized with a smile. He brought it back for a second blow.

Most of the punishment at Blue Diamond had been done by a female chimera named Tigre. Tigre had shown him how to beat women without seriously injuring them. He brought the belt hard against Persephone's buttocks, making the blow land in the same place. Persephone cried out.

"Do you remember Tigre?" he asked.

"Yes, sir," she said.

"Would you like to dance for her again?" he asked.

Tigre was dead, killed by ICON agents when they destroyed the Blue Diamond slave brothel. But it was better if Persephone believed the tiger was still out there.

"No, sir," she said. She cried out with the third blow.

His fly pinched the side of his penis. He thought about putting it back in his pants, but decided against it -- he liked having it out, in the forest, with no roof but the sky. It was usually locked away and it amused him to think that it liked being outside for a change. The air felt cool on it. He rubbed it against her fur; she didn't dare to move. Her fur was soft against him, warm when he let it rest.

"I can do that," he told her. "One phone call, and you'll be back in Blue Diamond with ten cocks a day and Tigre for inspiration."

Even as he said it, he knew he didn't want to give her up.

She shrieked with the fourth blow. "I'll do better, Master," she promised.

He hit her a fifth time. She was crying now, and he rested his free hand next to her head. She turned her face and licked his hand, desperate to ingratiate herself. He grabbed her hair, entwined his fingers in it and rested his weight against her head so he could make the last blow the hardest.

Persephone screamed on the last, and choked back a sob. Walton rolled her over onto her back in the grass and dirt. Her breasts bounced into view and he dropped the belt. She was crying and frightened and utterly desirable. Walton held her down by her upper arm, and with his free hand he flipped her skirt up; just like a dog expected food from its master, a lioness expected something from the man in charge.

Persephone quieted down. She was breathing heavily. She was just a chimera and she knew her place; it wasn't a *faux pas* to stare at her breasts and between her legs.

Persephone flinched, as though she were going to squirm away.

"Going somewhere?" He patted her crotch warningly.

He should have known better. She moved her muzzle to the hand holding her down. Her lips parted and her tongue, rough, danced on his fingers. She looked him in the eyes for a moment before turning away with a submissive smile. "You're my Master."

"Yes."

"Master, I'd like you to watch while I prepare for you. Master is *so* big," she explained.

He put his hand on her breast and stroked it gently. He loved its feel and its weight. He ran a finger lightly over her nipple. She licked her lip.

"You like that?" he asked.

She nodded. "Yes, sir."

He pinched her nipple and twisted. She grimaced, for a moment. "But it's not about what you like," he said.

"No, sir. I'm yours. I like that." She opened her legs.

He held her down by her wrists. Persephone didn't struggle. He rolled over onto her, and looked into her eyes. She gasped and he reached down to move the tip of his penis into position.

He could feel her tense up, either in anticipation, or she was bracing herself. Whatever.

She didn't struggle; she knew better. Slowly, he shifted his weight to his hips. She yielded slowly. He couldn't see her face, but he could hear her suppressing little cries as he moved deeper into her. She was warm and tight, and trembling under him. He moved upwards against her body, shifting his position to push it deeper into her.

She was tight and firm as a virgin bride. Walton lifted his chest and looked down at her face. Her eyes were closed, breathing in short pants, between her legs she embraced him warmly. She was a masterpiece of engineering, body and mind. He lay there for a few moments, savoring the sweet pressure on his shaft.

Her breath slowed, and she started breathing more deeply. Walton waited for her breathing to return to normal. Without warning, he pulled partly out and drove back home, hard. Her body shook, and she gave a cry halfway between pain and pleasure. Again, he waited just a moment.

Walton wanted to take this slow, to prolong the feeling of being inside her, but the urgency took over. His hips started to move, pulling out and slamming back in with a quick jerk. His new body *was* stronger; he could feel her body jerk under his thrusts, and he knew it was his momentum.

But as it went on, he felt her start to move under him. Her hips could barely shift position, but she found his pace and went with it. Her ankles crossed behind him, and she added the strength of her legs to his thrusts. She got louder, and her cries had less pain about them.

Her eyes were closed and she was panting. Persephone was entirely given over to pleasure. She struggled to free her arms, not to escape, but to embrace him. He denied her that, and he could feel her pleasure building. Something flicked across his lips; the tip of her ear. Walton took it between his teeth and applied pressure. She climaxed, her cry loud in his ears, her physical pleasure so plain that he felt his own build, intensify -- and then burst, a torrent flooding out of him and into her. He bit; her body twisted beneath him.

Slowly, he let her ear go, and she sighed with relief. He released her wrists, and now she wrapped her arms around him, hugged him to her.

"Master's stronger," she said. She licked his chest.

Walton chuckled and kissed her forehead. Persephone was a simple thing. He pulled out of her, and she sighed. He sat up.

She lay there for a moment, her breasts heaving. Without a word, he took her hair between his fingers and pushed her face into his lap. She performed her task quickly, sucking out the last drops of discharge and cleaning him so his pants wouldn't stain.

He got up and pulled up his pants. He opened the trunk of the car and reached in. No, he reconsidered: she shouldn't see him carrying something when she wasn't. "The case," he said curtly, and went inside the cabin.

The first thing he checked was the sharps locker. He opened the door and looked inside. There hung a hatchet, an axe, saw, cooking knives, forks, and various other essential but potentially dangerous tools. Each was on its hook, with a silhouette painted around it to show what belonged where. All was in order; she knew she would be whipped if it wasn't. He put the multi-tool in the only empty slot, took out a pair of manacles, closed the locker and spun the time lock all the way to twenty-four hours. He had a key to override that if she didn't have a chicken dressed. Maybe it was paranoid, but if ICON had gotten to Sentry they might have gotten to her.

He looked around. The cabin was small, but there were two beds: a large one she could use when he was here, and a narrow one up high in a loft, so she wouldn't have to waste wood or electricity for heating when he wasn't. There was a bookcase with her small, almost sub-literate library. It was mostly collections of comics, and a copy of *Crime and Punishment* that she had begged off him the last time he was there. There was a table, and a chair. He sat in it, and put the manacles on the table.

Persephone came in with the camera case. She had put her shirt back on, he noticed sourly. She looked at the manacles, put the case on the floor, and sat down in front of him. She lifted her foot. He put one of the cuffs around her ankle and locked it. When it was on, she gave him her other foot. He moved her leg so her thigh lifted her skirt, giving him a good view between her legs. The fur on her mound was damp.

"Leave the case on the table," he said. She came to her feet, the hobble's chain making the soft metal on metal hiss he enjoyed. He walked around her, and shook his head in disgust. "You've got grass in your hair," he said. "Go clean up. And don't use the hot water." The solar heater only gave enough hot water for one or two good showers a day.

"Master." She stripped, eyes averted, and put her clothes into a hamper by a washboard. She turned around, nude except for her fur, collar and manacles. Persephone opened a chest at the foot of the large bed and took out a bottle of special shampoo that he liked.

The chimera had to walk past him to get to the shower; the hobble limiting her to small steps. On a whim, he stopped her with a hand on her arm. He turned her around, and took her nipple into his mouth. Walton licked it once, sucked for a moment, and then gave her a playful nip. He let go and slapped her on her rump -- she flinched, probably because he had hit a bruise.

The lioness went into the shower and drew the curtain. That annoyed him for a moment before he remembered it would prevent splashing.

Walton leaned back in his chair and tried to think.

The Dopples were experimental. He knew that he was Doctor Travis Walton, but it was unlikely the courts would agree. When he had set this up, he had hoped the replacement could take place in secrecy. Ideally, he would die in his research lab, without anyone outside knowing he was even sick.

What he *hadn't* counted on was a very public murder that got police attention.

Now that Travis Walton was dead... Maybe a fresh start was what he needed.

There was a hiss from the shower and he jumped. Foolish. It was just air being forced out the shower head. Water sprayed for a few seconds; just enough so she could wet herself. Her silhouette squirted some shampoo into her hand.

"Open the curtain," Walton called out.

She obeyed, and stood facing him as she lathered up. It was a source of pride to him that she understood he wanted to look at her. Although hundreds of different engineers had contributed to the delicious creature soaping her hair in the shower, he was one of the most important.

It wasn't enough to duplicate the human brain; chimerae were product to be sold. You could beat a chimera until she screamed, and then fuck her and make her scream again. There was none of the tedious work involved in making a human woman climax, none of the drama about being a selfish lover, no need to feign interest in her opinions or personality. Persephone proved that; she was both insatiable and easy to satisfy, the perfect recreational partner.

She finished with her hair and started lathering her breasts. He moved forward, just a little.

Persephone trembled in the cold, making her even more enticing. Her breasts moved hypnotically. The cat watched him watch her and when he looked up at her face, she smiled. She leaned against the tile wall, closed her eyes, and put a hand between her legs to clean and pleasure herself.

"Hurry," he said.

She opened her eyes wide, and looked at the bulge in his pants with surprise. She was used to a Travis Walton in his fifties.

She rinsed and he fought to take his eyes off her.

He knew that he needed to *think*. But he was safe here. He got up and opened the chest at the foot of the bed.

Persephone was only to use the things in this chest when he was here. He lifted a bottle of cognac and looked at it suspiciously. He wasn't absolutely sure how much had been left, but the mark on the bottle matched the level of the amber fluid it contained. The shampoo, perfumes, cosmetics... but the bulk was clothing. 19th Century courtesan, French maid, bikini, an outfit made of chrome chains and black leather ... which woman would she be for him?

She came out of the shower, rubbing herself briskly with a towel. It was big and fluffy and she was probably cold. "Put that on," he ordered her. He took a leash from the chest and turned away. He waited, savoring his own impatience.

"Master," she said after an eternity.

He turned to face her. She was an African savage from Hollywood, animal teeth and lion claws and beads and hand-woven fabric in simple patterns. An ivory phallic pendant three centimeters long, perhaps a symbol of some heathen deity, dangled from a thong around her neck, nestled in the soft fur of her cleavage.

She lifted her breasts and pressed them together against the penis on her necklace. She looked at him and at the leash slyly. "Am I Master's captive?" she asked.

"Yes... yes, I think so," he said.

She stepped forward, lifted her chin so he could fasten the leash on her collar. He stood here, holding the leash as her eyes burned for him.

"Does Master want me to fight and lose?" Her eyes and mouth smiled; assuring him it was a game.

"I don't know if I want to play that," he said thoughtfully. "I've done that for real," he bragged.

She slipped a hand under her skirt. "Tell me, Master." There wasn't any jealousy in her, and she liked to hear him talk about other women. She worked at herself as he told her.

"There was a chimera in Blue Diamond," he said. "Her name was Chili, a Reynard."

"She said no, but Master persuaded her?" she asked. She looked at him steadily. "Lucky girl."

He laughed. "She didn't think so. They had to tie her up for me."

Persephone reached down, put her hands on his crotch, met his eyes sincerely. "She loved every second this was in her," she said with perfect confidence.

"Yes, she did," he agreed. He touched her forehead. "That's my gift to all of you."

"I know that, Master," she said. She rubbed his crotch through his pants. "This is the best thing in my life, Master."

He knew it was the truth, for Persephone and for Chili. Humans were gods to them. Except Chili didn't behave. And after, she signed a lying report claiming that Lilith had shot him. What had gone wrong with Chili? It was almost as though Chili resented him. He didn't know and it made him cross, an itch he couldn't scratch.

"You're too grabby," he frowned.

She snatched her hands away. "Master, you're exciting me *so* much."

Walton knew he shouldn't take his frustrations out on her. "Turn around," he ordered.

She hesitated, and with a sorrowful expression, turned her back on him.

"Are you afraid I'm going to hit you?" he asked.

"I'm afraid Master is displeased with me," she said. "The whip brings Master's forgiveness."

"Cross your wrists." Handcuffs went onto her, chrome metal to match the manacles on her ankles and the leash. Walton tugged the leash and turned her back to face him. The chains weren't necessary, he knew, but they were exciting symbols of her status; they made her more beautiful. He opened her top, and her breasts came out. Walton fondled them, felt her lean her weight towards him, enjoying his play. He pushed her top down her arms, stopping at her elbows. His captive breasts moved with every breath; her eyes were uncertain.

Part of him had wondered if he was wrong: maybe Lilith *had* killed him; maybe Deidre *had* left him. But this simple animal's response encouraged him. Persephone was as loyal as Lilith and Deidre; all she wanted for herself was a cock and some reassurance.

"You're a good girl," he said.

"Thank you, Master," she said, relieved.

"Chili wasn't. Isn't," he said thoughtfully. He stroked Persephone's breasts while he explained. "Even while I was inside her, even while she was coming so hard she could barely talk, she said she hated me." He put his hand on Persephone's face. "You could see it in her eyes. The anger, the sense of violation, like she was a human woman."

"Did Master have her beaten?" Persephone asked.

"Yes, before I put it in her." He shrugged. "Even that didn't settle her down."

"Poor Master," Persephone licked his hand.

"No, it was fun," he admitted. He scowled. "Chili's trash. She needs to be put into her place."

Persephone didn't respond. She was probably wondering if she was going to be a Chili's whipping girl. She tried hard not to show fear, but he could see it and smell it on her. He couldn't help but smile.

Walton touched Persephone's breast. There was something liberating in this woman, effectively naked while he was still clothed, her body his to do what he wanted. He could stare at her breasts, and she'd consider that something due to him, not a gift or favor from her.

"Beautiful, of course," he said, "you're all beautiful."

Persephone smiled. "Thank you."

"Beautiful but trashy. She looked like a chrome silhouette on a mud flap. How could she look in a mirror and *not* see what she was for?"

Persephone laughed at that image, and it lightened his mood.

"Her tits were bigger than yours." She swallowed, the sound soft in the cabin. Was she afraid she would be punished for not having large enough breasts?

"Almost *too* big," he added. "It was a pleasure to come into her and know how much she loved it, no matter what she said." He shook his head. "She never admitted it, though."

"Master could bring her here," Persephone suggested. "I'd like to watch Master force into her, and taste Master's seed in another woman."

Walton used the leash to draw her close. She parted her lips, and he kissed her more than once; quick and light. He put his tongue in her mouth, and she responded ardently with hers.

He couldn't remember when he had last been so excited. His penis was so hard it almost hurt. Was it the new body?

He lowered his hand, and she followed the leash down until she was kneeling. He undid his belt. It tried to push its way out, but got tangled in his pants. He worked at it awkwardly, while she knelt before him and watched, attentively, waiting for a treat she longed for. Finally, his shaft came free in front of her.

The chimera surprised him. Persephone moved up, letting his penis slide between her breasts instead of taking it into her mouth. She moved them the length of his shaft, her soft fur on his sensitive skin. "Master's so hard," she purred. It vanished into her mouth. Her mouth was deeper than a human woman's; she slowly withdrew it, making a soft "yum" sound.

Walton couldn't wait any longer. He pulled her over to the bed, attached the leash to the headboard. He arched his back to push his pants down, and held his penis up. She climbed onto him. Her savage costume had a skirt, and he didn't let her wear panties. The lioness moved forward and back, and expertly, without looking, positioned herself so his tip entered her. She slid down until she reached his fist. She looked at him, wondering what he wanted.

"How many men have you done this for?" he asked.

"I'm not sure, Master," Persephone said. "In Blue Diamond, there were hundreds." She smiled. "Master's the best."

If some human whore had told him that, he wouldn't have believed her. But Persephone and her kind were different. All the lies women told were true for them. She said he was the best, and he was sure she would say that to any man inside her. But there was no intent to deceive; it was an honest expression of how that moment moved her. There was nothing but the here and now for her.

She moved her hips urgently, reminding him wordlessly that his hand blocked her and she was impatient.

He took his hand away and placed them on her breasts.

She sighed as she slid slowly onto him, impaling herself as he pinched her nipples and squeezed her breasts. She leaned her weight forward, using his hands to help support her. She was chained, but desperate to satisfy him. The thought was almost as exciting as the warmth and pressure on his shaft.

"Get to work," he ordered.

The lion looked down at him, her eyes filled with longing. She moved her hips, slowly at first, her eyes on his, a naked, chained savage with nothing on her mind but the man inside her. She didn't speak, not in words. She couldn't keep her pleasure to herself; it escaped in little sounds that forced their way out of her.

It inevitably spread to him. He thought about ordering her to slow down, but instead let her speed up. She was delicious and he was curious; what would she do if he gave her her head?

Like a horse or dog born to run, she moved faster. Her hands were bound, but she put her heart and soul into pleasing him, and so pleasuring herself. She was tight on him, and all she wanted was the reward he would give her.

Was giving her. His climax was unexpected, intense, long. His eyes closed and his head lifted; he squeezed her soft breasts. She shuddered, cried out and bit her lip as she came.

Usually, when he was done with a woman he was done with her, but he was filled with a desire to have more of her. He turned his hips to get her off and stood next to the bed. She moved her head to his crotch, thinking that was what he wanted from her, but instead he stepped further away. She knelt on the bed, held by the leash, watching him, fatigued yet fascinated, as he stripped his clothes off and let them fall.

Naked, he returned to her. He pushed her down on the bed. She struggled to please him, but he didn't let her: instead, he kissed her. Her mouth, her neck, her shoulder, moving to the top of her

breast before he rested against her, arms around her, exhausted for the moment.

He closed his eyes and held her in his arms and thought of the other chimera women he knew.

Tiny little Deidre, licking his hand gratefully after he punished her for something. *Master's whip brings forgiveness.* Who wordlessly brought him to ecstasy every morning before making his breakfast. She was an amusing diversion; she never asked anything of him, and was always available and compliant. Why had his son freed her?

Tigre, a tiger taller than he was. He was proud of her; he had taken a stroke victim and turned her into the loyal right hand of Blue Diamond. It was incredible to watch the pain she could draw out of a chimera with a whip. He had seen chimera girls piss themselves when they were given to her for punishment. If humans were the gods of chimerae, Tigre was their Satan. He had never taken Tigre to bed, and now that she was dead, he regretted it. He had seen her eyes shine as she made chimerae lick her; he would have liked to make that light come to them himself.

Cheshire, a jaguar woman, about the same size as Persephone. Cheshire had been a stunt actress in video until her knee was ruined when a gag went wrong. It could have been a tragedy, but her owners sold her to Blue Diamond, where she was feared almost as much as Tigre. After Blue Diamond had fallen, he had seen to her getting a position where she kept order among chimerae. He wondered how she was doing, and if he could contact her safely. It was possible she was being watched.

Lilith. Deadly, submissive Lilith. A dark elf porn star's body, beautiful, sleek, naked, on her knees before him, her tongue moving from his feet to his shaft. Not a lover; a worshipper, shamelessly paying homage to him the way she had been taught, using her magnificent body to bring pleasure to those who created her. She could pass as human and she did. He had her groomed as a killer, a weapon he would eventually use against ICON, one that could strike and would die rather than compromise him. She had struck one blow for him, killing Mehta. They had celebrated that. The only reward she wanted was permission to touch herself after Walton had climaxed on her face and breasts. She had understood her place perfectly.

Poor, humble, unselfish Lilith. It had gone wrong. She was dead, and they accused her of killing the original Doctor Walton. That was nonsense. If a chimera could love, Lilith loved her master. She loved him, serviced him and served him, and now she was dead.

He knew how she had died: a grenade in the parking lot of a strip club in Atlanta. ICON said it was suicide, self-inflicted after she had been injured by an ICON operative. He wondered how much of that was lies. The grenade rang true; she was to use that to prevent her arrest. But why had she been fighting an ICON operative? Had she been trying to avenge him?

He wondered if he should have told her about the Dopples.

...Yes, but that was just hindsight. He hadn't *known* the Dopples would even work. It wasn't his fault, even if he was right.

How would he replace her?

He grimaced. Lilith and Chili, mirror-images. Lilith had understood what she was; Chili thought she was a person. A "free" chimera.

Ridiculous. It was like letting dogs run wild. Chimerae were better off with an owner to protect them. They needed a master, even if they thought differently. He had fun with her, she enjoyed it, just as she was designed to. Was Chili any happier for being free to say no?

Had she falsified the reports on his death, fooled ICON and even the police? Would she go that far? Could a chimera be that spiteful?

There was something he was missing. Something the last Dopple had missed too...

He squeezed Persephone. She moved in response, not to escape. Her tail brushed against his legs slowly, lingering and then wrapping around him.

Technically, Persephone was his son's property. The thought annoyed him at the same time that it amused him. If his son knew about her, he'd probably "free" her, let her "choose" what she wanted to do. Soft, warm Persephone. What a ridiculous name that was. *She should be called "Parakelsis." Comfort.*

"Stop squirming," he ordered her. "I'm going to take a nap."

It had been a long, exhausting day. Chain rustled as she moved to be more comfortable for him. He closed his eyes, resting against a living fur pillow that existed only for his comfort.

He dreamed of Chili's breasts surging, her muscles struggling against the chains, her face a mix of hate and ecstasy he had not believed possible. Sometimes a chimera who resisted copulation would play possum, and that wasn't satisfying. Chili had been whipped before he started, and he was driving her against raised studs. She couldn't suppress responding.

Chili was a tall woman, and he pushed her muzzle down sideways with his lips. Her teeth were tight on her gag, but they were parted wide enough for him to insinuate his tongue. Her ears flattened and her eyes screwed shut. His cock was in her, but the silly girl resisted a French kiss. She hated him, but she was bound for him, helpless and at his disposal. She was trying to resist a climax, but he wanted to see her come despite that. She knew it, she fought it, and she would fail.

He awoke. The sun had moved; Persephone had not. His dream had made him hard. He kissed Persephone again, and then harder. Her arms were bound, but she kissed him back.

The memory of Chili, under him, struggling against him, cursing him as he made her moan -- the memory was intense, real, and he imagined his cock in a defiant red fox. He'd make her come and beg for more.

"You like that?" he asked.

"Master's impatient," she said. She grinned back. "Who did Master dream about? Who was the lucky girl?"

He scratched her head idly, but didn't answer. Chili was his fondest erotic memory, difficult and even dangerous, like white water rafting, or, better, like riding a horse that was barely broken. Forcing her to come despite what she wanted was a challenge and a triumph; when Chili trembled in an orgasm under him, it felt like an accomplishment.

Persephone licked him. "Would Master like chicken for dinner?"

"I think so," Walton said.

"I'll need to start now," she said apologetically.

He was comfortable holding her, but she was right. He sighed at the inconvenience and sat up. The key was on the ring in his pants. He pulled her close to him by her collar, kissed her once and undid her leash; she stood and turned her back so he could remove her handcuffs. He pulled her top off her arms and lay it on the bed.

He pulled her into a hug from behind, one hand around her waist and another on her breast. He heard her lick her lips.

It didn't seem right that she was wearing more than he was, so he undid her skirt and let it drop to the floor. Walton kissed her back as he played with her breasts, heard her breath come deeper. He moved fingers between her legs. Persephone's fur was slick, wet with their fluids: he put a finger into her and raised it to her lips. She took his finger into her mouth and sucked it clean.

"Master," she said shyly, "I can't chase a rooster with these on."

He blinked and looked down at her feet. Of course, she was still wearing the manacles. He bent over. She supported him as he unlocked the chain on her ankles.

He sat up, and she knelt before him. She showed respect, touching her breasts to the floor and licking his foot. He touched her ear but instead of coming to her feet, she stayed on her knees.

She put her hands on him, squeezed lightly, and ran his penis between her hands. She leaned in and kissed his tip. It surged in her hands, grew and stiffened.

"Master," she asked. "May I have lunch before catching your dinner?"

He laughed, and opened his thighs wider to invite her. She took him into her mouth. He stroked her head, and closed his eyes as she went to work. He wasn't fully erect, but she could handle that.

Her tongue was rough and her teeth were sharp, but she was well trained. Of all the ways a man could use a chimera, this was probably the perfect symbol of the relationship. She was kneeling, and all the pleasure was his. Clients at Blue Diamond seemed to know that intuitively: it was almost always the first sexual act they would pay for.

And paradoxically, it was the one which offered her most control. She had nothing to distract her from the work she was doing. She had her arms wrapped around him, holding him still as she bobbed her head. There was nothing for him to do but lean back and feel her work on him.

She was making sounds of pleasure, muffled by what was in her mouth. Walton liked getting oral sex and she was good at it, intent on his cock and nothing else. He opened his eyes, knowing he was about to --

She took him out just as he came; mostly into her mouth, but splattering on her face. She held his penis as he jerked; in between spurts she squeezed more out onto her breast. Persephone looked up at him and swallowed theatrically; she licked him off the corner of her mouth, and with her other hand rubbed it into the fur on her breast, leaving a dark wet spot.

"Thank you, Master," she said humbly. "Master should sleep now. I'll get his dinner ready."

Walton stroked her head. "I need to start spending more time here. Maybe I'll take you with me."

She hesitated a moment, almost as though she were weighing options. "I'd like that, Master."

She showed respect, stood, and leaving her clothes on the floor, silently padded to the door, swishing her tail as she closed it behind her.

Walton lay there for a few moments. A cool breeze made him uncomfortable. He got up and pulled his pants on. He thought of Persephone, naked, chasing a rooster, and decided he wanted to see that.

No, he had to think. Who had killed him twice? He didn't know. ICON? Or was it Chili? Or was it his son? Could he trust Sentry?

Did Deidre leave him?

Sentry hadn't stopped him. Didn't that make the Fidelus innocent? Maybe. But --

Walton was identical to the first Dopple. Who hadn't even made it here. What had he done right? Was it his choice to leave Sentry? Or maybe it was luck --

He stepped out the door and froze.

Luck.

That was exactly right. He couldn't *figure* it out. If he used logic, he would follow the same paths and whoever had killed him before would kill him again. The only way to be sure he was trying a different strategy was to randomize.

He took a coin out of his pocket. *Heads, I trust Sentry. Tails, I don't.*

The coin went into the air just as the knife went into his neck.

Persephone had made the knife from flint, and kept it on the roof. She jumped off and used her momentum to sink its entire length into him. Her weight crushed him to the ground. Claws weren't for cutting; they were for grappling: her claws latched into his skin. His eyes were already glazed as her teeth found his Adams apple and sank in, closing his windpipe. A lion kills by strangulation.

His arms were held tight to his sides, and he struggled, but not for long.

Persephone held him several minutes after he stopped kicking. She withdrew the flint knife. Half had snapped off inside him.

Tentatively, she relaxed her bite, and the rest of her knife flashed across his throat. His heart had stopped and blood pooled, weakly, in the wound. Persephone tossed the knife into the grass, stood, and brushed herself off. In the chicken run, a rooster wearing her collar chased a hen.

Persephone looked at the car. She had driven the first one off a bridge; she didn't want to risk that a second time. She would drive this one within walking distance of a bus station a few towns away, then take a bus back. The nearest station was twenty clicks distant; she could walk it, or call Mike (her phone was hidden on the roof) and sweet-talk him into giving her a ride back here. Of course, she'd need to get rid of the body first. Then a shower. A *hot* shower.

Persephone looked back at her cabin with a grimace. She could handle one bad day every month or so, but staying *with* him... no. She had a good thing going here; a lot of work had gone into the chickens and vegetable garden. But more Dopples would be coming and it was time for her to leave. She didn't look forward to pulling up stakes, but she couldn't keep this up forever.

Still, she wished she knew why he always flipped a coin.

The Leather's Always Blacker
by Whyte Yoté

The unassuming whitetail buck in the back room of the Crossroads Cafe warily watched two otter boys run past the entrance to the secluded alcove in which he sat. When their screams had receded to a safe distance, he let out the breath he didn't know he'd been holding. Turning his attention back to the laptop in front of him, he fished his slender length back out and resumed a languid but increasingly desperate stroking.

Beep.

ass_o_nine had typed, "I run my hands over your tight fluffy body, all the way down to your new curly tail. When I slide underneath to feel your knot, I watch your little hole twitch." Rike shuddered. First an hour of leather play and now this unexpected transformation. He was starting to regret choosing the Christian coffeehouse as his roleplay spot for the night. The threadbare donation couches and recliners hid his activities from anyone walking down the hallway thirty feet away, but back at his noisy cramped apartment he at least would have been able to moan. Still, he was slick enough that it wouldn't take much now anyway.

"Your husky pup strains at his leash, humping your hand, eager for something to breed," Rike replied, hoping to move the action along a bit quicker. Droplets of pre added a dull shine to the more worn keys on the board.

In the chat window, the nude donkey leaned back and crossed his arms over his broad chest, the tube of his cock just visible in the lower right corner. The buck hoped to have his lips around it in a week's time if all went well. Though the donkey was Sir, and if Sir forbade it, then Rike would just be shit out of luck. But even then, any orders were sexy when the donkey gave them.

ass_o_nine's muzzle turned up at the corners before he leaned over the bulk of his belly and tapped away. If merely looking at the donkey was enough to get Rike hard; reading what he wrote next sent him straight to edging: "Good boy, tho your purpose is not to breed, but be bred." He presented his cockhead to his webcam, an appreciatively sticky sheen spread all around the blunt head.

Rike didn't even have time to think about how it would feel to have that flare spread him open. God knew how many times he'd fantasized about it. But just seeing how much he turned on his master—and, concurrently, how good of a boy he was—pushed him past the summit. With one final, furtive look for interlopers, he grimaced, grunting quietly as he sprayed the carpet between his legs.

When his vision cleared, he noticed the chat window blinking. He had been too busy spasming to pay attention. "You lose it?" the donkey had typed, referring to Rike's load.

"Sure did, Sir," the buck henpecked with his unoccupied hand, making sure he hit the shift key for that second S. Sir didn't like it when his moniker wasn't capitalized. And when Sir was displeased, Rike was punished. Sometimes it was a string of chastising slurs, but other times the donkey would just sign out of chat, leaving the buck high and dry, so to speak.

It wasn't like the buck wore a sheath lock or anything, at least not yet. At first he had balked at the idea of denying himself after he'd pissed Sir off. He would just open up his porn folder and set a slide show until he got his satisfaction. Over the past few months, digging deeper into the world of The Service Sector had changed his perception of satisfaction. Getting off didn't seem to be enough anymore.

"Good boy," said Sir. "I can almost see that ass wiggling around right now." That would have been the truth; Rike couldn't wag much but he could approximate it by adding his hips to the limited movement of his tail. The praise was such a Pavlovian trigger by now that he had to restrain himself or be surreptitious in public. It wasn't that uncommon to see an average whitetail in an average coffeehouse, but it *was* uncommon to see one wiggling around like a puppy with a laptop in front of him, webcam clipped to the top of the screen like it was now.

Rike smiled at the lens. "Awwrrruff!" he typed. "*Giraffe?*"

"*Giraffe,*" Sir replied. The safe word—more of a role-play trigger by now—had lost any trace of the silliness that Rike had felt the first few times he'd used it. Once invoked, the world around Rike mostly ceased to exist. It was just him and Sir, and Sir could do anything he wanted until one of them closed the session by restating the word. On this day Sir had deigned to slowly turn Rike into a dog, and the buck had lasted all of ten minutes before blowing.

"That was pretty damn awesome," Rike said. *Giraffe* also meant the end of silence; once in the role play all talking was forbidden. At first Rike didn't believe it made a difference, but the separation of communications had added to the realism, as real as it could be through the Internet. "I don't know how you do it, Bill." Sir's real name was Rufus Williams but he made it clear that anything but "Bill" would get Rike punished, role play or no.

"I'm not the only one doin' it," the donkey said, smiling. "I can supply the material and the leadership, but the rest is in your head. You might not think it but your brain is doing most of the work here. I can type words all day long, but you're the one rubbin' that cock."

Rike sat back on the couch. "Pretty soon I hope to be rubbing yours." It hadn't taken long after he'd met Bill that he'd figured out "ass_o_nine" referred to species and cock length, respectively. Bill had verified this with a tape measure one night during a strip tease for Rike's benefit, out of character for once, and ever since then the buck had wanted to see it for himself. That date was quickly approaching.

"Pretty soon," Bill chuckled, showing his oversized incisors. "Though I still don't think you know what you're getting yourself into."

"Do I still sound naïve?"

"Sometimes," the donkey said, leaning back, the old La-Z-Boy creaking under the weight of his frame. "I don't doubt you have the passion and the interest, but it takes a special kind of person for this. I'm not sure you fully understand yet." He crossed his fingers over his belly, twiddling them slowly.

Rike stared at the screen for a moment, thinking. Bill was watching him with his familiar mix of respect and skepticism. Even after their conversations and Rike's soul-searching, the donkey still didn't seem convinced of the buck's conviction.

"If I didn't want to take it seriously," Rike said, leaning in, "I wouldn't be wanting to meet you and see for myself."

Smiling, Bill replied, "Alright, I have to give you that much." But then he turned serious: "Just don't blame me if you get in over your head. Once you get in that door the only thing that'll bring you back into the real world is *Giraffe*. I know what you're thinkin', but you might have to use it anyway."

"I understand." Rike nodded, a bit downcast. Though he implicitly trusted the donkey, he understood the need for such measures.

"I just want to make sure you're prepared," said Bill.

"I don't think anything could really *prepare* me other than hands-on experience."

"No, I know you're right." The donkey leaned back in toward the camera, the end of his muzzle bumping it and sending the image off-kilter before he straightened it back up. "And I trust that you're in a place mentally where you can process what's going to be going on. I don't want to have to deal with another Andrew."

Rike remembered how hesitant Bill had been when talking about Andrew. A former pet, the macho wolf had flipped out in his cage, requiring tranquilizer darts so the EMTs could extricate him. Andrew had disappeared, as had Bill from the BDSM scene for a few years.

"No way," said the buck, his face set. "I wouldn't do that to you. I respect you too much to not know myself going into this."

"You better respect yourself first," Bill said, to which Rike nodded. Bill always knew what to say. Always in control. "Okay, I need to turn in. Up before dawn again you know."

"Okay. I probably won't get to talk to you again before the weekend, but I have your address."

"Only if you're sure about it. I need you to come prepared." Rike thought about making a joke but it would have been tasteless at best.

"If I'm having doubts I'll let you know." Bill seemed to be evaluating the truth of the buck's words, but he finally nodded back.

"Good. You have a good night now," the donkey said just before the window went black. Rike closed his laptop and sighed. Just thinking about the weekend was causing his sheath to rise once again. Swearing under his breath and getting to his hooves, he checked for stains and inappropriate bulges. Finding neither, he packed up and headed for his car, grinning at the unknowing people around him.

***

Over the next week Rike forced himself to be celibate. Exceedingly difficult at first, the buck quickly grew used to the building anticipation and eventually came to like the pleasant, constant arousal.

Rike packed his bags Thursday night. Clothes would be optional, but still necessary. Toiletries were a given, but beyond that the buck decided it wasn't all that different from a weekend visit to a friend's house. He even considered his modest collection of toys before deciding it would be better to leave things to the capable care of the donkey.

Friday passed quicker than Rike expected, his anxiety tempered by anticipation. So much so that all he could think about as he pulled up in front of Bill's nondescript ranch house was being tied up and going down on that massive meat.

As Rike gathered up his bags and locked his SUV he noticed how quiet the neighborhood was, and how unassuming. The sun, little more than an hour from setting, cast long languid shadows over the street. The voices of playing children wafted from around the corner, and the buck could almost feel what the first residents here felt when they moved in back in the 1960s. All he had to do was imagine smaller trees and bigger cars. Even now it was peaceful and organized.

Rike heard the familiar Westminster quarters chime within the house when he pressed a fingertip to the button. Moments later a shadow appeared through the translucent amber glass, approaching the door. Then the door opened and Rike's heart leaped up from his chest into his throat when he saw the donkey in real life for the first time.

"Hi!" the buck said, feeling his lips stretch in an involuntary smile, and before he could say anything else the donkey stepped over the threshold and enveloped Rike in a tight bear hug that squeezed the air right out of his lungs.

Bill pulled away and grinned back. "Hey there. I see you found the place okay."

"Yeah, it was easy enough." Rike shifted his duffel higher up on his shoulder. The donkey was shorter than he had imagined but it wasn't really a surprise given how hard it was to judge height over a webcam. Even standing in the doorway with his bulk filling the frame, he exuded an air of authority, something subconscious that made the buck aware of choosing his words carefully. This time he didn't have a backspace key. He stood there shifting from hoof to hoof, looking down before he realized how transparently submissive he probably looked.

Thick-nailed fingers lifted his chin to meet the donkey's gaze. "Hey."

"Hm?"

"If you're not ready, Rike, I'll understand." It was so unexpected that the buck actually had to catch himself twice before knowing how to respond.

"I didn't come this far to back out without even trying."

The donkey's grey-hazel eyes locked on his own. "I know you didn't, but I need you to be sure you know what you're giving up once you step into this house. You get inside and you belong to me for the weekend. You are not your own man. I think for you, I make decisions for you, I control every part of you."

"That's what *Giraffe* is for, right?"

Bill shook his head slightly, grinning again. "Sure, but it's the end of the weekend. You say that word and you go home. It's not something you can use to take a break when you don't feel like it anymore. That's the difference between a fetish and a lifestyle."

"I need to find out at least. This is the only way I can think of."

Bill patted the buck on the shoulder that wasn't holding his bags. "Alright. I trust you, but you're going to have to trust me in everything I do. It's for your own good." Rike swallowed and nodded, his smile never faltering though his nerves were making it difficult. "Then come into my world," the donkey said, stepping aside with an open palm toward the door. And the buck walked right on through.

The first thing he smelled was tension, pungent and bitter to his muzzle. He could smell sex too, but even that was tinged at the edges with a certain unease. Rike was in the middle of a spacious living room; he could see the kitchen up ahead and an open door that seemed to lead down to the basement. The decor was a few years old but inoffensive, and kept up nicely.

After the tension and sex, there was tiger. Rike could smell it even before he made the full turn back to the door and saw the orange and black fur. And leather, lots of leather. Harness, mitts, a pup mask, and little else. Bill had made no mention of having someone else over for the weekend, and it kind of pissed him off. He wasn't really in the mood to share his fantasy with another "pet," not for his first time. The tiger just stood there with a thick collar in his paws, from which dangled a shiny bone-shaped tag with "Rike" engraved on it.

"Who's *this* guy?" As soon as the words came out Rike caught movement out of the corner of his eye just before his vision exploded in a sea of stars and pain. The world spun, the buck moaned, but his voice was a million miles away. He thought he heard Bill saying something, garbled and unintelligible through the ringing on the left side of his head. When he felt finger pads on his neck he opened his eyes. The tiger was kneeling over him, taking his pulse.

"Oh, don't bother, he's fine," Bill said dismissively, closing the door and stepping over the buck before addressing him. "Who he is, is none of your fucking business at the moment. You stepped over the threshold and you talked out of turn."

"What the *fuck*? What happened to *Giraffe* starting things off? Don't I even—" Rike was cut off with a hoof to his chest, right over the diaphragm. Air left his lungs in a deep *whoosh* and he lay, curled up and wheezing, clutching his gut.

"Get him ready," the donkey said to his accomplice, who reached behind the buck's antlers and snatched something from the table. Rike couldn't do much in the way of moving, which wasn't necessary as the tiger brought a pair of scissors to the buck's belly and began cutting his shirt right up the middle. Soon it was nothing more than rags, and the tiger started on his jeans. Rike considered asking for an explanation, but thought better of it. Somehow, he knew he would only get more pain.

"I warned you," Bill said, his voice something completely different from anything he'd used in their online sessions. It was cold, domineering. His face was drawn downward in a leering smirk. His eyes were still warm behind it all, though. "After you get in my house, you belong to me. You already know Rule Number One: you *don't* talk unless you are given permission. You don't eat unless I give you food. You don't drink unless I give you water. You don't *anything* without my say-so. Just like in our little role plays. Except it's a lot more real, isn't it?"

Rike nodded and said nothing as the tiger cut down to the end of his jeans and they fell away from his body in tatters. His boxers came next, unceremoniously, and he found himself feeling humiliated by being exposed so quickly and emotionlessly. He would have worn less expensive clothes, but there was no way he could have predicted this. *Any* of this. He certainly hadn't expected to be on the floor of the donkey's home, coughing and naked as his bags and clothes were gathered up by a tiger in pup gear and taken away. The collar was all that was left, and Bill picked it up.

"Now, come here," he said. Rike started to stand but the donkey shoved him over with a hoof. His rack slid along the table's surface, leaving deep scratches. "Rule Number Two, or at least it'll suffice as such: nobody walks on two legs in this house but me or those I give exceptions to. That's not you right now." The buck nodded. "So come *here*."

It actually took some effort to get back onto all fours, gasping through tears and snot. But he was already learning lessons and he didn't want to think about what would happen if he couldn't make it over to Bill. The donkey was kneeling with the open collar in his hands, watching Rike for what he would do. Drawing in a deep breath (as much as he could, anyway) he crawled slowly over to Bill, his head hung low, his mind racing at a mile a minute. When he reached the donkey he stopped, and the next thing he felt was a gentle constriction around his neck and the decisive *click* of a small padlock at the back.

"Good boy," Bill murmured as he drew the buck up close and held him, stroking between his ears and down his back.

Rike broke down. He just couldn't help it, and he honestly didn't know how else to process his emotions. In the space of five short minutes his life had been turned completely upside-down. And he was mad at himself for blubbering like this because it meant he *hadn't* been prepared after all. Not for this. Bill had been right: this really *was* nothing like their Internet chats.

In spite of his inability to process everything as quickly as it came, Rike was learning things about himself he never could have known without Bill's help. Like how, when crawling the length of the living room the buck not once looked up into his new master's eyes. And how he knew he deserved the punishment he'd gotten for his insubordination. And how despite his crying in the donkey's thick arms, he was immensely turned on just from the close comforting contact. He realized his hips were rolling slightly and stopped, though there was no way Bill couldn't have noticed.

"I felt that," the donkey said, reaching around Rike's belly and down between his legs where he found the hard, thin shaft already protruding. The heat of a blush burned the buck's cheeks, drying the tracks of his tears there. "What, you thought it *wasn't* going to happen? I thought this is what you came here for." Rike wanted to qualify that statement; it wasn't the *only* thing he'd come for, but he'd rather have the donkey's words in his mouth than be punished again. And he'd *much* rather keep that hand on his cock, stroking as gently as the words coming out of Bill's muzzle. "When was the last time you came, boy?"

Rike was afraid to say anything.

"Speak, boy."

"Monday," the buck croaked instantly, eager to comply with the order. A rush accompanied the word, as if he were free for just that moment, and passed just as quickly. He heard Bill rumble low in his gut, felt it all through his own skull.

"So, this is feeling pretty good for ya then." Rike nodded emphatically. He wanted to come badly, but if the donkey decided this wasn't the time for it he was prepared for that too. It just meant a bigger payoff later. But Bill cupped his sheath and stroked it back and forth, solidifying his squeezing, making the buck moan and open his eyes. Though his vision was half-obscured by the donkey's chest, he could see the pup-tiger across the room, leaning against the corner of the wall.

The donkey's left arm held the buck in a kneel, his legs spread, his other hand milking Rike's erection. "I know you've had a long day, Rike, but do you think you could come for me? Before I put you down for the night, I'd like to get some of that tension outta you so you can sleep well. Sound like a plan?"

Rike nodded into Bill's big round belly. Bill's pace increased and the buck shuddered bodily.

"Then come, boy." Time ceased to have meaning as Rike closed his eyes and focused on exactly what was happening. His first official action as a new "pet" was to sit there in the middle of the living room and bust his nut. Pleasing his master was as easy as his own pleasure, at least for now. Bill's strokes were a bit rougher than what usually got him off, but it was Bill's hand getting him closer to climax. Bill was clutching him, watching for his body to tense before he shot, controlling damn near everything.

The donkey was interminably patient. Each time Rike reached a new plateau, he was given murmured encouragement, never forceful. And when the buck felt the donkey's other hand move beneath his tail and apply pressure there, it was over. He writhed and bore back onto the intrusion, wishing it would go in but shooting all over Bill's carpet before it did. It was just too much. Afterward he collapsed against the donkey, panting and sweaty.

"That was quite impressive," Bill said, standing up. "I think that's more than I've ever seen from you. Good job." Rike got a pat on the head for his efforts and he smiled, too tired to do much else. "Pup, could you put him to bed while I clean up?"

There was no answer save for the light clinking of metal as the tiger came over to them. A flash of orange and white, and then he was hoisted into big, strong arms, the scent of feline and leather replacing Bill's earthy musk. He found himself vaguely aware of his own legs bouncing limply as they descended a staircase into the basement, which was darker and cooler than the upstairs had been. A wire mesh door was opened for him and he crawled through, too tired to process any of it. The door latched shut and he was down for the count.

***

Rike's sleep was deep and dreamless, and when he woke up it took a few minutes for him to realize two things: he wasn't in his own bed (or any bed, for that matter), and it was the first time he'd woken up naturally in quite some time. No alarm to jar him awake. He blinked twice and was conscious; it was a nice change.

It was still dark outside but the buck's night vision showed him fuzzy details in the dim blue-grey hue from the partial moon outside. He was curled up on a soft bed within a cage just large enough not to be cramped, but too small to do anything but crawl around. So small, in fact, that when he tried to lift his head his antlers rattled against the bars. Rike froze at the sound, repositioned his head and tugged again, but the cage gave no ground.

"You're locked in," came a deep voice from a few feet behind him, followed by rustling. "Sir doesn't want us moving around down here." Rike's hands ventured up to the top of his head, and after a bit of feeling around he realized the tiger was right: his rack was shackled at the base, attached to the cage by small chains. After a bit more squirming he knew his hooves were the same way. He found it odd that he would be bound inside a cage he couldn't escape anyway. He also found it odd that the tiger was talking to him.

"So you *can* speak." The buck turned his head toward the tiger but only moved a few inches before meeting resistance, and so he just gave up.

"Not when Sir is around," the tiger replied. "But I had to say something before you woke him up." Silence for a moment, then: "I'm Tenso. But Sir calls me Pup."

"For obvious reasons."

"Mhm." Tenso stretched and groaned, shaking both cages, which Rike decided must be attached somehow if it wasn't all one piece anyway. "Are you the new pet?"

Rike nearly answered before he actually stopped to think about the ramifications of that seemingly simple question. It wasn't necessarily hard but the way Tenso asked hinted at more to this weekend than the fun and games the buck had expected.

"I'm just here for the weekend."

"Oh. Sir said I was going to have a new pet to play with."

"Well, Bill didn't tell me anything about that. I'm new to all this."

"He's probably just trying you out then." Tenso's words were muffled by the mask but far from garbled. "Trying out" wouldn't exactly be the term Rike would use, but the mere mention of it caused the buck to doubt why he was here in the first place. The buck's purpose here was a hands-on, real-life experience. And here

he was, chained to a cage next to an actual "pet," and it didn't get any more real than that.

Already Rike questioned his dedication compared to Bill's and Tenso's, the likes of which he hadn't seen before. Hell, he'd never seen or read about *anything* like this, which led him to believe that either what went on in this house was rare or he hadn't delved into the subject nearly deep enough.

"Are you here for the weekend, too?" Rike asked, speaking up slightly to compensate for his awkward position.

"I'm the pet," the tiger said, the smile evident in his voice. "I live here."

"So, you're Bill's boyfriend?"

"No..."

"Husband?"

"No, I'm the pet," Tenso repeated. "Sir takes care of me, and I live here."

Nonplussed for a moment, Rike gathered his thoughts and formed his question carefully. "All you do is live here, and... what... serve him?"

" I... don't really serve. I just be the pet. You know, do pet things. Sleeping, and eating, and... you know... other stuff." The naïve act was starting to get on the buck's nerves.

"Playtime."

"Yeah, there's that too."

All his chats and reading aside, seeing an actual permanent pet was still disconcerting. Everything that had been so hot to him now seemed unreal up close. "Why'd you decide to do it?"

"Well," the tiger said, moving as close to the buck as he could, "I just like it. You know, no worrying about bills or clothes or food. I just worry about being good and giving Sir what he wants. A lot of the time, that just means me."

"And you're okay with this? You gave up your life for this?"

"I didn't give anything up," Tenso said. "This *is* my life." Rike fell silent after that. Not just because of the tiger's nonchalance, but because he absolutely meant every word. It just sounded so easy coming out of his muzzle. The implications behind that simple blanket statement left the buck with nothing more to say. Rike hadn't gotten all he'd wanted, but it was enough.

Tenso was quiet, and soon Rike could hear him rumbling softly as he slept again, and he wondered how odd it would be to have a leather pup purring contentedly at one's feet. The sound soothed his taxed mind and the next time he opened his eyes the basement was illuminated with the weak glow of the approaching sunrise. Sounds from above told him he'd been woken by Bill's plodding hoofsteps as the donkey wandered about. Most of the time they were centered around the kitchen tile, but occasionally they would move over to the carpeted hallways and what the buck assumed were bedrooms and a bathroom.

Just as the first rays of sunlight came through the basement window, casting bright bars onto the wall across the room, Rike heard the clink of a key rotating the tumblers of a lock and the creak of the door. One step at a time the donkey descended the stairs, the buck counting the first seven before he caught movement. They stopped right in front of the cage and Bill squatted into view. He was nude, and smelled of coffee and bacon.

"Mornin'." Rike knew better than to respond, but he could at least look up most of the way to meeting the donkey's eyes. He still felt uneasy about the whole situation but he remembered last night and couldn't help grinning. "Looks like the pup did a good job getting you all secure, didn't he?" Bill reached over into Tenso's cage and the purring grew louder.

"You ready for me?" Bill stood and walked to a support beam well out of reach and took a key ring from it, kneeling down and inserting a key into Tenso's side of the cage. Beyond that Rike couldn't turn his head enough to see, but he heard other locks being opened, the jangle of chains and shackles, and Tenso's constant purr. And then the tiger was out, crawling around Bill's legs, trying to act canine while his feline tail all but gave him away. As Tenso made his way over to a wrestling mat a few feet away from the cage the donkey turned to the side, giving Rike a clear view of his growing erection. Only then did it dawn on him what they were about to do.

Tenso spread his legs and raised his tail, making for quite the oxymoron with his muscular build in such a position. It was actually the first time Rike had seen anything like that. Bill picked up a small black bottle from a shelf next to the mat, went to his knees behind the tiger and applied a liberal amount to his fingers, then Tenso's hole, then his own shaft. Aiming himself with one hand and holding the tiger's cheeks apart with the other he pressed forward, the flare of his head disappearing into the valley of white fur.

From the cage Rike had a perfect view. The basement was suffused with the gentle glow of morning, throwing everything into a kind of soft focus as the buck watched Bill mount his pup. It was unceremonious without being rote, loving without being sappy or feral. Bill's thick legs flexed with his thrusts, his belly pushing the tiger's tail up over his back. Tenso was quiet at first but as the pace quickened, he had more and more trouble keeping his moans and barks (which he was pretty good at) in check. Rike ventured a hand down to rub himself with no intention of finishing. He felt like that decision was the donkey's now.

Less than ten minutes later Bill grunted and held the tiger to his hips as he came. Rike found himself quite jealous despite being so turned on, mitigated by the fact that he would need serious prepping before being able to take that hefty member. The thought was just as hot as it had been in his role playing with Bill.

Bill pulled himself from Tenso's backside with a groan, a puddle of cum appearing between the tiger's calves. "Good boy," he said, patting one firm buttock, then leaning over to whisper something in Tenso's ear. The tiger nodded and stood, stretching his bulk before taking off the mask, along with the rest of the pup gear.

"Christ Bill, you weren't kidding when you said you were saving up!" he said, spreading his cheeks and wiping up the mess with a towel. "Well, never mind. That's pretty typical for you."

"I got big balls, what can I say?" the donkey replied. "I don't exactly hear you complainin.'"

"Never." Tenso cupped Bill's scrotum and hefted it. "It's better when I can actually feel you shoot," he said, smiling and leaning in to kiss the tip of the donkey's snout. And Bill actually *blushed*. Rike watched the exchange, confused and flabbergasted. What, exactly, was their relationship?

"Uh-oh," said the donkey, looking over at the poor buck, "it looks like the new guy's confused."

"Looks freaked out to me," Tenso added.

Bill placed his hand on Tenso's shoulder. "Why don't you do your routine and get ready while I take him out and feed him? You got a big day today." The tiger nodded before both males left the basement. More steps, all around the upper floor, then they both came down again, Tenso in a jock strap and Bill in a plaid robe that didn't really hide anything. After cleaning up the mess on the wrestling mat the tiger began to do yoga poses, and Rike watched that perfect body while Bill opened his cage, released his hooves and antlers, and attached a leash to his collar to lead him out.

***

It surprised Rike how free he felt after getting used to walking naked on his hands and knees through the house and into the backyard. He could actually use his hooves too, for the most part, once he found out how flexible his legs were in a quadrupedal position. Squatting in a corner of the backyard, however, was more difficult with Bill watching. Eventually the donkey had to turn his back while Rike did his business, fighting his sense of shame by telling himself this was what he was supposed to do.

When they returned to the basement Tenso was on his back on a bench press, lifting what looked to be an impossible amount of weight. As the buck passed he watched the tiger's arms flex and curl with the strain, and the bulges they made, as well as the bulge of sheath under the fabric of the jock. He could hardly believe their pre-dawn conversation, watching the feline as he was now.

While they were outside Tenso had brought down bowls of kibble and water for Rike. The tiger finished his set and went upstairs to shower, and it was only then that the buck felt comfortable with taking a couple bites of the dry, artificial-tasting pellets. He managed to choke down a few mouthfuls with the water but Bill chuckled and said he could stop if he didn't like it. Still, Rike felt ashamed for not finishing his meal.

"How do I look?" Tenso's tenor echoed down the staircase. The tiger stepped onto the basement floor, transformed from the cat he'd seen yesterday. A smart charcoal suit with a navy shirt and black tie covered his substantial frame. Rike finally got a good look at his face, which wasn't as young as it was young-looking. His green eyes sparkled as he smiled at them both, his tail curling lazily behind him.

"Smart as always," Bill said, reaching over to adjust the Windsor knot at the tiger's neck. He turned to the buck. "Can you believe they're making him show up for jury duty on a Saturday?"

"It's a murder case, and it's my civic duty. Not my fault if they closed arguments at the end of the workweek and had to send us to deliberations the next day. Mind if I take the Prius this time? I found out I get free parking with the hybrid sticker thing." Tenso rolled his eyes, jangling the keys in his pocket.

"Sounds like you picked 'em up off the table anyway," the donkey chuckled, "so I don't really have a choice, do I?"

Smiling, the tiger replied, "I knew you would say yes." Bill gave him a lighthearted punch in the shoulder as the feline turned to leave. "I'll text you when I'm on my way back. I'm gonna be horny, just so you know."

"I'll see what I can do!" the donkey chuckled after him, winking at Rike. The basement door closed and the two were left in silence. Bill looked down at the buck, naked and leashed beside the still-full food bowl. He sighed.

"You wanna talk to me, don't you?" Rike nodded, though he found himself more interested in the floor than Bill's face. "Alright then. *Giraffe*, for now." The word struck deep down, stronger than Rike thought it would. Even though he knew it wasn't the end of the trip, that feeling of failure came back on him like a rush of blood in his ears, bringing heat to his face and tears to his eyes.

"I didn't... expect a lot of this. Especially him."

"Are you jealous?" It sure sounded like jealousy, as much as Rike didn't want to admit it. But he hadn't been prepared for Tenso, and what Tenso was to Bill. He still didn't actually know the specifics of that yet.

"Kind of. He lives here?"

"He does. He's lived here for about six months," Bill said as he sat down beside the buck, the end of the leash still in his hand.

"Is he your partner or something?"

Bill smiled and looked off into the distance. "Far from it. Partners are equals. Tenso is my pet. Subordinate, obedient, dependent. He's a dedicated lifestyler. Took me a while after I met him online to take him seriously when he told me he always wanted to be a permanent pet. But I've lost count of how many times he's proved it to me. You see how he is."

"But you let him out?"

"You can't shirk jury duty. It's a civic requirement. Anything like that—voting, Christmas, renewing a driver license—he gets to go out for. Some things you can't avoid. Everything else, it's handled. He wanted someone to take care of him, and in return, he's here for me as a pet. It can seem kind of extreme but we're used to it." Bill reached out to scratch between Rike's ears. "You think you're in over your head?"

Rike didn't want to answer right away. He didn't want to admit it, and he didn't think he *was*, exactly. He just didn't think he could be as dedicated as Tenso... not nearly. The buck just couldn't square the idea of giving his life and independence over to anyone else, not even a guy as good as Bill. Not because he wasn't strong enough, but because... because he couldn't give Bill what Tenso already did.

"I don't want to disappoint you."

"Oh please." Bill waved it off. "Andrew disappointed me. You slept through the night. I halfway expected you to run right back out the door, naked and all, after I decked you!" The donkey's deep belly-laugh shook the robe loose before he caught the buck's deep blush. He narrowed his eyes. "You tellin' me you liked it?"

Rike hadn't allowed himself to think about it, but Bill's question brought the image into the forefront of his mind once again. Up against the coffee table, his back throbbing, his face stinging from the impact... and the tightness in his pants that hadn't been apparent until Tenso had scissor-stripped him. The buck finally looked up into the donkey's eyes, which held a shining determination that demanded an answer of him.

Bill's hand was faster than his patience was long, and in a split second the fingers that had been rubbing him between the ears were balled up and sailing through the air toward the side of Rike's muzzle. The connection was solid but not damaging, sending the buck onto his side against the cage, rattling it. No way could the buck hide his excitement, and right now he didn't want to.

"Looks like you liked it." There was no hiding that boner. "Lucky for you I take a bit to recharge. Now that I know, I can have more fun with ya." Bill tucked himself back into his robe, thought for a moment, then asked, "Can I pose another deep question to you?"

Rubbing his nose and not-so-secretly enjoying the pain, Rike said, "Sure."

"What're you here for? I mean, why're you visiting me? Really, I'd like to know."

"I... thought you wanted me to see the lifestyle for myself." By now, "lifestyle" had mostly lost its meaning.

"Yeah, that's what *I* wanted. But what did *you* want to accomplish by coming here?"

"I thought I wanted to be a pet. But... I didn't know how far it went."

Bill sat cross-legged on the floor, turning the buck's face to his. "You've gone a lot farther than most people," he said. "It takes a lot of self-knowledge to do what you've done without breaking down. I'm pretty proud of you."

"Yeah, but... I'm not like Tenso."

"You say it like it's a bad thing," the donkey said, planting a rubbery kiss on Rike's black snout. "Tenso is one kind of pet. You don't have to live in my basement, you know... I could keep you if you feel it's where you want to be. You can be my second pup for as long as you're here. You might even learn to like the food, heh."

Rike looked toward the bowl, recalling the texture in his mouth. "I can try," he said. "Do I get leather gear like Tenso?"

"Tenso's the only one allowed to wear his leather," replied the donkey. "But... " Bill stood and walked to the far corner of the basement, digging around in an old dilapidated chest of drawers. Consternation clouded his features while he searched drawer after drawer until he shouted, "Aha!" Turning around, the donkey sauntered back to the buck, whose eyes widened when he saw what Bill held. "I haven't done this in a while, but I may have the next best thing."

"Is... is that an airbrush gun?" Rike asked. Bill just grinned.

"*Giraffe.*"

***

Bill wouldn't tell the buck what he had in mind, and Rike couldn't have asked if he'd wanted to. When the donkey snapped a pair of sunning goggles onto the bridge of Rike's muzzle, he began to get the idea.

On all fours with the goggles blocking most of his vision, Rike could only stay as still as possible while Bill gave him orders to lift this arm or that leg. After a while the buck lost track of the time and began to concentrate on keeping himself still, a difficult task because of his position and his anticipation. Whistling as he made his way around Rike's nude body, Bill grinned the grin of an artist satisfied with his work.

A ventilation fan dried the paint quickly, mingling the scents of acrylic and horny buck. Bill sniffed and growled at intervals while fine-tuning his details, and the fact that he was getting worked up further heightened Rike's arousal. The goggles came off only long enough to paint the buck's eyelids, so he never got a chance to even glance down the length of his own muzzle.

"Alright, I think I've done all I can do here," Bill said. He brought the fan closer and turned so that the buck got the full force of the air stream. "That should only take a few minutes to dry. In the meantime, we have a few more things to do." As the fan did its job Rike heard the donkey storing his equipment, then rummaging through the chest again. "Dammit, hold on," he said, and clomped upstairs.

Rike enjoyed the few minutes of solitude before the donkey came back down, feeling the air in his fur, flowing over its surface, fluttering his ears gently without making him overly cold. He felt like himself, like he was in his element, no longer torn between worlds. Like he fit in. In any case, he was having fun.

Bill came back into the basement, braying triumphantly. "I *knew* I had these around somewhere! Christ, I should have looked for these before I started. I lucked out." The donkey secured something around each of his hooves, then asked him to raise a hand so he could slide a mitt over it. Inside was a small round grip that forced his fingers to curl. Once they were on, he would have to crawl on his fists. Finally, something soft was shoved against his tail and clamped around his waist.

"I think we're done here," said Bill. "You wanna have a look, pup?"

"Rawrf!" Rike replied without even thinking. It just... seemed like the right thing to do. Bill led him over to the corner with the chest of drawers, next to which sat a tall wardrobe.

"Ready?" Rike nodded, and Bill opened the doors. Inside, a husky stared back at him from a full-length mirror. A husky with antlers.

"Whoa..." murmured the buck, before remembering his place and cringing, waiting for the blow to come. But the donkey let it slide this time, and Rike got a good look at what he'd become.

With the exception of his antlers and the anatomy of his lower legs, the buck could pass for a blue-and-white husky in his summer coat. The dark patches on his muzzle had been turned a greyish-blue and white. The pattern ran down his torso, more or less mirroring the transition of his normally brown-and-beige fur. The dapples on his rump were nothing but a plain blue field, as was his tail, which blended almost perfectly with the strap-on tail Bill had latched around him. His hands and hooves were encased in matching paw-mitts, completing the ensemble. He was, for all intents and purposes, a dog.

Bill appeared behind him, looking deservedly proud of the job he'd done. He patted Rike on the head and asked, "You like your new look?" Before he could really think about it the buck started panting, his tongue lolling to the side, grinning a shit-eating grin and actually wagging for the first time in his life. The husky tail moved with his rear, fanning from side to side. The donkey smacked one of those cheeks, making Rike yip and moan all at once, and it looked fantastic in the mirror.

A door slammed upstairs. "He's home," singsonged Bill. "That went quicker than I thought."

Claw-clicks approached, stopping at the basement door. "You guys still down there?"

"It's like we never left!" replied the donkey. "Come see what I've been making all afternoon." The door opened and the tiger came down. "Was the guy guilty?"

"Hell yes, he was. I don't think there was any way we could... holy *hell*, you've been busy." Tenso stopped two steps from the floor when he saw Rike, eying him appreciatively. "You haven't done any painting in a while. You haven't lost your touch, either. That's... that's hot, Bill."

"You think so?" asked the donkey, pressing down on the buck's lower back. "Sit." He complied, sitting on his haunches and exposing his half-hard sheath to the tiger.

"You taught him commands too?" By this time, Tenso had a paw between his legs, massaging.

"No, he's pretty good about figuring them out himself. I would ask him to roll over and beg but I don't want to ruin the paint job I just did."

"I think that's an eventuality, not a possibility," said Tenso. "If it doesn't rub off on the floor it's gonna get messed up by something else." The tiger winked lewdly, the bulge beneath his paw growing.

"Jury duty really gets you worked up, doesn't it?" Bill asked, pacing over to the stairs and leaning in close to whisper in the tiger's ear. Tenso nodded and visibly deflated into his former weaker, simpler self. "Now go get ready so you can join me and we can break this pup in."

Rike whimpered. They were talking about *him*. He suddenly realized how horny he was; now that he had an outlet, the need was fierce and building quickly. Rike the buck was gone for the time being and in his place stood Rike the submissive pet husky, obedient and willing. It was a part he vowed to play well.

"I think it's time I made good use of you," said Bill, leaning to grab a sawhorse near the bureau and dragging it over to the wrestling mat. "Get over here and bend yourself over this thing." Rike moved, but slowly because his balance was thrown off by the odd surfaces of the paw-mitts. Halfway to the sawhorse the buck slipped and sprawled out on the floor. Before he could get up the donkey belted him one, sending him back down. The pain was a flash in his mind, brilliant and sharp, and it felt damn good. He tried to hide his pleasure behind a wince the same way Bill hid his behind authority, but each was enjoying himself immensely.

Smiling away from Bill, Rike crawled over to the sawhorse, which had been modified to half its original height... the perfect height for suspending a willing bottom. "Giyyup!" Bill ordered, pointing, and the buck lay face-down, his chest along the length of the wooden rail. Clinking from behind him told of Tenso's return to puphood, and to the basement. "Oh good, you're just in time. Down! Good boy, now grab some spreader bars and help me." Rike wished he could see the look on Tenso's face at the command, but he imagined the flush behind the black leather and the tiger's secret enjoyment. The donkey continued, chuckling: "And take that lock off; I need your cock tonight."

Rike's backside clenched in response. Bill's tone was urgent but not forceful. He was a man who knew what he was doing and how to get what he wanted. And he had two perfectly capable pets to assist him, at least for tonight. When the donkey doffed his robe, revealing his half-hard shaft, the buck began to whimper and wag his two-tailed rear. Whatever was in store, he'd enjoy it.

A set of paws spread Rike's feet apart so his hips dropped off the edge of the sawhorse a bit, exposing his hole. Cool metal snapped around each ankle, and then the tiger came around to the buck's front, doing the same to his wrists. Rike wasn't secured to anything but he didn't have to be. He wasn't going anywhere, and if he tried he wouldn't go far. In a bold move, Tenso grasped the buck's white rack and pulled him forward to meet the tip of his leaking sheath, which Rike did not hesitate to lick. He glanced around the tiger's hip; they both watched for Bill to turn around.

Rike got off only a few licks of the barbed head before Tenso pulled away, smacking him across the face for the donkey's benefit. Spittle, and probably a little precum, flew off of his lips and onto the mat, followed by a groan that was more of a moan anyway.

"He ready?" Bill asked, kneeling down to inspect the tiger's handiwork, giving Rike a close-up view of his thick buttocks and the thin tail sweeping from side to side between them. It wasn't the donkey's heft that attracted the buck, but his unwavering and effortless domination had kept him coming back online for more. Seeing it acted out in person, unrestrained, was ten times as hot. Bill patted Rike's side and got to his knees. The sawhorse matched his inseam perfectly.

Nine inches of donkey dick dangled right in front of Rike's flared nostrils. A nod. "I think y'are, pup." The buck shivered and stuck out his tongue.

It wasn't sweet nectar, but it *was* the distilled musk of the combination of scents that made up Bill. Heady and earthy, clean but not sterile, it was just a very manly combination. Rike's tongue made quick work of the pre that drooled from the donkey's uniquely flared tip, and his lips drew in the head after that. He earned a grunt of appreciation and fingers around his antlers, always a good sign that someone enjoyed his efforts.

From behind him Rike could hear rustling and the creak of leather. He clenched again, just from the thought, and hoped Tenso could be gentle. It had been—forever, really—since he'd bottomed, and that distinct kind of pain wasn't something he could turn into pleasure. At least not right away. A paw reached below his tails and spread him while another applied a generous amount of lube, a claw penetrating slightly to ease the coming entry.

Bill gripped Rike's rack harder and began a slow thrusting. The girth of the donkey's member stretched out his cheeks but it wasn't long enough to trigger his gag reflex, so the buck had ample opportunity to use his tongue and throat to coax out more fluid.

"Damn... that is *nice*," said Bill, suppressing a more feral sound. All Rike could see was the donkey's navel, but if he squinted he could see out to the edges of those meaty thighs, or he could close his eyes entirely to concentrate on the feel of those balls, black and smooth, bouncing against his chin. Behind him he felt Tenso's knees between his own, and the heat of another shaft begging for entrance to his body. He was in no position to deny it, nor did he want to.

Tenso's head popped through with little effort due to its tapered shape, but after that a pleasant thickness stretched Rike a bit more than he'd been expecting. But the tiger was gentle and let the buck acclimate before moving more. Soon Rike was wiggling around, trying to wag but failing, so he just braced himself and bore down until he felt the tiger's belly on his lower back. Tenso moaned as he bottomed out, his claws grasping at the buck's rump to hold him close.

Bill turned out to be a bit too thick at the base for Rike's narrow jaw, so he settled for steering him with one hand while the other went to the base of his cock to stroke what remained outside of the buck's lips. "It's... too bad you... don't want to be more of a pet," the donkey managed between thrusts. "You... would make a great friend for Tenso. You're a... good dog, a very good dog. I'll take... what I can get for the moment." If this was consolation, it was one hell of a consolation.

The sun was beginning to set and the south-facing windows let in the glow to cast a warmth throughout the otherwise dingy basement. Bill's browns mellowed to umbers, Rike's new colors turned an odd shade of yellow-grey, and Tenso glowed even more orange. There wasn't much noise, save for the soft *shh-shh* of fur on fur and a grunt or vulgar word from Bill every so often. Tenso did his best not to say anything out of turn, lest he be punished by not being allowed to finish what he'd started.

Once the tiger's paw reached below Rike's belly and grasped his arousal, the pace seemed to quicken by leaps and bounds. He'd been so wrapped up in servicing the other two that he'd almost forgotten his own needs. The moan that escaped his throat added a gentle vibration to his fellatio that Bill appreciated. A fresh volley of pre coated the buck's tongue.

Tenso's pads were slick and soft, caressing his flesh just the right amount to pull him to the brink and keep him there. Soon he was thrashing as much as the bars would allow, trying to get as much cock into either end of him as possible. Even Tenso's teasing eventually proved to be too much and with only a whimper, Rike sprayed across the mat for several feet, the rest of it dripping into a puddle beneath him. He kept his muzzle open, but mostly he was just hanging in there for the ride.

Without the constant tension of needing to climax Rike could focus on other things, like opening for maximum penetration on Bill's end and clenching against the tiger's withdrawals so he could hear the desperation in Tenso's purrs. The feline's thrusts became erratic, and soon he was fighting back a mewling moan as he unloaded himself into the buck's rear, holding his shaky position while the donkey worked himself to the end.

"You want it, boy?"

Rike nodded.

"You want my nut?"

Rike nodded emphatically, barking around his mouthful of cock and wagging the tiger with his motions. He looked up into Bill's face, trying his best to make puppy-dog eyes. Bill watched him, his face screwed up in concentration, the whole of his body tensed up. It was easy to tell when the donkey realized he couldn't stop himself: he relaxed, pulled out of Rike's muzzle and set his tip on the buck's snout for the best aim. A few seconds later, he cursed and grimaced while his seed made small parabolas in the air before coming back down all over Rike's head. He was soaked, but he didn't mind one bit.

After that, silence. Tenso eventually went soft and plopped out of the buck's backside, staggering back on his knees before giving up and crawling on all fours into his cage where he proceeded to clean himself. Bill recovered enough to release the spreader bars and, after hearing the buck's stomach rumble something fierce, led him over to the food and water the buck had passed by earlier. Nothing could have tasted better at that moment. Rike scarfed it up like a starving stray, taking the moment to relish the feel of seed in his hole and on his face.

But the most satisfaction came when he caught his reflection in the bureau's mirror: his paint smeared, the claw marks on his legs, and—most of all—his cum-soaked muzzle, the mark of his position.

"You're pretty good at that," Bill said, leaning down to wipe some of the fluid away. "I'm usually a one-shot-per-session guy, but I might be workin' up to a second." The donkey licked a runnel from above the buck's left brow before it could get into his vision.

Rike looked back at himself, a cum-covered husky with antlers and a lolling tongue. Right now he was everywhere he wanted to be.

***

"You had enough?" the donkey asked, grinning that sinister big-toothed grin of his. "Speak, boy."

"No way," Rike replied. "I don't think I could ever get enough."

"Now boy, I thought I taught you about thinkin' before you speak. You see, there's this deer who thought he was all ready to be a pet, but... "

Rike sat back against the headboard and rolled his eyes dramatically enough for Bill to see them clearly in the webcam. Bill still liked to give the buck a rough time even though they'd hashed out their feelings before Rike had left his house.

"*Giraffe*, already. You ruined it."

"Me? I'm not the one with a crotch covered in spooge here. At least you got off already!" The donkey was laughing so hard he nearly toppled over in his chair, and Rike couldn't *not* smile at seeing his friend (and sometimes master) so pleased with himself.

Rike hadn't played the pet since the visit to Bill's house, and he found that the break had done him a world of good. He'd been too close to the problem to realistically consider his options, so when Bill had thrown *Giraffe* out prematurely on Sunday morning at breakfast he'd had a good reason.

Saturday evening had been a blast for all three males. Spit-roasting Rike had only been the start of a long evening of play, and as time went on Rike had felt himself slipping deeper into his canine role. Eventually it had become second-nature, and he nearly forgot his true species. When he later described it to Bill the donkey had said that was exactly how it was supposed to feel when one was lost in the role play But deep down, the buck knew he was no Tenso. After a surprise morning session where he was allowed to mount the tiger (and lasted about five minutes, he was so excited) Bill had used *Giraffe* on Rike and whatever word he reserved for the feline, which was apparently a very secretive and personal thing.

Over breakfast they had discussed Rike's concerns, with Tenso jumping in here and there whenever he could help. The buck admitted he wasn't ready and he might never be. And when Bill brushed it off and said he already knew, it was a huge weight off of Rike's shoulders.

"The problem is, you let your expectations and ego get the better of you," the donkey had said. "You can't force it no matter how much you want it. I happen to think you make a damn good husky pup, and if you can only come over for a weekend here and there I think that's where you belong." And that word *belong* mattered the most to Rike. He'd had time to think on the drive home, and between then and tonight's role play he'd decided he had nothing more to add. It was exactly what Bill said it was.

Rike smirked at the donkey in the video window. "Well, you already said the word, so I can't do anything to help you!" the buck said to his webcam as the donkey's laughter settled down.

"Nah, you're okay, I had the tiger's muzz between my legs before I logged on, so I'm good." Just the mental picture was enough to stir Rike's sheath all over again.

"I just wish I could keep up with you guys."

"Now, what does that mean?" Bill asked. "Don't you tell me you're having doubts again. Don't make me beat it into that hard rack cuz I'm getting' tired of it." So tired, and yet he smiled.

"I gave up on that days ago," replied the buck. "You give me a hard time about not making the cut, I give you a hard time about my feelings of inadequacy."

Bill moved closer to the cam. "Well, you can take that to a couch in some doc's office, unless you wanna pay me a bunch of money to draw in a notebook and nod my head." They both laughed at that and the tension broke. "Seriously though, when do you want to come over next? Tenso's been kinda lonely."

Rike's tail started to wag against the sheets, at least as much as it could. "I'll have to check my schedule, but I'd love to. Do I get to be a husky again?" It was refreshing to not have to take things as seriously as he had been. He could finally just *talk* about it.

"Actually, I've been at my sewing machine making some new things I think you'll like. Got some new paint too. I think you'd make a good Doberman." Rike's jaw dropped, and it wasn't the only thing. Bill laughed. "I guess that's as good an answer as any!"

"Yeah, my schedule can wait... that sounds pretty damn important," the buck said, pulling his erection from his belly to show the donkey, who nodded, licking his lips.

"You keep that thing nice and hard, and I'll make it worth your while. Until then, I have some sleep to get. You do too."

"Yes, *Dad*."

"I can do that fantasy too, if you want." Rike waved it away with both hands, shaking his head frenetically. "No, no, one at a time! One at a time!"

"At least it's an idea," replied the donkey. "You take care."

"Night." Bill's cam went dark and it occurred to the buck that he hadn't used "Sir" all night long, nor had the donkey mentioned it. Perhaps the rules weren't hard and fast. Rike thought that whatever worked would be fine between them. They both agreed that fun was the first priority in anything they did. And there was nothing wrong with that.

Rike leaned over to grab a washcloth from the nightstand and wiped himself off. He envisioned himself with black and tan markings, his tail bobbed and rounded off, his hands and hooves bound into paws again. He had to stop or he'd never get anything done, so he sat up straight and stretched out beneath the covers. Bill had an early bedtime, but the buck still had work to do.

As he got down to business, Rike reached over to the nightstand and grabbed a handful of kibble from the bowl he kept there. He smiled to himself as he flicked a few pieces into his mouth, the texture still foreign but palatable. These were chicken-and-rice flavored, much better than Bill's brand and oddly enough, they went great with orange juice.

He might grow to like them yet.

Attachments
by H. A. Kirsch

"I have a surprise for you. Still coming over @ 6."

The message's sender was a Doberman-like dog whose head sidelined the text bubble, with the name "Dary" underneath it. Leo tickled inside as he looked at the suave, rakish dog, even as a tiny headshot on his cell phone.

The red fox had an hour and a half to prepare himself and his condo for his third date with the dark, towering dog. The first two had been to a restaurant and a dessert bar, both with extended heavy-petting goodbyes at the Beauceron's apartment. Maybe the surprise would be something more fitting of the stunning leather-clad photos on Darryl Springer's KinkFest web profile.

Leo put on an old set of yellow and white biking gear while he worked, a running black mustang emblazoned in a full gallop across his slender pecs. Half an hour after the message, and just as he was about to start the kitchen floor, someone rang the doorbell.

He muttered under his breath, then padded over and answered it without even looking. He opened it to a tall sharp-eared canine in a charcoal frock coat, black leather dress gloves, dark slacks, and what looked like retro black dress shoes. "Aahh, Dary? You're really early." Dary had a black leather duffel bag with him, large and almost stately.

The dog smiled. "Surprise. No, this is the surprise." He hefted the bag. "Could you put it over onto the sofa?"

Leo took the heavy, boutique-fancy bag and groaned as it almost toppled him forward. Surprise? Leo had a surprise, too. He scooped the bag in both arms and carried it over to the sofa, then set it down on the middle cushion. "I really wasn't expecting you yet, so I was, uh, cleaning. Sorry for the attire." My surprise is right on the front of me, Dary. It's right there, Leo thought to himself.

Attachments

Dary gave Leo a dog smile as he stepped across the room. "Why would I complain about a fox in spandex? You look great."

"I look like I should be in the Tour de France," Leo said, dodging Dary and grabbing the mop, running it over to the utility closet. When he turned around, Dary was right there. The fox yipped and backed up into the closet door. "Hey, don't sneak."

"This isn't the surprise, either," Dary said, muzzle tipped down, growl in his voice but a grin on his muzzle. He swung his coat off and handed it to Leo, who took it like a rack takes a towel. When Dary had his hands free, he unbuttoned his shirt stripper-style, pulling the cowboy shirt snaps apart and exposing a black leather polo shirt with a lace collar.

Leo clutched the dog's coat in front of his own groin. He smiled. "What're you going to do now, take off your pants?"

"No, you are," Dary said, stepping forward to nudge his sharp muzzle against Leo's ear, directing the soft directive right into Leo's blushing flesh.

The fox gulped and reached for Dary's fly. Not only was the dog hard, but he wasn't wearing a belt. He gave a testing pull and, just like the shirt, it popped apart with almost no effort. Underneath, yet more leather. Leo's hands shook as he felt around, black fingertips gliding over the body-fit black hide. Riding breeches, unflared, reinforced seat, double-zip sailor front. Leo's hands tingled and he momentarily lost control, towel sliding off his tilted forearm and puddling down at the floor. He grappled with the rest of the dog's pant leg and it opened up just the same way down a hidden seam, revealing a pair of knee-high riding boots with a laced instep. "I really wish I had clothing like this," he said, talking down to Dary's boots.

Dary reached forward and tickled at one of the screen-printed galloping hooves of Leo's shirt horse. "Put all your pocket change in the piggy bank." That hoof happened to be right over Leo's left nipple, and the fox reached up to push Dary's hand out of the way. The dog snatched it away, then patted the fox's hand down against his chest. The two met eyes for a few long seconds, and then Dary grasped Leo by the wrists, spreading them apart and leaning forward. Leo froze and slumped back against the cabinet, instantly panicked by the firm grasp. Dary nosed into his ear again. "Tell me you want your surprise."

"Please," Leo whimpered, ears swinging back. He almost said, Please Stop, but his erection made him reconsider. "I want... my surprise?"

Dary let go and stepped back, then pointed his gloved hand over to the sofa, still staring at Leo. He furrowed his brow but kept the grin. "Sit."

Leo quickly padded over, heart pounding in his chest. Not only was Dary wearing extremely hot leather gear - the boots and gloves alone would have stirred him until he toughened up - but the dog was playing a little tough. If only Dary knew what would happen if he played too tough with the fox, though... Leo lost himself as he thought of what he would eventually have to tell his dark canine lover, and sat down on the duffel bag by accident. It was lumpy and clunked inside, and Dary didn't look very concerned. "I'm not a dog," he said, watching as Dary strode over. With his regular clothes on, Dary had looked a bit yuppie-ish. With the leathers on, he moved with a calculated shoulders-back strut.

"Mmm-hmm. You're a fox. Open the bag."

Leo rubbed at his upper arms, nerves wound up enough to give him butterflies and the dull ache that replaced the prickling 'cold feet' most would get. He used the spandex cuffs as an excuse to fiddle. Dary stared at him, then at the bag, arms curled in front of his tight chest, gloved fingertips drumming at one arm. Leo gave in and unzipped the bag.

Inside: more leather, more black. Cuffs. Cuffs and straps and some other unidentifiable things. Rope. A gag or three. Metal clips. Gauntlet binders. Enough gear to tie up everyone Leo knew personally, all at once. No wonder it was heavy.

The fox bit his lip, inhaled, and rocked back. "I... I..." His erection drained to nothing, cold water ran down his spine. It was exactly what he thought it would be, feared it would be.

Dary frowned. "I'm sorry, I thought..."

Leo swallowed hard, then milked his upper arms again, blood vessels confused with what to do. "I.. I don't know if I can do that kind of thing, Dary."

Dary sighed and sat down, then reached forward and put a hand on Leo's thigh, leather toying only with the fur forward of the shorts cuff. Leo's tail hugged against his leg on that side, and the dog gave it a gentle brush out. "I thought you'd like it. I thought it came with the territory, the leather and..."

Leo put his hand on top of the dog's glove leather and felt his cock swell again. "No, I don't mean... that I don't want it. I mean, I don't know if I can. I don't know if it's safe."

Dary put on his best warming smile, but it just exposed teeth. "Of course it's safe. I'd never do anything stupid... or hurtful, not to you." The dog tipped his muzzle down and to the side when Leo still didn't seem to accept Dary's interpretation.

Only two dates, and words like that? Leo let out a soft whine and smiled, rolled his eyes. "Come on, Dary, I'm not... I mean, I physically don't know if it's safe to tie me up."

The Beauceron cocked his head to the side and let out a chesty rrrh, then blinked. "I have a lot of practice, Leo. It's mostly leather gear, too, and that's easy to adjust. Not like rope. I-"

"No no no, I can't..." Leo huffed and palmed at his muzzle, fox-purred into it, and then stood up. "Dary, two can play at this game." Leo practically jumped up from the sofa, turned one way, then the other, black hands held up in front of his ribs. Embarrassed but determined, the vulpine marched through the kitchen into the back hallway, into the master bedroom. Dary brought up the rear with the hollow clop of fine leather boot heel.

Leo rooted in his closet, hunkered down, tail waving as he cleared some fallen shirts off of his version of Dary's toy bag. It was more of a flight case, aluminum edge wrapping and rubberized black skid panels. "I didn't mean I was afraid you would hurt me, like you would go too far. I'm afraid you'll accidentally break me." All of Leo's attention focused on his tool case. His life-tool case. "Dary, I'm reconstructed. I told you that, right?"

Dary squinted in thought. "Rec." His eyes popped open and he leaned back, hand reaching out to grasp onto the back of Leo's writing desk chair with a squeak of leather on leather. "What? No, you didn't."

Leo shut the case and turned around, something in one of his hands. "Well, I am. It's a long story. It's not very sexy. But, now that I know you want to tie me up, you get to know more about me. You like gloves, take your right one off and put this on." He handed the dog something that looked like a skintight spandex gauntlet, with flexible glossy parts down the underside of the thumb and index finger.

The garment had Dary's interest in a second. He skinned off his glove and took the new one, sniffed it, looked inside, snuffled again. "It's certainly... interesting." He pulled it on, flexed his fingers out into the very tips, twisted his hand around. "Hmm, nothing's happening. I was expecting it to do something to me? Like maybe a superpower?"

Leo stuck his left arm out, palm down. "Grab my arm, kind of run your thumb up from the wrist, along the underside, along the.. vein, or tendon, or whatever. You'll feel kind of a soft spot all of a sudden, press in a bit. Then, grip and turn, and then pull."

Dary cocked his head again, but squinted and twisted. The look said that Leo was crazy. "Uh, sure," Dary said, flexing his fingers in the new, black glove. He did what Leo asked, snatching at the fox's wrist the way he'd done before. "This is kind of turning me on. So, sorry if you weren't wanting that."

The fox half-grinned, knowing what was about to happen in front of the clueless dog. Half grin, half grimace. Surprise, indeed. "I figured it would, but just you wait. It's nothing like what you brought... ohv... ah, hnf."

Dary's thumb pressed in at the aforementioned spot, prompting the fox's wincing grunt. Leo's hand, which had been slightly twitching and feeling at the dog's furry forearm, simply held fingers out straight. Dary looked down at it, squinted, held his other hand out flat. Leo recognized it as a twitch of a puppy-slap reflex, the ground smack that playing canines used.

The Beauceron twisted and pulled until something clicked inside the fox's arm and the entire forearm came off in his newly-gloved hand. "Holy shit!" He dropped the synthetic limb and Leo caught it with a swipe of his hand. Leo's stump had a vaguely electronic look, metal with a seal around the very rim, pins and contacts and tubes and clear things that looked like fiber cable. About three quarters of an inch around was something squishy, and then fur on the outside that matched the orange-red of his elbow and upper arm. The now-frozen arm had the matching 'plug' to Leo's socket.

Dary looked ready to faint, ears trembling, tail swung under his legs enough that it actually curved out by his leathered knees. His breeding still came through, body looking more like he'd just taken a beating instead of shrinking back in horror, chest compacted, shoulders lifted, neck corded and taut under the black shiny fur.

"Surprise," Leo said, forcing half of a smile. "That's a key glove. You need it to take these things off," Leo picked up his arm and used it as a prop, black-furred forearm and hand looking like nothing more than inert demonstration parts. "So, uh, they don't come off accidentally. The only other way is the strain relief, which is further back in the joint. It's... it's built into my upper arm bone, and it's stronger than I am, so if you.. if you work it too hard, or at the wrong angle, it can crack the bone real easy and that's a huge, huge problem to fix." He stopped forcing the smile and just grimaced, then shrugged.

Dary sat down on the bed with a rough thump, slapped his hands at his thigh, one leathered, one still in the key glove. "It... cracks...what?" The dog gave Leo's separated body parts a thousand-yard stare.

Leo sighed and held his synthetic forearm up. "The cybernetic parts are stronger than the rest of me, so if I put too much strain on it, it'll crack right here." He tapped his elbow with his own fingers, using the stiff digits to point. "I don't usually tell people about it because it freaks them out. But... you can't tie me up, because it might strain it just the wrong way." The explanation did nothing to mollify Dary's horror. Leo inhaled and sighed. "It won't kill me. It's mostly inconvenient, and expensive to fix."

Dary's look of horror drained away into rapt fascination, muscles tight at the chest as he leaned down and pushed his head forward, watching Leo wave his detached arm like it was part of a mannequin. "Such a fragile little fox," he finally said, eyes looking up from the mechanical connection that moved when Leo presumably flexed his now-disconnected forearm.

"Hey! If you break the joint, I have to go in and get it all refitted. I have spares, but it's a big pain in the ass and refitting hurts. They have to reprogram the nerve interface, which is like... Is this really interesting to you? I mean, you came over here to... to..." Leo stopped as he realized that Dary had come over to tie him up, with the promise of a date as bait. He hunkered forward and huffed lightly.

Dary rubbed at his face with his leatherclad left hand, leaving the one in Leo's key glove to rest limp on his thigh. "When you said you had your own surprise, this isn't really what I was expecting." He squeezed out a chuckle, almost a wheezing bark at the start. "It's not really a turn-off. It's just unexpected. I guess you have to tell me at some point, huh? I'm sorry if I offended you. I really like bondage. I really like bondage. Even the littlest bit, like if you're taking your shirt off and it gets tangled around your arms. I don't need it, though. Mmm?"

Leo smiled back. "In hindsight, maybe if I was... wasn't me, I'd have taken my arm off and pulled a prank with it, or maybe I'd have just put it on my profile, but it didn't seem important in that way, you know?" As Leo talked, Dary looked anxious and excited, ears up straight but eyes flicking around, body moving, constantly. So doggish, Leo thought, for someone who had minutes before played Master and ordered the fox around.

The dog settled his brown eyes on Leo's groin, then perked his ears up, forming a thought quickly enough that he sniffed. "Wouldn't it be crazy if your..."

"Oh yeah, it's crazy," Leo said, wagging his tail as he pulled his shorts down, unable to resist pushing the situation into joyful macabre. Out flopped one uncut mostly humanoid dick and a pair of cream-furred balls. "It's... it works great. You'd never know unless you tasted it, or sniffed I guess, or looked real close." Leo tucked his muzzle down. "The last time, when I was grinding on you and we were making out, I came all over the inside of my jock. It felt great. I just pretended I was turned on by that specifi-"

"You're kidding. That's not real?" Dary took a huge breath, then let it out, tilted his head to the side like a listening dog.

"Uh-huh. Scout's honor. My head's real, most of my internal organs except my kidneys, most of my fur and skin... that's all prime fox meat, lips to ass. Everything else... It was an accident. I was in a fire." Leo braced for the inevitable flashback, only to let out a held breath in a sigh when he only got a twinge. The actual accident was just a flash, a jumble of things happening. The trauma was delayed and extended afterwards.

Dary gave Leo a good, firm squeeze around the shoulders. "I'm sorry. You really made lemonade out of it, though, huh? I never would have guessed. Especially not this." The dog traced his black fingers over Leo's cock, thumb tip sliding around the fox's cock tip as it peeked out from under his foreskin. Within seconds, a lot more than just the tip was showing, fox flesh swelling hard into a pleasant-sized erection. Only it wasn't fox flesh at all.

Leo groaned and leaned his head on Dary's shoulder, tucked his muzzle down against his chest, and arched his back to press into the warm, leathery grip. "I have an idea. It's a really, really... it's really really really really extra filthy, but maybe you'll like it if you like leather and bondage and c... control."

"Is it where I take all your limbs off?" Dary spoke very gently, but kept his body at canine attention even while he leaned in close.

Leo sputtered. "What? I'm not into being an amputee, not really. I met this guy once, he told me he wanted to see me without all of my limbs. He got my legs and one arm off and... I freaked out, I kind of attacked him. He was going to leave me helpless, for the rest of the day, but he wasn't expecting me to beat him up with one arm." He brushed his head fur back, then massaged an ear. "But, I... well, you, will have to take them off. I just can't do it all myself. You have to promise not to do anything stupid like that."

The Beauceron's face lit up. "Trust me." Dary leaned in and puppy-nuzzled Leo.

"Don't do that, you look like a puppy! You're a police dog!"

"No, I'm not," Dary said, sitting up and brushing over his ear. "I'm a security consultant. That's like a desk job. I don't even work for a public group. So... what do you want? I mean, if you need me to take them off, but you don't want them to stay off, I don't really see what options there are."

Leo looked Dary in the face and squinted. The dog's expression was entirely too bright for someone who had no idea what Leo really wanted. "Well, go into the closet and get the big trunk out, and open it up."

Dary got up off the bed and set himself on his task. While he moved things around to retrieve the big black plastic trunk, something fell on top of it with a thump. The dog took it in hand and turned around, holding it up for Leo to see. A full-head leather bridle harness, complete with a metal bit, blinders, ear splints, and a black faux mane up top and down the back. "I thought you couldn't do any bondage because it'd break you. This is a bridle."

"Uh-huh," Leo said, crossing one arm, his stump pointed in the appropriate direction while his actual arm sat fingers-up on the bed. "My head's all natural." Dary's response was to just stare. Maybe the dog's a little slow in some respect, Leo though. Maybe he's overwhelmed. Maybe-

"Well, you can't really do pony play without getting tied up in a harness, and arm hobblers, hoof boots... I assume that's what the bridle's for, I can't think of what else you'd do with it." Dary set the bridle down and pulled the big trunk out, then opened it up. "Oh my god," he barked, then immediately laughed as he stared down at the contents of the trunk. "You've got to be kidding me. You've got to be fucking kidding me." Dary lifted out a similar part to Leo's detached arm, only the new one was furred in black, shiny horsehair except for a little dusky blending near the connection, and featured an extremely realistic black equine hoof instead of a hand or foot.

Leo blushed, and it hurt a little. "This company, Animalogic, makes that stuff. It's pretty expensive, but it's pretty awesome, too. I've heard of guys who... who get themselves chopped so they can wear those. I could never do that. Let me tell you, I'm glad I'm alive, but sometimes it's really, really hard to be glad, and I don't just mean survivor guilt. I'd never, ever get any of my parts cut off just for fun. But since I kind of had to... well, lemons out of lemonade, right? Like you said?"

Dary continued taking things out of the trunk. Three more hooves, two slightly larger, with a more pronounced ankle joint in the 'digitigrade' style.

"They have all kinds. Digitigrade ones for every animal species, paw hands, human hands for those few guys who have the weird cross paws naturally, metal, leather, rubber. Put 'em up on the bed," Leo said, setting his own arm on the nightstand.

Dary stayed dead silent as he continued emptying the trunk. Next: a spandex bodysuit, shiny rubberized spandex that matched the horsehair when one squinted right. Then: a horse-tail. "You better be telling the truth about your head. I don't think I could handle that. I'm not sure I can handle this, but I guess I'm handling it pretty well, huh?" Dary waved the horsetail around. He went to grab the final item, a velvet drawstring bag. He turned it around and went to open it, then froze. He looked at the bag, then at the fox. "Ohhhh no. Really?"

"Really," Leo chuckled, then reached over to take the bag. "I told you, that's not real either." The fox opened the drawstring closure and reached inside, then drew out a mottled pink and black horse penis, complete with quite natural black leathery balls. Leo had been in the same situation before with another man, right when he'd gotten the toy. The previous time, his prospects for playtime - even getting off at all - ended when the horse cock came out. He braced for the impact of rejection.

"That's amazing," Dary said, eyes wide, ears so erect that they almost tipped forward instead of just facing off to the side. Dary then stood up, leather creaking, and fondled himself through his breeches. His erection curved off to one side, towards the outside of his hip. He stroked it with the fox's key glove, spandex against black leather.

Leo watched Dary's reaction, took a deep breath, and let it out along with all of his sexual rejection anxiety. "I don't like my body, in that it feels wrong, I can always tell I'm not normal." He immediately held up his remaining fingers in case Dary was going to scold him for being angsty. "So, I love to wear spandex, tight clothing, leather, rubber, things like that. To cover it, but always make me feel something. Like I want to have a... new skin, or new everything. Then I realized that... I could actually be something different, something new. I've always loved horses, in this kind of low-level way. They're just beautiful. Beautiful and really, really sexy. So..." He took a deep breath to replace the air he squeezed out with his words.

"You want me to turn you into a pony," Dary said, closing up the empty trunk, then sliding it off the bed.

Leo didn't answer, instead grabbing for the horse-dick. His faced burned so hot that he had to squint his eyes and lean back, like he was wielding something hot. "I'm going to put this on myself... let me have that glove back?" The fox motioned for Dary's right hand, and the dog held it out. Leo peeled the glove off his canine partner and slid it onto his own hand. He reached down, massaged around the base of his cock, and let out a soft yelp, face wrinkling up. "It's just like my arm. You just need the key glove on, and you hold it at the joint, then push and twist."

"Does it hurt?'

"It feels like I'm having a urology exam," Leo said as he put the gloved paw on his cock.

Dary turned away with a cluck in the back of his throat. "Sorry, I don't think I can watch that."

"It's okay. I have nightmares about it sometimes myself," Leo said, and when he was done told the dog. "You can look now."

Dary turned around, then stared at Leo. The fox's new cock drooped to the side and swelled up, sank a little, swelled up, bobbed. The balls gently shifted in their sack. Dary repeated his cock-milking from before, grunting as he massaged his bulge with leather-on-leather from his dress gloves. "That is the most amazing thing I've ever seen. Wait, did I say that already? Maybe the second most, I mean, after..." The Beauceron mimed the action required to unlatch Leo's arm, the one he'd just learned but five minutes earlier. "I feel like I'm inside of a movie."

Leo peeled the key glove off and handed it back. Dary had put his own back on, and this time just slid the spandex on over his black dress leather. Leo's newfound cock throbbed up to a full, unflared erection as he watched the Beauceron fiddle with leather and stretchy fabric. "Go on," he urged, gaze constantly dropping to watch his equine cock throb and swell, then droop back down. "Dary, I need your help. I can't-"

Dary had gone back to his masturbatory reverie when he'd slid the glove on, but snapped back out without any warning. He leaned down and felt around at the fox's left calf, trying to find the equivalent special point. His thumb sank against a weak spot and he twisted, then pulled. He set Leo's left foreleg aside. "I can't believe I just took your leg off. Every time you do it... I do it... you wince. Does it hurt?"

"Not bad, just like when you hit your funny bone." Leo scooted back on the bed, now missing both left limbs. When he had tilted back against his row of pillows, Dary crawled onto the bed and grabbed for his second calf. "Hey, you're pretty enthusiastic for this. I thought your eyes were going to pop out of your head when I first... showed you..." Leo said, swallowing as he watched Dary's eyes fixate on his remaining arm. Dary had said to trust him, just minutes before.

"I can't imagine how it feels. I can imagine how you feel, though." Dary set the fox's second leg aside, then reached for his arm.

Leo immediately tensed and reached forward, then clutched out at the dog's gloved fingers. The stroke of leather on fur and finger pad made his cock twitch, but the panic made it stay mostly soft. "Dary, maybe you should... try putting one on me first? So you know how to do it?" Leo stared at Dary's face, at the dog's sudden determination, sudden change in attitude. Dary was no longer startled but tolerant; he was the same dog who had shoved Leo up against his linen closet just rough enough to scare him.

"Maybe you should ask me for what you want." Despite Leo's clutching fingers, Dary maneuvered his thumb into the right place, pushed in, and twisted. Off came the final limb, leaving Leo completely helpless.

Leo collapsed in on himself. His entire ability to do anything by himself was contained in RFID tags woven into the spandex fabric of that key glove, now on his supposed new boyfriend's right hand. "Dary, please." Leo's gorge rose and he panicked, feeling like he was sick and strangled at the same time. He went to grab for his throat out of instinct, but all he did was bring into view his stump's glittering metal computer and bio interface. "You know what I want. I told you. You told me, you figured it out."

"Ask me for what you want, Leo. You, say it."

Leo, body rendered useless, wondered if he'd screwed up. Maybe he had somehow glossed over Dary's interests on the online profile. Leather, roleplaying, a few real hobbies - no mention of bondage, but it was implicit. It had to be, on a website like KinkFest. No mention of pony-play.

He stared up at Dary and the dog stared back, gloved hands at his hips, key-glove mocking him as it gripped at the dog's polished leather basket-weave police-issue belt. Leo's dissociative pondering crumbled back into creeping panic. He needed his limbs back. He'd do anything to get them. "I want you to turn me into a pony, Sir."

"I thought maybe I could tie you up, that you'd warm up to it. Just start off a little slow, a little rope, maybe just a pair of handcuffs. Then, a gag. No, you don't want to be just tied up. You want to be a pony." Dary stayed there in his patronizing pose, cock straining so hard into his leathers that his knot began to add a second lump above his balls.

"Dary, please, please please please," Leo whined, eyes closed, face staring up at the ceiling. He opened them again to Dary standing over him, bridle in hand.

"You are not going to speak once I put this on you. You are a pony." The statement was meant to be a reminder, but it turned into a warning. The Beauceron fitted the bridle into place over Leo's face, bit stuffed back into the hinge of the fox's jaw. "You're my pony." Dary picked up one of Leo's arm-hooves and looked around at it, then mated it up with the corresponding stump socket. After a bit of twisting, it clicked into place. Leo yelped and swatted his hand - instead of fingers slapping against Dary's wrist, his hoof swung and thumped against it.

The fox stared down at himself as Dary readied and applied the second hoof, spasming again but with less of a body shock. His hand felt like it was balled into a fist, comfortable but useless. He tried to move his fingers, but they just stayed balled up, at least from the sensation. To the outside world, there was only a gleaming hoof. Dary smiled at it.

Dary worked on Leo's equine calves, ducking away from a couple of leg-kicks out of the fox as the sensations plugged in and evened out. When the second hoof was in place, Leo kicked and rolled right off the bed, bolting up with his arms raised like a begging pup, hooves dangling.

"Whoa there, I'm not finished!" Dary barked, then lunged right after Leo, crowding him back onto the bed. The next item took the most effort, the black spandex bodysuit which zipped up the back but needed Leo's limbs fed into it first. Thankfully Leo was helpful, offering a token struggle before straightening his new-found limbs into the black, almost iridescent fabric. The final touch: Dary got the key glove back, unplugged Leo's tail and attached the horsetail, black strands taped halfway, coming to life like a snake as he fitted the contacts into place.

Leo's initial freakout seconds earlier came from overstimulation at having his first full-pony experience. When Dary helped him into the spandex, Leo's fearful arousal of New Things faded away. He felt like someone else, something else. No longer was he a fox: he was a pony. He carefully climbed off the bed and stepped around the room, tossing his head back and snorting, drool collecting onto his lip and flinging away in a wet strand whenever he tossed the bridle's faux mane attachment. Somehow, swallowing didn't come to mind.

"You make a great pony," Dary said, stroking the bridle's mane brush back, then hooked two gloved fingers around one of the rings where the leather straps met up. "How about you come out here?" Dary backed up out of the bedroom, lightly tugging Leo along.

Leo didn't have anything of the guidance, putting up increasing resistance the closer he got to the door. When Dary readjusted his finger grip, the pony-fox bucked back and clopped over to the wall, then backed himself right into a corner. He pranced in place, whinnied as best he could, and started trying to circle the room.

Dary grabbed onto the bridle's reins and clutched them both up in a gloved hand, then petted down Leo's muzzle as he again tried to drag him to the exit. "You keep holding up, and I'm going to have to slap you."

Leo flicked his tail up and followed along as Dary tugged, hooves held up in front of him, still dangling forward. He reared back and let out a sputter, then slowly clopped into the other room on his feet. On his hooves. The fox had worn the leg hooves many times before, and had clopped over every inch of the resonant hardwood floor in them, but no one else had ever been around to hear. Now, he had an audience, and that attention sent the vulpine Leo somewhere else. In his place stood a shy, but aroused, pony. His teeth worked at the bit, his hoofed hands hung useless with his forearms held up in front of his chest, his tail lashed instead of curled, and his dick bounced and bobbed like never before.

"I think you need some water, pony. C'mere," Dary said, leading Leo to the sink. The clop changed from hollow wood to the sharp click of hoof on hard stone tile in the kitchen. Dary stood by the sink, patient but alert, chest ruffed out into his leather shirt. As the fox approached, Dary opened up the cupboards and very obviously fingered through a number of cups and saucers.

Leo's bad horse behavior died back, replaced by a wide-eyed stare at the dog's gloved fingers rooting through his belongings. The pony-fox huddled against the fridge. He chuffed and mock-whinnied, then clopped up to sidle against the counter, back bent slightly, tail arched, legs constantly shifting inside the spandex, two hoofed feet even clopping in place. He was curious what Dary would do, curious but scared. He tried to bounce on his toes, but only paced his hooves in place, brain impulses meeting the lack of appropriate parts.

He knew exactly what Dary was going for, and let out another sputter as the dark dog's fingers seized on a water bottle. It looked like the generic condiment bottles that restaurants used to spurt decorative sauce onto food; Dary filled it up from the sink and then upended it. The dog squeezed the bottle, squirting water into Leo's mouth, aiming in to the back and side so he didn't choke the poor fox.

The vulpine gagged and swallowed hard, head bucked to the side since he couldn't suckle his lips around the squirting water. The bestial treatment humiliated him so much that he felt like his pelt was on fire, pawing out with his hooves but never quite bashing them up against the dog's forearms. Dary used up a whole bottle, but Leo got barely a third down, the rest wetting his face and making a puddle on the floor.

Dary refilled the bottle and squirted more, petting down the fox's very real mane ruff. After another whole bottle's worth, the pony fox bucked back and whinnied. "Okay, okay, guess you're full up now. Good pony. Now, can you really walk like a horse?" Dary said, holding the reins close up to the pony-fox's forced-open muzzle. He slowly led Leo out of the kitchen, as much to tickle the vulpine's ears with the slow clack of boot heels and leather squeaks as to be relaxed about it.

The pony-fox twitched and squirmed, clopped in place, then gave a double clop of one hoof. Leo knew exactly what Dary meant, and he desperately wanted to try it. He just wasn't sure if he could do it.

Leo walked out into the dining room and squatted down, then sunk forward. Like a real pony. He crouched down onto all fours, then took a tentative few steps with all four hooves clicking against the hard dining room floor. It was hard, very hard, and his nervous shuddering gave way to muscle quivers from bodily strain. He drooled because he couldn't be bothered, because the exertion made him breathe hard, because he wanted to stare at the floor, because he

couldn't close his mouth. He managed to circle the dining room table twice before collapsing over against the wall, tail slapping against the hard surface. Dary moved in to help, but Leo flicked his tail against the dog's thigh and squirmed around, hoof knocking forward at the dog's chest.

Dary grabbed onto the hunkering pony-fox's wrist, then started fondling him. Leo nearly kicked, whinnying out, the sound unwavering and real as he reacted to the electric tingle of the glove leather on flesh. It wasn't his cock flesh, it was something else, and he had to take the prosthetic sensations no matter what. "See? It's just your reward. It's your reward for doing a great job out here. You made it around two whole times! That's a long way for a new, fresh pony." Dary used a bit of what hybrids called 'dog voice', the patronizing speech humans tended to use when talking to domesticated animals.

Leo stared at Dary, even as his cock throbbed in the sudden, leather-gloved milking. He tried to flare his lips, but there wasn't much to flare. Pony Leo was terrified. Fox Leo wanted to get off so bad his balls hurt. He squirmed away, only to stand up, reaching a hoof out to nudge Dary, then leaning forward to nuzzle at him.

Dary let go of Leo's pendulous horse dick and took the reins again. "And now, the thing everyone wants a pony for," Dary said, leading Leo into the bedroom, shoulders now confidently square away from the pony-fox. "A ride."

The big dog nudged Leo up against the bed, body crowding up from behind, throbbing package getting Leo in the lower back. The fox immediately kneeled down, flicking his faux-mane around as he hunkered with his hooves facing out along the sheets. Dary groaned and ground up against Leo's spandex-clad ass, then leaned over, gloved hands stroking the body suit.

Leo's body twitched and his horse-grunts took on a distinctively high tone, body breaking character as he overfilled with stimulation. A wave of pleasure crested and left him bleating and slobbering all over his bedsheets from pleasure, then sunk into stinging humiliation as he realized that Dary could very well be simply turned on by the aesthetics.

Dary sighed with the tone usually reserved for that moment just after breaching through someone's warm anus. The dog spread his fingers up and down Leo's spine, stopping to stroke around the tail base. He slid up and drew the spandex suit's back-zip down, exposing some real fox fur again, along with the pink pucker under Leo's new tail.

The shepherd unbuttoned his own leathers and fished out his swollen sheath, milking at it with his gloved fingers until his dribbling sloped cock head slid free. Like most domestic dog hybrids, his was feral-style, as opposed to Leo's more human unsheathed length. He untucked it from the sheath, then stepped over to the nightstand and lubed himself up from the pump bottle so carefully laid out in the open there. Leo stared ahead as he kneeled at the edge of the bed, fore-hooves planted flat on the sheets. He stared as if the dog wasn't there, only to slowly turn and acknowledge the canine with a groan as he watched Dary slick himself up.

The dog took his place behind the newfound pony, spooned cock head nudging at Leo's ring, slimy with collected precum. He leaned in and stuffed right up the shelf, penetration bringing a sharp faux whinny from Leo, but no kicks. He gripped onto the reins and pulled back, forcing Leo to back up and squirm. "Whoa there, stay put. That's good. That's good." He sunk forward and drew back, then groaned at the warm, clinging pleasure.

Leo swooned and dropped his head, snorted and grunted, sputtered and even whinnied when it suddenly hurt for a cramping second or two. He'd spent quite some years playing with himself under his tail, but Dary was rough, rough for real, confident and not over the edge, but hardly considerate. Ponies were tools, ponies were toys, ponies were domesticated for riding and hauling and carrying and serving people, and taking their master's cocks even if it burned for half a minute - Leo's head swam, but all that came out of his mouth was a dull groan.

Dary ground his knot forward harder and harder, breath catching in his throat as he tried to reach ultimate pleasure. Leo shifted subtly but stayed in the same pose, feeling the heavy pressure but still grinding backwards more than trying to buck away. Soon, the pony's asshole was milking and kissing at that bulge, then engulfing it. Leo let out a big, shuddering whinny. Dary nudged forward and Leo nudged back; how could he resist? The black and umber dog lost his hold on his pleasure and roared over the edge of climax, cock throbbing as it tied into Leo's squirming hole, seed emptying in as he groaned and whimpered and licked his canine chops.

Dary started nudging his knot back out, then slid forward, letting the last few squirts come out as he nearly knot-fucked the pony, bringing another round of whinnying out of Leo. The leathered dog slipped free and his cock slopped down, spent, body sagging back.

The rush of pleasure left him buzzing, suddenly affectionate. "Now, it's time for my pony to relax," Dary said, then stepped over to the closet. He moved like slow motion, cock still burning inside, tingling with the aftershocks of a profound tying orgasm. When he crouched down to root around, his dick tip dragged on the floor, shaft loose as it flopped around out of its sheath, still tingling and bloated. He found what he was looking for, a fleshlight toy with the asterisk of a snug asshole at the wide end. He took it and trickled some lube into it, then brought it back and stuffed it underneath the pillow top cushion on the mattress. He put a pillow on top, then tapped at it. "Hooves up, pony."

Leo stamped his hooves onto the pillow and started immediately trying to hump into the makeshift artificial mare, precum-slick cock skidding sideways and up onto the pillow on purpose. When Dary clutched his shaft tight and aimed it just right, Leo took off, hammering into the slippery fleshlight with no moderation. The fox swept his ears back as he listened to the wet claps of his leathery cock plunging into the lube-wet silicone rubber, squelches and slurps as the hard fucking slurped air in around his sizable shaft.

The new-found pony whinnied out and bucked into the toy, hooves stamping at the bedroom rug, tail arched up, head bucking upwards and sending some slobber flying out of his bitted mouth as he blasted his orgasm into the toy, actual twinges of pain crushing into his prostate as his muscles clamped down so, so hard. He pulled out and splattered the toy with a shot before Dary guided him back in, then bucked his last few out before tugging back again. The orgasm was a complete shock, so satisfying but so sudden, body fulfilling its needs and leaving Leo's mind behind to stare in the afterglow.

Dary grabbed Leo around the shoulders and hugged him from behind, limp cock tucking back into its sheath as it nudged against the open gash in the fox's otherwise glistening black stretch suit. He guided the pony to kneel up onto the bed, then lie down on his side. Dary went for the key glove, while Leo curled up in an equine fetal position, sinking into the dark place that sometimes follows an orgasm.

The dog felt up one of the hoof arms, tickling enough that Leo contracted tighter, then stretched out as he realized what was coming. Dary squeezed and twisted, and off came the hoof with a sort of a faint sucking sound. One by one, he restored Leo's real parts, ending with the tail and leaving the cock to the fox. The last thing he removed was the bridle and its slobbery bit. Dary worked quick, concentrating on freeing Leo.

Once Leo could talk and use his arms to himself, he grabbed Dary down into bed and clung onto the leather dog, burying his slobber-matted face fur against Dary's chest. He immediately started to whimper and sob, foxtail limp against his back leg as his human emotions overrode the vulpine need to tuck the brush under. "I don't know what's wrong with me," Leo whimpered, body shivering for a moment as he clung onto the dog's muscled arms. "I don't even feel sad. I don't know what I feel. This is so weird. When you... when you..."

"Did I force you?" Dary said, stroking his gloved hand up Leo's black spandexed back. "I was so turned on."

"What? No," Leo chuffed, then chuckled, the sound interrupted by a post-sob heave. "I slipped out of who I was, I wasn't me anymore, I was a pony. I was a pony toy, for you to use, and that's so strange," Leo whimpered as Dary gave him a gloved scruffle to the head. "I was still in there somewhere, but I couldn't... I've just never done that. I was scared. I'm sorry I'm crying like this," Leo murmured, then took another huge shaking breath. His clutch turned into an affectionate squeeze, then the relaxed slump of someone burning in both sexual afterglow and post-sob euphoria.

Dary's face twisted with a hint of pain and the sour realization that he'd overwhelmed Leo. He cradled the fox, moving his gloved hand further around, across the fox's back, down his spine, tickling at his side until Leo squirmed and gave him a rotten look. Red-eyed but now smiling, drowsy. "I'm sorry I scared you. You moved like a horse. I can't describe it. You even sputtered and snorted when a horse would, and you never let anything else slip past it. You were a good pony."

"I loved it. I really did. I guess I just got a little worked up just now. This is... this is hard to deal with, these are," Leo said, holding a hand up, then pawing over at one of the hooves. "It's a lot of trust. I have to trust doctors, I have to trust myself, I have to trust other people. There's always something between me and the rest of the world. I..."

"You want to put something there that you want, not something you didn't ask for. Right? I think I've been there, in a way. I didn't start off on top, you know." Dary smiled, then cocked it into a grin.

Leo looked up at Dary and his worried calm dissolved into wonderment and bliss. "Oh my god."

"Yeah, yeah, just imagine me bound up and squirming on the floor while some big wolf wallops my butt." Dary dropped his muzzle and rubbed an ear. "I can't imagine what you've been through," Dary said, shifting away so he could truly sit on the bed, gloved hand reaching over to stroke Leo's naked leg. "What... happened, anyway?"

Leo swallowed. "Well, do you remember when they rebuilt the Carson St. bridge? You were probably in middle school. I was in third grade." Leo stood up and started to pace, both to help his feet 'wake up' and because he couldn't sit still and stare Dary in the eye. "I was going into town to go to the museum with my aunt. The bridge gave way and the train we were on derailed right into an oncoming freight train. We were going backwards, you know? Like the engine was pushing us so there was nothing in front. Our car was the one that hit the other train first. Right into an ethanol tanker."

Dary stared.

"I managed to get out of the wreck, and it was winter so I was all bundled up. Suddenly it felt like I was wet, like I'd fallen in a river. But... it wasn't cold. I just took off and ran, like two blocks, three blocks, then someone mortified at the... at me running along... on f-fire, they tripped me into a puddle. It was mostly my hands, my feet. Thank god it wasn't my head. I ended up getting a staph infection, that... I lost my hands because of that... Then..." Leo gestured to his horse cock. Then he stared at it, realizing it was the remainder of his behavior. "Oh shit, let me take care of that." He turned away, snatching the key glove off a startled Dary. He yelped as he unplugged one set, then caught his breath in his throat when his own dick and balls snapped back into place.

"I don't want to know what happened to that part," Dary said, forcing a chuckle and motioning towards the fox's groin. "No offense."

"Trust me, none taken. You don't want to think about it. I was just a kid, but still. I was in bad, bad shape. I have memories of that awful shit, while other people my age just remember crying at their birthday party because they didn't get a pony."

Both of them twisted to make eye contact at the same time after what Leo said.

"I didn't want a pony when I was a kid. It just took a while," Dary said.

"I guess it's a neat trick," Leo shrugged, rubbing at the back of his neck, then his shoulder, with his almost-natural fingers. "I'm still a freak."

"Don't say that. I mean sure, it's weird, but... you're not a freak. You can do something awesome. And I mean full of awe, not just..." Dary offered.

Leo smiled. "Yeah, I guess." His stomach growled. "We can... go out if you want."

The Beauceron closed himself around Leo, swiping the fox up in a hard bear hug, then loosening his grip into a much more intimate embrace. Leo clung onto the leather like he was kneading an enormous dick. "You're amazing. I don't want to sound like one of those guys who just fawns all over you because you got him off. You did get me off, though, and you better do it again, pony." Dary gave Leo a hard nuzzle. "I really mean it. Look at you. You got lit on fire, and not only would I never have guessed, but you look great, and you can become a real pony fox." The dog sat up, slapped his leatherclad thighs. "And yes, we can go out. I'm thinking... Brazilian steakhouse."

"Mmm. You just want to put warm cuts of meat in my mouth." Leo thought about his words as they fell out of his muzzle, and quickly scooped at his snout as if to shovel them back inside before Dary heard them. "I can't believe I said that. I'm not really like that!"

"Yes, I do want to watch you eat delicious steak. I want you, to come out with me. You'll have to be a little social."

Leo sighed and leaned his head on Dary's shoulder, then slid back and started looking for a respectable set of clothes. "Mmm."

"You'll have to be social so you get used to the attention," Dary said. Leo just looked at him, taking his turn to head-cock. "For when you wear those hooves out, eventually."

Leo's eyes turned from slits to gaping black pools with gold rims. "You..." He started to fur-fluff from panic.

"Not tonight." Dary grasped onto the fox's arms, then slid down to hold hands, tender and almost romantic. Leo still kept his hackles up, imagining that Dary's smile only came from the unique knowledge that the black hands the dog was caressing were not at all real fox paws. Dary squeezed and brought Leo back. No, the dog was serious.

"Thank you," Leo sighed, then let his arms go a little limp before he pulled them back. "I think it's time for those warm cuts of meat I mentioned."

"Such words from a pony, huh?" Dary smiled. Leo smiled back.

About the Authors

Kandrel
A writerly fox from across the pond, if you enjoyed his story here, you can find many more over at SoFurry or FurAffinity, both under the username Kandrel. He also maintains a twitter feed (@Kandrel) with many musings on vulpine nature and authorly pursuits.

Ianus J. Wolf
Ianus lives in Seattle with his mate, where he writes whatever happens to come to mind. He is currently working on a few other projects including a potential anthology and a novel. He can be reached at ianusjwolf@gmail.com

Mangi
Mangi is tiger and a new writer to the fandom, this is his first published story. You can find him on Twitter and FA as MDMangi and SoFurry as Mangi.

Sparf
Chris "Sparf" Williams has been writing, off and on, for years, and finally decided to start seriously honing his craft once he found a place where he could present the kinds of stories he wanted to tell. The story in this anthology is his first erotic story, and given the feedback will likely not be his last. In addition to writing, he is a professional actor and voice actor, finishing up his MFA in Acting at a university in Washington, D.C. Some of his voice work can be heard in the fandom on the AnthroDreams podcast. He can be found on furaffinity as "sparf" and on Twitter as @Sparf.

Eli Lapso
A writer from the state of Illinois with a penchant for poetry. , when he's not writing, he is generally being lazy, random, and sociable. You can find his writings at furaffinity.net/user/lapso

Rechan

Rechan has had several erotic stories published in Heat, along with the novella "Handcuffs & Lace" through Fur Planet. His stories can be found at SoFurry and www.furaffinity.net/user/rechan

Ashe

Ashe is known for the leading the Anthrocon Writing Track for the past several years. He's back from a long break for this anthology, with more work to come. Currently, he resides in Seattle with his partner, Ianus (who is also featured in this anthology).

Tarl "Voice" Hoch

From the frozen north that is Calgary, Alberta, Canada where he spends his days, Tarl writes erotica and horror to stave off the Canadian winter. When not writing he's scaring small children with his spider-folf awesomeness, researching Lovecraftian horrors, or simply driving everyone else insane. This is his first published piece.

http://www.furaffinity.net/user/voice/

Nathan Cowan

Nathan Cowan is the penname of a guy who doesn't get enough time to write. You can find him at:

http://www.furaffinity.net/user/nathancowan/

Whyte Yoté

Whyte Yoté has been writing for the furry fandom since 2000, his works having appeared multiple times in *FANG*, and also in the anthologies *ROAR*, *X* *The Fortune Teller's Poem* and *Holidays* in addition to issues of *Heat* magazine. He lives in Sacramento, California with his forever-boyfriend Tym, juggling multiple short-story projects as well as anthology and novel work.

www.furaffinity.net/user/whyteyote/

whyte-yote.sofurry.com/stories

H. A. Kirsch

H. A. Kirsch usually (but not always) writes gay, BDSM and fetish-themed erotic anthropomorphic fiction. He can be found at:

http://www.hakirsch.com

About the Artists

<u>Kadath - Cover</u>
Is a furry artist who runs on coffee and giraffes.
http://www.furaffinity.net/user/kadath

<u>Tim Dzon - Interior Illustrations</u>
Is a comic book artist whose work has been seen in The Flash, Doom Patrol, and the Suicide Squad from DC, and in Avengers West Coast, Spiderman Unlimited, Fantastic Four Unplugged, What If?, Ironman, War-Machine, and others from Marvel Comics. He is now back into the field as a full artist not just an inker, and his artwork can be found at *http://www.furaffinity.net/user/tkddbull/*

About the Publisher

FurPlanet Productions is a small press publisher serving the niche market that is furry fiction. We sell furry-themed books and comics published by us and most major publishers in the community. If you can't get to a furry convention where we are selling in the dealers room, visit *www.FurPlanet.com* to shop online.

www.ingramcontent.com/pod-product-compliance
Lightning Source LLC
Chambersburg PA
CBHW071834020726
47502CB00004B/1348

* 9 7 8 1 6 1 4 5 0 0 4 9 0 *